WHAT MAISIE DIDN'T KNOW

Judy Upton

WHAT MAISIE DIDN'T KNOW
Judy Upton

ISBN 978-1903110812

First published in this edition 2021 by Wrecking Ball Press

Design: humandesign.co.uk

Supported using public funding by
**ARTS COUNCIL
ENGLAND**
LOTTERY FUNDED

CHAPTER 1

Who'd you give your last half-hour of telly to? It's a tough one that and I've never been good at making big decisions. Helen's already taken her sleeping pills so it'd be wasted on her. Jayne and Marjorie One have visitors so don't need it either. Jill gets scandalised by stuff in 'My Weekly', so watching 'Love Island' might be a sensory overload. That only leaves Marjorie Two, to benefit from the gift of my pay-to-watch TV card. I'll break the news to her when her catheter's been changed. I hope she's grateful.

"I've got something for you," Masoud announced as he plonked himself down in the chair beside my bed. I was glad of the visit, but desperately hoping he hadn't brought me chocolates as they're banned by the regime. Look, don't worry, right? For anyone new to my ramblings, I'm not some plucky heroine living in a future world where the government's almost as crazy as ours. This ain't 'The Hunger Games' – well not quite. I'm in Brighton General and it's the nurses who are watching me. Watching everything I eat.

Masoud's the assistant manager of Pizza On The Pier. He also has a sideline as a street photographer. He takes those shots of blokes skinning up in the skate-park and Staffies cocking their legs up a post box you see in the free magazines. He makes sales through an online agency too, though not enough to trade in his delivery moped just yet. The pictures that sell best are the ones that illustrate concepts. They can make seriously good money. So if someone is writing an article called 'you are what you eat'; a banana with a smiley face drawn on it, next to a burger with a ketchup-painted scowl, might be what they're after. I come up with the ideas and Masoud takes the pictures. Gingerbread men are brilliant for this type of work. Once I iced three as gingerbread women, then made the faces of two of them look like they were laughing at the third one. You ice their eyes carefully, putting the little blobs for the pupils to the side. It makes them look sly see? I gave the third gingerbread woman a sad face and crumbled her slightly. She was emotionally crumbling – get it? A woman's magazine certainly did and bought the photo for an article about how women judge each other. Masoud and me shared the fee and the gingerbread. Win - win.

As Masoud opened his pizza satchel, everyone at the nurses' station was instantly agog and poised to pounce on a flat, cheese-covered item of forbidden fattiness. Instead he revealed an empty-looking jam jar with small holes punctured in the lid. The nurses rubbernecked, but I knew they weren't gonna see anything from the other side of the ward. "I managed to catch her. It was quite easy." I'd have given him a hug if I hadn't got my reclining bed stuck in an almost flat position. There she was – an Araneus Diadematus – or Garden Cross Spider. Mrs Webster, as you, and the rest of her two hundred thousand, one hundred and forty three Instagram followers know her, was hanging on to the jar lid.

Hadi messaged Masoud to tell him to collect his next delivery so he couldn't stop for a chat, even if chatting was his thing, which it ain't. We've become friends of sorts over the past year, but I wouldn't say I know him well. We really only talk about photography, pizza toppings and the outside world. When I was bed-bound, Masoud's photos of the seafront, piers and the beach were all that kept me from going fruit-loopy. The view from my flat's window was never the most inspiring, in spite of Mrs Webster spinning her web across it. I overlooked a weedy concreted yard; the café next door's fly infested bins and the houses in the street behind. It could've been a 'Rear Window' situation if I'd seen a murder happening in the house I looked out on. Instead there was a thick net curtain that badly needed washing, and a solitary dead pansy in a cracked window box. Since I've been on this ward, things have looked up in the view department. I'm not on the sea-facing side of the building, but I can see the racecourse and the Downs. There've been some sunsets to treasure, and that's saying something, as I'm not normally a treasurer of sunsets. I've a whole collection of them on my phone now. There's even a rainbow over the Number 2 bus going up Race Hill. Masoud and most of my Instagram followers are envious of that one.

I wonder how Mrs Webster feels about leaving her web behind. She can build a new one of course, but it takes time. She's probably pretty pissed off cos on a fine evening like this she should be catching a late supper of gnats, mosquitoes and the odd moth. I had a plague of moths a couple of months back - little brown bastards chomping their way through Mrs Latimer's manky carpet. When I opened the window, some flew out straight into the web. I didn't used to like watching Mrs Webster catch her prey or wrap it in silk, but I've got used to it. It's no good being squeamish, as she can't become a vegan even if she wanted to. Even in Brighton there aren't any vegan spiders yet as far as I know. I didn't used to like them that much - spiders I mean, not vegans. I was never scared, just not keen. Accidentally walk through a web and it don't half make your face itch. Not to mention the tiny dead flies and bits of larger insects that stick to your cheeks and eyelashes. Yuck!

It was Orla who made me see the light so to speak. She left her glasses behind at my place, after she'd got me up and made my breakfast one morning. I tried them on, just to see what I look like in glasses really. I suppose I was hoping for a transformation – to see someone I liked looking back. In fact the ruddy things hardly fitted round my face and I was scared the arms were gonna to snap off. But they did magnify everything and that was amazing. It was like becoming 'Antman' or 'Mrs Pepperpot'. It was 'Honey I Shrunk The Maisie' – or is that just wishful thinking? I could see all the dandruff on my hairbrush and the choco-milk stains on the duvet left by escaping Coco-pops.

When I looked at the spider on the window, the first thing I noticed was the pattern on her back. In the middle was a big white cross, like a crucifix. Her body was light brown with two thick squiggly dark brown lines that travelled right down to her bum. And I could actually see her face – really see a spider's face for the first time. Her eyes, all eight of them, were in two rows of four and they were oval, black and shiny. They were looking at me, as they glinted, I was sure of it. Plus her tiny feelers, or palps as I've since learnt they're called, were moving very slightly, and almost trembling, as we eyeballed each other. I lifted and wiggled my little finger at her and her palps waggled more energetically looking almost like she was knitting. I had waved and the spider had waved back. Man had been to the moon, DNA had been discovered and I'd communicated across the human-spider species divide. I'd met Mrs Webster and it was about to change both our lives.

Tonight Mrs Webster is in her jar on my table beside the jug of plastic-tasting water that I reluctantly take the odd glug from, since running out of Capri-suns. All I need is a doctor to turn up and sign me off and I can be on my way to my new home. For a while last week, my chances of heading anywhere apart from a shop doorway, cardboard box in an underpass or my mother's least favourite sofa weren't looking good. I was officially classed as a bed-blocker while my Primary Care Team bickered with the housing department about exactly where to park my sorry arse.

My landlady Mrs Latimer hadn't believed her luck when the whole bariatric rescue happened. She'd been trying to evict me for decades, having successfully rid herself of all her other housing benefit tenants. With me though it was different. I presented her with a challenge. A thirty-five stone challenge. I was way too heavy for any bailiff to woman-handle out of there, so Mrs Latimer had to let me be. Until the unhappy day I fell off the bed that is, and had to be hoisted out of the first floor window by a bloody great crane. That was her opportunity – the evil old witch. I'd barely been plonked on an extra large bed in this ward before her lawyer was arguing the flat was "unsuitable for my complex needs". Total bollocks but the fuckwits at the council and DWP bought it and let her evict me.

I was only supposed to be in hospital for a few days, but they went and stuck me in a bed next to a snot-monster. So I caught her cold, my asthma got worse, and what was supposed to be some routine tests followed by a bit of outpatients' physiotherapy, turned into the full 'Grey's Anatomy'. Mrs Latimer got shot of me and the council, NHS trust and social services have been playing pass the fucking enormous parcel with me ever since.

Finally though I have a place to go. It's a housing association flat on the first floor of a house conversion in a seafront square. When I had a gander at it courtesy of Google Earth, it looked like it had seen better days. It's one of those old houses with cracks in the render and rusting railings with half a bike chained to them. I was supposed to get a ground floor place, but guess what, I've stairs to deal with once more and steps up to the front door too this time. Mind you, thanks to the dogged efforts of Justin and the rest of his torture team, I can again walk a short distance with the aid of a stick. I've practised the stairs in here and while it's not exactly a piece of cake – note to self, stop using that expression – I can manage. At least being a house split into flats will mean I'll have neighbours. Hopefully among them will be other younger people like me. We'll be able to lend each other cups of sugar, pass the time of day and do other neighbourly stuff. I'd really like to live somewhere like in 'Friends' where people pop in for a natter, a coffee and a laugh now and again. Knowing my luck though it'll be full of anti-social freaks and past-midnight-death-metal-fans. No doubt that's why it's available to a housing benefit and Personal Independence Payment receiving person like me, but hey, I can dream.

So any time now it'll be goodbye to my ward buddies: the two Marjories, Helen the Snore, Jayne the Night Wanderer and Jill the permanently constipated. It's also farewell to Lin the Wise Taker Of Blood Pressure and Neve the Selectively Deaf Ignorer Of The Emergency Buzzer.

Today has been the first time Mrs Latimer has let Mum into my old flat to collect my belongings. The spiteful old hag had kept making excuses for why it wasn't convenient. I'd half suspected it was a delaying tactic while she stuck all my stuff on ebay. Mum's bagged and boxed everything up for me, but she had to call Masoud to collect Mrs Webster, as she's scared of spiders. I knew as soon as my things were out of that flat, Mrs Webster would be in mortal peril. Even before, I was a bit worried. What if Mrs Latimer was snooping around up there and decided to knock the web off the window? Or even fumigate the place with my belongings still in there? An eight-legged influencer would've been murdered.

Masoud would've given me a lift to the new Chez Maisie if he could, but Pizza On The Pier's van is currently awaiting a new exhaust. I should be back on four wheels soon myself though as I've a new mobility scooter on order. Melanie, the social-wonder has arranged it. It's a refurbished one, she said, so I won't raise my expectations too high – it'll probably be a heap of shite. Most likely it'll drive me in circles if not a round the bend, but let's hope for the best eh?

*****

I've now lost my bed to a hippy. I mean a woman who's just had a replacement hip, and so I'm chair blocking rather than bed blocking. I'm out in the foyer, freezing my arse off. For two hours I've been overhanging this hard, plastic insult to the word seat, right next to the automatic doors. They keep opening and closing, mostly for invisible people or ghosts. Each time an icy blast of air threatens to freeze me rigid. For some reason Mum forgot to bring me a pair of socks with the clean laundry so I'm relying on my holey slippers to save my toes from frostbite. It's almost nine pm.

Mrs Webster is motionless in her jar. It's in my holdall on top of my pyjamas, crossword magazines and toothbrush, so she should be getting enough air. She's still clinging to the lid, but hasn't moved so much as a leg for over an hour. Spiders are cold-blooded so if the temperature's low they're not active. Back at our old flat she'd be tucked up under the window frame at this time of night.

She had a little white scrap of thickly woven silk and she'd climb inside, pulling in all eight legs to escape the draught. It was just like a hanging sleeping bag. If I moved the curtain and looked for her at night she'd only be in her web if it was mild with very little breeze. If it was cold, blowing a gale, or pissing down I'd have more chance of spotting a unicorn.

I hope the hospital transport people haven't forgotten me. I've tried ringing but keep getting stuck in a queue. This is despite the stuck-up sounding robot at the other end assuring me that my call is important to them. I don't understand why they still have lying answer-bots in the 21st century. I mean we all rumbled it years ago. We know our calls aren't the tiniest bit important to them, or they'd fucking well answer them. So why don't they just tell us the truth? "We can't be arsed to employ enough staff to answer your call, as to do so would mean we'd make less money for ourselves." Do they really think we'd be angry if we heard that response? I don't think we would, cos we've always known this was what was going on, haven't we?

There seriously needs to be a vending machine near the exit doors. I don't mean one selling overpriced chocolate bars either. I mean hot soup, or teas and coffees at the very least. I'm sure I passed a machine on my way down here. It was in the adjoining corridor I think, but I was being pushed in a wheelchair at the time and I don't think I could retrace my route and find it. 'Kin 'ell! I just broke wind and the automatic doors slid open again. If they're gonna do that every time I fart, I'm gonna die of exposure. Definite.

*****

"Maisie? I'm Donal. Your lift this evening." About fucking time, I thought as I forced a smile. Thankfully he'd managed to pull up right outside and it was one of those mini-buses that look like burger vans with windows. As I stood, taking the weight on my stick, my legs creaked. Just like an old tree – you'd have had to hear it to believe it. Donal had a wheelchair onboard but I'd been fixed in one position for so long, I needed to stand. Although the physio sessions have got me walking again, Justin has stressed the importance of making sure I keep doing it. If I don't, I'll be back in here again. There was already talk of sending me to some extreme weight loss boot camp. 'Kin 'ell. Just the thought of that bollocks is enough to keep me putting one foot in front of the other.

The hospital transport bus had space for seated people as well as those in wheelchairs. I sat as far forward as I could so I could back seat drive if Donal needed directions. The upholstery was a welcome refuge for my sore arse. Did you know you can get bedsores from sitting in a chair? That's why they're calling them pressure sores now. It's not some politically correct thing to stop blaming and shaming beds, in case that's what you were thinking. I'm a mine of useless information, me. I soak it up like a sponge. After a couple of days on the ward, I'd know when Marjorie Two's catheter was blocked before she did. And I'd impersonate Doctor Macdonald's deep voice to tell Jayne "Shall we try another gentle enema?" That used to crack up Marjorie Two. She'd have laughed 'til she pissed herself if she wasn't plumbed to avoid it. I was also the one who noticed Jill hadn't had her stretchy stockings put on her legs when she returned from having her operation. "You don't want her developing DVT, do you now?" I said to Neve, who pretended not to hear me as per usual. "I'm sure her family will go for compo if she suffers a stroke. I've seen them eyeing up the personal injury claim leaflets in the day room." By the time I got back from loo, Jill's leg coverings would've made an Egyptian mummy proud.

Talking of DVT, there was plenty of legroom in the mini-bus, which meant I could practice my ankle flexing, and foot gripping en route. If I was rich I'd have one of these four-wheeled wonders myself, complete with a personal driver naturally. A uniformed chauffeur, that's what I'll have when Mrs Webster's influencing makes both our fortunes. She surely can't need many more followers before a talent manager comes calling. She's way ahead of Tracey The Tarantula, despite the fact the hairy one lives in San Francisco, and George The Bird Eating Spider posts so rarely now he's no longer a serious contender. In fact I reckon George has probably gone belly up and his owner's not letting on, to try to stop his income stream going the same way. There's a certain amount of ruthlessness in the world of animal influencers I can tell you. I mean we all know a certain hamster who seems to have been alive for ten years now, don't we?

Donal does two days a week as a hospital transport driver. Well, when I say days, as often or not, it's nights, as they tend to disgorge patients at all hours. I wonder how many eerie figures end up shuffling down Race Hill in their nightclothes like escapees from a zombie apocalypse? He does hospital driving 'to give something back' he said. It's always the people who owe society least who give the most back. Like my best friend Abby – always crocheting, knitting or collecting for one cause or another. At the moment she's making stripy jumpers for rescued battery hens. And what has life given her in return for 'giving back'? She has M.E, poor kid.

I could tell Donal's into his music, by his jaunty grey quiff. Rockabilly is his thing he said, with a "side-helping of skiffle" – whatever that is. "It's Lonnie Donegan. 'The Rock Island Line'." Honestly I was none the wiser. I told him about the hospital radio station. I'd asked them to play me anything by Rag 'n' Bone Man and instead got some old song called 'My Old Man's A Dustman'. Donal chuckled and said his daughter used to listen to Garbage. They are a band too apparently. I wonder if anyone's ever formed a group called 'Recycling'? If they have I bet they're rubbish.

When he offered to put the radio on, I said that would be great, but don't think it's cos I'm not chatty. When I meet someone new I always try and have a natter with them, if only to give me something to tell you. The radio station was one of those playing old pop. It was probably 'Heart Sussex And Surrey' but I didn't catch a jingle so who knows. They were in the middle of Beyonce's 'Crazy In Love'. I sang along, replacing the word 'love' with 'Hove'. We started doing the same to other song titles, as you do, when you've nothing much to talk about. "I'm Not In Hove," suggested Donal.

"I feel Hove."

"All You Need Is Hove."

"The Hove Cats." That one cracked him up.

"Hove Will Tear Us Apart." Whilst we were heading in a westerly direction, my new place is definitely still in Brighton, rather than over the border. "Hove Is A Battlefield."

"I'll Never Fall In Hove Again." Donal reckoned he'd sing that one next time he's on his way home from the pub after one too many.

I'm gonna have a flat warming party. Donal's only the third person I've invited, after Masoud and Mum. He brews his own beer and will bring some bottles. He also makes something he called a 'sweet perry' – out of pears of all things. It sounds fucking disgusting but his wife and her friends prefer it to Prosecco. I told him his wife can come too. The more the merrier.

As we pulled into the square, a fox trotted out into the road, a half sausage from a communal bin hanging from its mouth like a huge joint. Donal braked and its cold amber eyes stared right through me before it headed on its way. Some foxes have a seriously bad attitude.

The outside of the new Chez Maisie looked even shabbier than in daylight on Google Earth. Who knows when their all-seeing camera car last filmed down here? Something I had noticed though, when I panned around the square were the two police cars that on that particular day were parked just up the road. Not a very positive sign regarding my new neighbourhood, but as we drew up it all seemed reassuringly quiet.

I'm actually extremely glad to have been offered a flat at all. At one point someone from the assessment team – they're always teams, although you never see more than one of them at once – suggested I'd have to go into an old folk's home. "At thirty one!!! Fucking hell!!!" We then had the usual, "no I'm not swearing at you, I'm just expressing a heartfelt opinion on my situation" argument. I was told my mobility problems mean I need to be somewhere with a hoist, and at least two care visits a day, which my current care provider could no longer provide, or care about. In the end I lied, well to be more accurate, I stretched the truth a little bit. I said I was now confident I could live independently. I knew even if Justin in physiotherapy didn't agree with my assessment, he'd be overruled. The thing is they don't listen to the experts these days. They listen to the person who's telling them what they wanna hear. And what they wanna hear is always the thing that costs them the least. Putting me in a granny farm would be expensive for them, so of course they wanted to hear I can cope, even if I can't. It's a juggling act for me, avoiding incarceration while not losing my Personal Independence Payment. Hopefully, if they do cut my carers, Mum'll just have to help out more, hopefully with less moaning than usual. In fairness, she does my washing, sends back parcels and brings in anything I can't buy online, but she does go on about it, like she's trying to earn sainthood or something. I can stand long enough to cook a ready-meal in my microwave and just about manage to wash myself all over.

After I'd headed off the threat of the old folk's home, there'd been talk of me having to stay in a B&B hostel. That had also filled me with the deepest dread. I used to pass one on my way into town from my old flat. Its steps were always draped in drunks or junkies shouting and spitting at each other. "Get a job, you fat cow!" shouted a spotty druggie before the effort of insulting me caused her to cough up half a lung. "Get off and milk it!" an elderly alkie skeleton cackled as he indicated my previous mobility scooter Bessie. In another quick recap for those who are more recent followers of my adventures, Bessie was stolen and later found in the marina, hanging out with the super yachts. She was only dredged to the surface when an oligarch weighed anchor. The police had to identify her barnacled remains from her serial number. As he tossed her in the back of his truck, the scrap dealer told me I should see metal recycling as a kind of reincarnation. Now every time I guzzle a can of Fanta I think of her.

My new street has so many parking meters it makes me wonder if they've found some way of reproducing. Anyone ever seen a baby one? No, don't tweet me, please.

Donal was hopeful that he wouldn't have to pay to park at that time of night, and I wished I hadn't lost my last two quid in the faulty vending machine in the next ward, while struggling to stick to my new diet. I didn't want Donal to be out of pocket; after all he is a volunteer. It ain't right. Then I remembered the meters round here have all gone remote or "too posh to accept coins" as Mum puts it. According to her, you now have to pay by phone or "the web-thingy". She makes this little hand gesture when referring to doing anything involving a website or contactless, as if she is a magician magicking her payment from here to there. Not a great fan of "the online" is Mum.

Donal opened the van's doors for me to clamber out and as I did so, a young woman click-clicked past on heels, wearing a fun fur coat so thick and huge I couldn't see if she even had a head. If they do those in Primark or anywhere cheap I think I'll get one in readiness for my next wait at the hospital's sliding doors. A key flashed in the streetlight as she entered my house, closing the door behind her before I could even sing her the first bar of the 'Neighbours' theme.

Donal wasn't supposed to come up. His role is to drop off the patient at his or her front door. Having heard he was taking me somewhere I hadn't seen the inside of though, he offered to see me safely in. Melanie the social wonder had given me the keys when I was on the ward, but the housing association rep works nine to five, so wasn't here to show me around as planned. I'd been told it was furnished, so arrived hoping that meant more than a broken table and piss-stained carpet square.

The stairs are steep and the screws of the handrail coming out of the wall, so I took Donal's arm for safety. It felt very regal, as we slowly ascended together. If he wasn't married and old enough to be my dad, it might've even appeared romantic. I opened the flat door and switched on the light. I was pleasantly surprised. It didn't look too bad. Best of all there's a bay window that gives – I can hardly believe my luck – a partial sea-view! The sea was the thing I missed most during my long months stuck indoors. Now, even if I lose my mobility again, I can see the sea. I love it here! I love it!

The room also has a high ceiling, which means it won't be dingy like my previous place, though the threadbare red rug on bare boards and 'slug snot' coloured walls are hardly exciting. Thank fuck it's a double bed even if it does have a suspiciously thin mattress. Not a smidgen of memory foam here by the look of it. There's a big saggy sofa and a reasonable sized TV. The kitchenette has cracked tiles and chipped cupboards with missing handles. At least the separate bathroom has a mercifully clean toilet and a mould-free shower. My arse won't fit into your average sized bath, nor can I get down to that level. "S'alright eh?" Donal said approvingly.

I asked him if he could open the sash window a crack. "You sure it's warm enough for that?" I said I needed to release Mrs Webster. I'm hoping she'll spin her new web on the back window of the flat. I've chosen the rear of the building as it's more sheltered. I don't want a gale blowing in from the sea and blowing my poor spider to fuck knows where. You might've thought 'Incey Wincey Spider' was just a nursery rhyme, but it's actually a health and safety warning. I know spiders travel on the breeze when they're young, but being blown from a web is highly dangerous. A fallen spider might be trodden on, eaten by a bird or drown in even the tiniest of puddles.

It's Mrs Webster's choice as to where she builds her new web of course. I can't force her to construct it where I can still see her. She might crawl off and start spinning it on another part of the building. I know she's used to me, as back at our old place, if I put my hand out the window she'd long since stopped freezing, curling up her legs or racing back up to her hideout under the top ledge. It's probably stretching things to suggest she enjoys watching me as much as I do her, but I'm sure she's learnt I mean her no harm. Whether this is reason enough for her to stick around, we'll have to see.

As it turned out, Mrs Webster wouldn't even come out of the jar. The stubborn little madam folded her legs, dropped to the bottom and played dead. Donal thought I should tip her out gently, but if I'd turfed her out the window she could've landed on the ground below. It seemed best to leave her in the jar 'til morning. At least she'd be safe for the night, even if she did get a bit peckish. Mind you, by that time, she wasn't the only one with a rumbling gut. I'd ordered my evening meal at the hospital, but was chucked out before it arrived. Either the woman with the hip replacement ate my Cumberland sausage with mash, and low fat Greek yoghurt, or it all went to waste. Why they don't send it after you, when you've been moved down to await collection, I don't know. I'd have had plenty of time to eat it while waiting for my lift.

When I opened the kitchen cupboards, they made Old Mother Hubbard's look well stocked. Donal frowned. "They've not even left you a few teabags and some afterlife milk?" I think he meant long-life, but didn't bother correcting him. There's a 24-hour store nearby and he's insisted on going to get me some milk, teabags and a packet of cornflakes too, so I've my breakfast sorted. There are kind people out there. With my online diary or 'vlog' I encounter so many trolls and fat-haters that occasionally I forget this fact. I've asked him to get some bread, a pot of spread and some bog rolls too. I've been left an old toaster, but no toilet paper. Pretty fucked priorities, but there you go. As soon as he gets back, which is hopefully any minute, that toaster's gonna see action.

Donal turned out to be a real treasure. He added a packet of plain chocolate digestives to my shopping and wouldn't take the money for them. "Flat warming gift." He apologised for having to buy apricot-coloured bog roll as if that's something that matters. Why does it come in colours anyway? He left me his phone number and promised he and his wife Sarah will come to my party, with their home brew and perry. "Who's Perry?" Even as I asked, I remembered it's the fermented pear piss. Honestly, you can tell I'm dead knackered can't you?

I'll love you and leave you for now, as my bladder's full to bursting. It's time to officially christen my new toilet. For months I've relied on shee-wees and bedpans, so it's a privilege to walk into my own bathroom and perch on the pot. I'll have to sit down carefully mind you, as the wooden loo seat has a hairline crack in it. Have you ever sat on a cracked toilet seat and had that chasm in the wood open like a mini pair of jaws, only to snap shut, trapping a piece of your most tender flesh in its splintery vice? It's an experience never to be forgotten, trust me on that. I'm gonna be lowering myself very gently indeed.

'Kin 'ell!!! Thank fuck for the light of this little screen! I just pulled the light cord and the bulb shattered. I'm now sitting here in darkness. It's not only the light here in the bog either - the light in the main room's gone too. Course I did my business before updating you on this sorry state of affairs. There's no way I'd pee on camera, even in the fucking dark. I'm always modest and respectable me. If you're looking for cheap thrills, fuck off and follow someone else. Once I've pulled my keks up, I'll have to find the fuse box by the light from my phone. What a crap night this has turned out to be.

There has to be a fuse box somewhere. Only I can't find it. Mrs Latimer's was a regular shithole, but at least you could switch on one bloody bulb without shorting out the National Fucking Grid. When I walked in here all the paperwork had been left on the kitchen bench showing that the wiring and appliances meet current safety standards. Boxes had reassuringly thick biro ticks in them. Not that that means shit, as I discovered while I was in hospital. A guy turned up once a day and took the file from the end of everyone's bed out into the corridor beyond. "He's a box ticker." Helen The Snore in the bed next to me explained. "That's all he does, I'm sure of it. Takes our files out into the corridor and ticks a lot of boxes, then puts them all back." She reckoned there was something decidedly dodgy about it all. "Bugger my angina, I'm gonna find out what's going on," she hissed determinedly. So the last time he turned up, she got up and followed him out on her walker, holding a copy of 'The People's Friend' like she was on her way to the day room for a read. "Spy craft" she said it was. It made me suddenly wonder about what she did before she retired.

Anyway, regardless of her prior level of experience in the world of espionage, Tinker, Tailor, Soldier, Snore was on the case. The suspected box ticker had retreated to the corridor and opened the first file. His pen was raised, hovering over a box, when he spotted her, doing her best to discreetly observe him from behind her magazine. Quick as a flash he beckoned to the nearest nurse and Helen was bustled back to bed and distracted with the news that the tea trolley was on its way "with some bourbons too if you're lucky". So the great NHS Box Ticking Mystery has been temporarily filed as 'unsolved'. Next time you're in hospital, see if you can solve it.

If only flats came with instruction sheets pointing out where everything is. Back at Mrs Latimer's when the tap started dripping the plumber wanted to know where you turned the water off. I hadn't a clue. I mean if you need to turn off the water that's when you call a plumber surely? I'm almost starting to get homesick for that crappy hovel. I suppose there's nothing for it but to go to bed, once I've unpacked my pyjamas by phone light. I can call out an electrician in the morning. Mum's sure to know a cheapish one, though no doubt he'll be some drinking buddy of Shaun's. I did try giving Mum a quick ring, but it went to answer so she must've already gone to bed. Hang on; I can hear a noise on the landing outside. Either this place has got rats, or there's a neighbour about. A helpful one I hope.

"John?"

"Err, no, I'm Maisie."

"Gotta torch?"

"No."

*****

My heart's still ping ponging. Did I mention it can be a bit irregular if I get stressed? I'll try my inhaler, cos I've got a bit breathy too. Give me a minute and I'll tell you what I've just seen.

*****

So, this is what's gone down. Hearing someone on the landing, I opened my door. The hall light wasn't working, so I'd clearly fused the lights in the whole place. Not the best start to my tenancy. There was a trickle of streetlight filtering up from the panel in the front door below. It was just enough make out a figure on the landing, fumbling to open a small wooden cupboard on the wall. Clearly this was where the elusive fuses lurk. Anyway a floorboard must've creaked as I opened my door cos the bloke span round with a startled gasp. On discovering I was neither someone called John or currently in possession of a torch, he grunted and hurried down the stairs and into what must be his flat, the ground floor one.

The geezer returned with a decent-sized flashlight and I could make out he had curly dark hair, and a face that was all angles in the torchlight. He located the latch, opened the cupboard and flicked the switches on the fuse box. It was that easy. Once again we had light. Then at exactly the same time, we both noticed the same thing. Lying on a greasy rag, on a shelf below the electricity meters, was a gun.

CHAPTER 2

Do spiders suffer from insomnia? I've not slept, in spite of the bed not being quite as hard as it looked. Try as I might, I simply couldn't nod off. In my mind I kept seeing the eyes of that fox crossing the road, and the eyes of my new downstairs neighbour when he saw that I'd seen that gun too. "Must be John's." the guy had said quickly, – too quickly.

"Right... err okay." I'd said. My mind was racing. "Who's John?" His dark brows raised, quizzically.

"You came out of his flat."

"He used to live here?"

"Still does. Far as I know." The bloke had turned to go, then hesitated, picked up the gun. As he weighed the pistol in his hand, I flinched back into my doorway.

"Look, err did you ought to pick it up? I mean if it's a real one, it might go off or something." He checked the part where they stick the bullets, the way only an actor in a TV thriller or someone used to handling guns does.

"Not loaded."

"So it is a real one then?" He laughed suddenly. He was probably around my age. An earring glinted in his ear.

"Apparently."

"Did we ought to call –" His jaw tightened in a way that stopped me from finishing the sentence. He wrapped the gun up in the rag that it had been lying upon.

"I'll drop it in at the nick in the morning."

"So this bloke John, who used to live here..." I fished. The geezer shrugged.

"Not seen him in weeks. If you've moved in, maybe he's moved out."

"Without his gun?"

"If it was even his. There're always plenty of comings and goings." He looked at me, something akin to mischief in his amber eyes. "Perhaps you're gonna be a slightly quieter neighbour."

"Yeah, no worries. I hardly see anyone."

Immediately I wished I hadn't said that. It made me sound needy and vulnerable when I'm anything but. Also it might not have been wise to let my neighbour know I'm gonna to be living here alone, not until I know him a little better at any rate. I can't make my mind up about him. Sometimes I get a vibe about people, good or bad. Not with him. Nothing.

"I'm Reuben." He shook my hand firmly. "Need anything just knock okay?"

When Shalamar sang 'Let's Make This A Night To Remember' I'm sure this wasn't the kind of thing they were talking about. Still, it's time to get on with the most important business of the day – releasing Mrs Webster. If I stand my phone up against the window ledge hopefully that'll let her admirers see all the action as it unfolds.

"Oh come on!" She's not moving at all. I hope she's not sick. Anyone know a vet who's gentle with spiders and dirt-cheap? She's taking no notice of me tipping the jar and tapping on the glass. Would it be wrong to give her a gentle poke with the end of a biro?

Hang on, she's moving. I'm gonna try and shoot some of this in close-up. Might put some music behind it later. I'd thought of 'I'm Coming Out' but she's crawling so slowly it needs to be something less upbeat. My arm's aching holding the jar. Come on, Mrs W! Get your silk-spinning arse into gear!

Finally Mrs Webster's onto the wooden window frame, waving her palps are she tastes the fresh air. She must be hungry but it's not possible to feed her — I've tried before only for her to cut my pork scratchings and pepperoni slices out of her web and drop them in disgust. And now of course she don't even have a web, thanks to me. I hope it's not long before she's made a new one. I did check there were no spiders already in residence on the window. Spiders like their own space and see neighbours as a potential meal. They definitely don't do friendship and I'm sorry to say Mrs Webster killed and ate the only boyfriend who came her way. Spider males are smaller and have to be very skilled in the art of lurve. Get it wrong, like the potential Mr Webster did, and she'll be chowing down on your head while you're still doing the do.

Imagine if there was a Tinder app for spiders. She'd be scrolling with one leg while the other seven continued their multi-tasking. "Nope, nope, err definitely nope, yum, yum, ooh sexy... no on second thoughts – yum!" You wonder why male spiders still bother when it can all get seriously grisly. And are there gay spiders? Note to self: google that later. Shit, the phone's camera is telling me the battery's low and there's nowhere near the window to plug in a charger. I can't live without my extension leads. I hope Mum's rescued them from Mrs Latimer's.

*****

It's been decided I can survive with my Primary Care Team visiting only once a day. It's true I can now make it to the kitchenette to get my own breakfast. There's a fridge freezer with the fridge on top which means I don't have to bend to grab the milk. There're two bar stools at the breakfast counter, though there's no way I can perch on a bar stool. I wonder if they belong to the flat's owner or could I flog 'em on ebay? Until Mum gets round to delivering my stuff I don't have a bowl for my cereal. It's so frustrating. She simply doesn't seem to realise the urgency of my situation. I've found a plate and there're two chipped mugs hanging over the sink. One has a brown flower design that looks like it belongs in a rip-off retro shop and the other says 'FBI – Female Body Inspector'. Probably belonged to 'John'. At least it's a big mug, as I'm gonna have to manage with Cuppa Cornflakes, if you know what I mean. Hopefully I'll have my microwave back before dinnertime.

If I sit on the saggy sofa, will I ever rise again? For the moment, I'm not risking it. The TV works, which is a nice surprise, but there's not much on, apart from DIY bores and shouty cops nicking people for swearing. Still at least I'm no longer paying to watch this crap on a tiny, scratched screen, dotted with other people's phlegm. On the property show they started playing that Destiny's Child song about being an independent woman. I mumbled along through a mouthful of cornflakes. Today I depend on me.

Abby and me have arranged to natter in Hangouts, so I'm awaiting her call. She likes to get changed and do her make up before she sees her mates, the same as if it involved going out.

"Hey Mais.

"Hey Abbs."

"How's it going, girl?"

"Mustn't grumble."

"It's like sooo amazing – you're already in your brand new –

"Whoa!"

"What?"

"Shhh!"

"What? What is it?"

"Listen."

"I can't hear anything."

"Someone just screamed!"

"Oh my God – where?"

"Upstairs, I think."

"Oh my God! Someone is being murdered in your actual house! Oh. My. God!"

"Shhh, Abbs! There. Did you hear that?

"Like um no."

"I'll try to angle the mic so you can hear it."

"Sorry, still can't. Is someone still screaming?"

"Nah. They're not screaming. They're coming."

"They're like what?"

"Orgasm, Abbs. Someone upstairs is having an orgasm."

"Um right. You're sure?"

"You want me to go up there and ask her?"

"I mean you are like totally sure she's not being murdered?"

"I'm sure. It's all 'Oh, yeah, oh ahhhhh, baby! Oh yeah, bay-beeee!'"

"Um isn't it kind of wrong, listening in?"

"Like I have a choice."

"Sorry, I wasn't judging, Mais."

"It's not like I'm enjoying it or something."

"No of course not. Sorry."

"I mean it's just rubbing my face in it, if you know what I mean."

"Yes. Um no. What do you mean?"

"I mean I'm never likely to do that am I? Faking it or for real."

"Course you will, Mais. You just need to believe..."

"...I can fly? Yeah, whatever. Anyway she's stopped now. Come to a sticky end."

"Urgh, Mais, that's so gross."

"Fine, moving on. Just give me a moment to get up on my feet... and here we go – here's the virtual tour as promised."

"Whoa, slower, Mais. Hold your phone like steady or something."

"I'm trying okay. I'll do a slow pan around the room so you can see it all."

"Urgh... I feel a bit sick."

"It's not that grotty, is it, Abbs?

"No, sorry, it's um your camera shake. I'm watching it on my desk screen and it's like giving me like nausea, sorry. Could you just like grab a few still shots for me instead?"

"Yeah, yeah. I'll do that and call you back."

*****

Abby agreed with me that my slug snot décor is mega-boring, but she reckons "neutral is a positive" cos I can stamp my own personality on it. She'll be sending me a list of ideas from Pinterest for paint colours and furnishings. I did try to discourage her, but she weren't having none of it. That's the thing with Abby. She always talks about finding yourself and doing your own thing, but then some fucking influencer or other influences everything she does. "Katy K says citrus tones are directional", or "Esme G says forget colour, think texture". The last time my walls had texture was after I'd had that projectile vomiting bug. Mum brought it back from her last river cruise. The one where she swore she saw a crocodile in the Rhine. "Think minimalist luxe," says Rosie B. I mean what even is that? "That's not a thing, Abbs trust me," I said. "It's just yadda yadda yadda – and oh clever me for getting paid to advertise this wank."

Nobody asks me to advertise anything; well apart from pile cream and I told them where they could stick that. No, not where you're supposed to put it. I came up with a more original insult, give me some credit here. The point is, I'm not gonna be nudged into buying some old bollocks just cos some skinny bird from Clerkenwell in colour-blocked cashmere tells me "it is so having a moment right now". If it's cheap, it does the job and there're no delivery charge, that'll do me, thanks very much. I mean I'm not planning to be photographed in my beautiful home for 'Slimming' magazine until

I've lost another twenty odd stone – in other words never – so why worry about citrus and textures? I didn't say this to Abby, and I'm certain she never watches any of my videos, as I'm not one of her wellness gurus with their 'happy places' and empowering words chalked on pebbles. Lighting a scented candle has never done much for me, apart from neutralise an eggy fart before a visitor turned up.

It wasn't until Abby had finished her design consultation, and I'd stopped dozing through it, that I told her about the bloke downstairs, the cupboard and the gun. Abby thinks I should ring the police later to check the gun's been handed in. I'm not so sure. If he's kept it and the cops get into a right old panic about it, they might come rushing round here with their semi-automatics and get me caught in the crossfire. Innocent people do get shot by mistake and I do present a large target. Also you don't wanna make enemies where you live, not if you're pretty much housebound and living alone. I'm lucky to have got this place, there's no way I wanna risk losing it, by making trouble for myself. Abby said I should have a look online for reports of previous suspicious happenings in the neighbourhood and that's a good idea. "And Maisie, you won't post online about any of this? You won't mention the gun in the meter cupboard? Or the woman upstairs' love life?"

"Of course I won't. What do you think I am, stupid?" I assured her, cursing the fact that as you, me and the rest of the world know, I uploaded my report on last night's escapade shortly after it happened. Oh well. I wouldn't imagine Reuben downstairs follows me, or Mrs Webster for that matter. Me and Abbs wittered on for a while, mainly comparing various supermarket-brand malted milks. If there's only one cow on the biscuit, the general advice is to put the packet back.

Mum's texted to say she's packing a cab with all my belongings and will be round with them shortly. About fucking time. I know she had the day off today, so what on earth's she been doing, while I've been bravely coping without my torch, bowl or jar of sugar-free toffees?

"How on earth did you collect so much clutter, Maisie? I don't know why you didn't have a good old clear out before moving." That's what Mum said after she'd collected everything from Mrs Latimer's. It's what I like about Mum. The way she can rewrite history in a blink of an eye. She'd conveniently forgotten I'd been subject to a Section 21 eviction while in hospital. If you're a person who can plan for unexpected shit like that, you should be running the country, that's all I can say. You can't do worse than the fuckwits currently in charge. I've only the bare minimum of possessions anyway – and I strongly dispute that any of them are the 'c' word – 'clutter'. When you're unable to get out, internet shopping passes the time. You buy stuff to give you a parcel to open, a jumper to send back or a bottle opener to break and complain about. Then there are the hobbies you think you might get into – felting kits, calligraphy sets and teach-yourself bloody-anything books. And I confess I keep buying things for my kitten, the kitten I still don't actually have.

I was glad Mum got a taxi round here with my stuff rather than relying on Shaun. He's probably at work anyway. He works at a place that makes injection mouldings. I've no idea what that even is and no desire to find out, so don't you dare tweet and tell me. I don't like Shaun. There're like a zillion things about him that rub me up the wrong way. Chief of them being he's not my dad. Not that anyone else could be Dad. I know it's a bit unfair and despite being an utter plonker Shaun makes Mum happy, but there you are. For what it's worth Shaun don't like me either. He makes sure Mum has no inkling about this, so I always get it in the head from her for slagging him off, "when he really respects you, Mais." She didn't even notice him singing 'Three Times A Lardy' on my birthday. Actually he shouldn't have turned up at all cos he wasn't invited and Mum wasn't offered the option to bring a 'plus-one toy boy' on the invitation. In fact Mum and Shaun were the only guests I had, as my sister is working in Australia and all my friends are online. Apart from Masoud that is, who brought me a card when he delivered the pizzas.

When the door-buzzer buzzed, I managed to walk down the stairs and open the front door. As I did so I heard Mum yelling, "guys like you make me bleedin' livid!" It was the cabbie she was hollering at. "Says he don't do unloading, Mais. Says we shoulda called removals or a man with a van." I started down the front steps using my stick but she waved me back. "Nah, nah you can't help." "Straight outta hospital she is, my daughter," she added for the benefit of the lazy sod who hadn't left his car. "And you bet he's charging us for just bleedin' well sitting there too." I could've pointed out that, as it was a mini cab it wasn't on the meter, but before I could say anything, Reuben had arrived behind me.

"Is there a problem?"

"Just trying to get my stuff unloaded..." I started to explain, but then a weird thing happened. The cab driver finally got out and started unloading my things onto the pavement. I can't be sure, but I don't think anything more than a look passed between him and my neighbour.

"Careful!" Mum shrieked as the mini-cabbie plonked a box down on the pavement. Presumably it contained something fragile. I'd no idea what she'd put in where. Reuben passed me with a pile of boxes. Mum followed him indoors, straining to lift some bag-for-lifes bulging with the contents of my old kitchen. I made my own way over to the cab and took a couple of bags from the back seat. While I was working out how to manage them and my stick, Mum returned and wrenched them from my grasp. "Oh no you don't. We've got this." I'm sure she said this just to show off to my neighbour. "Go stick the kettle on, girl. Me throat's parched."

"Maisie's making a brew," Mum called down to Reuben as he headed down to collect the last box. "He's nice." She gestured his departing back, all gym-honed muscles under a black t-shirt and tattoos down both arms. "Shame he's a bit of a looker, you're not likely to be in with much of a chance there."

"Mum – behave!"

"I'm only saying."

"Well don't. Anyway, as I keep telling you, I'm ninety-five percent asexual."

"Asexual my arse. And is that even a real thing? It's like the school used to tell me you had ADHD when you were the most sluggish kid in class. ADHD – you were practically a sloth."

I only had the flowery mug and the one that had held my Cuppa Cornflakes, and that needed a wash up. Luckily Mum remembered which box she'd stashed my china in and had even had the sense to wrap it in newspaper. Considering she don't read papers this was a fucking miracle, but as all the pages seemed to be from the same dated Brighton Independent, I'm guessing she'd grabbed a big pile of free papers from one of those stands you get outside newsagents.

In the top of a box is one of Mum's Mexican Hat plants. Tiny miniature versions of itself are lined up along each leaf edge ready to drop off and be trampled into the rug. I don't do houseplants, but she's always trying to foist them onto me as "they make a room more healthy." I was trying to find which box or bag my own kettle was packed in, praying that it hadn't by some tragic oversight been left behind. That's the problem when someone else has to pack for your move. Hopefully she'd instead assumed everything not nailed down was mine, and nicked Mrs L's carved teak bog roll holder and bath mats. Brighton has hard water. I mean real, seriously 'Oi, you want some do ya?' hard water. The kettle left here's so furred up that every cup of tea I've guzzled so far has contained more white flakes than a football team with scalp issues. Never has a decent kettle been more desperately needed.

"I love your tattoos" Mum gushed as Reuben lifted his tea mug. "You're obviously into wildlife aren't you?" I wondered what on earth she was on about, and then noticed the twisted vines of his sleeve inkings contained lifelike insects and reptiles lurking among the leaves. "Me, I've just got a woodpecker." She dragged down the shoulder of her fluffy pink jumper to show him. "I said I wanted a bird. I wasn't too fussed about what kind." She's got a peeling plaster on her arm, just above her HRT patch. Not a winning look, in my opinion.

"Looks like a Great Spotted Woodpecker."

"Is it really? You're sure the spots aren't part of me?" Admitting you've back acne isn't how I flirt, but in Mum's defence she's out of practice. Reuben laughed.

"No, I recognise it – black and white with a patch of red on the back of its head. When I was a kid, there was a tree-covered hill at the end of the road. Woodpeckers used to fly out and knock holes in the telephone poles."

"Did you grow up locally?"

"Just off Sutherland Road."

"On the way to the hospital, yeah? I got the bus up there, visiting Maisie. She was in there for over two months this time. I'd started to think they'd never let her out." She babbled on, without giving a thought as to whether I wanted him knowing all my business. It's always been like this with Mum. She tells everyone all about me. I wouldn't mind if it was all positive stuff, but no, I've caught her telling a meter reader about my bad circulation and the plumber about my bowel movements. If she'd started telling Reuben about my IBS, I swear that mug of calcium-infused tea would've scalded more than her woodpecker.

To distract myself from Mum's ramblings, I went to check if Mrs Webster had started on her new web. She hadn't. In fact I couldn't even see her. I felt a wave of panic rise inside me.

*****

Mrs Webster's Instagram's had a flood of enquiries about her health and current whereabouts. Normally I post at least one photo a day, but with no spider, there's nothing to tell people. After our chat, Abby scanned and emailed a card she's made to celebrate our move. She's collaged a cheery cottage with a flower garden. It has a happy, waving female figure and a smiling spider standing in front of it. It's all horribly out of scale. For a start the girl is slim and the spider is larger than her head, with googly eyes and black fur. Neither could fit in the cottage either, but hey, it gives me an image to post and tweet across all our platforms, for which I'm grateful. I start to feel uneasy whenever the clamour stops, the 'likes' dry up and even the trolls disappear between their own haemorrhoids. If my number of followers goes into a decline I start to feel physically sick. "What did I do? What the fuck did I do! Why don't you still like me?" I need you lot out there, every single one of you, okay?

Earlier, while Reuben and Mum were finishing their tea, a noise started upstairs, a rhythmic bed squeaking noise, if you catch my drift. We all looked at each other. Mum sniggered. Then the woman started her loud moaning again. "Adelina." Reuben grinned. While he'd been chatting to Mum, his eyes had been scanning the room, sharp as a hawk's. I wondered if this was to do with the previous tenant John, who was probably the owner of the gun. I've decided not to ask Reuben whether or not he's handed it over to the police. I'm not sure it's really my business.

After Reuben and Mum had gone, I spent over an hour on the phone to utility company cyborgs. It's all part of the moving flat ritual. I've been here before and would've bought the t-shirt if they'd one left in my size. The only interesting thing was Kelsey at the gas company, who seem to think, when I finally got through, that I'm some kind of idiot. Turns out she's right. I've an electric cooker rather than gas and the radiators are electric convector ones too. Who knew? So the flat's gas-free until my IBS flares up. I'll be glad to have the wi-fi on. Keeping on uploading from my phone has sent me well over my data limit. Thank fuck Mrs Webster is a monetised spider. If it wasn't for the adverts on her accounts, I'd be reduced to eating flies myself.

I'd imagined my care team visit, despite being scaled back to one a day, would still involve Orla and Tiffany. But it seems I've now become the responsibility of a new 'team'. Orla and Tiff used to come in twice daily to wash, dress me and prepare my meals while I was bed-bound. Now I've what they call limited mobility I'm visited instead by a woman called Elaine. She's jolly enough but nearly as large as me. She thinks her role is all about 'enabling and empowering the client'. This means her sitting there getting paid while I get my own lunch. She told me handrails are arriving next week for my bathroom as if this was a miracle on a par to the raising of Lazarus. She wasn't interested in the rail on the stairs that's falling off though, cos it's a communal area and so someone else's responsibility. If I fall down the stairs and break my neck a couple of times then it might get looked at. I'm offered a raised loo seat but Mum's brought my old one from Mrs Latimer's so I don't need another. Elaine seems unimpressed when I tell her of my problems with the shower. I unhooked the head this morning and it suddenly developed a life of its own, writhing and fighting me as if it was an anaconda trying to escape the grasp of Tarzan. That's why the towels and my bathrobe are currently hanging on chair backs in front of the convectors.

I asked Elaine if she could help me hang my pictures on the wall. There's a rail so it don't even involve banging nails in. I've even got the hooks all ready. It's a quick, simple job but if I stand on one of the bar stools guaranteed it will break. Elaine though had already checked the clock on her phone. It was time for to visit her next client who "currently has more urgent needs." What she really meant was they'd dock her wages if she fell behind schedule.

"Fine," I said, slightly snippily, "I've got your number if I fall off a stool and die." Rolling her eyes, she departed. I hate eye rollers and wonder if there's a way of getting Orla and Tiffany back. Tiffany was pretty much a waste of oxygen, but Orla looked after me. With Orla visiting I felt secure.

*****

I was still unpacking mid-afternoon when I noticed it. A long single strand of silk stretched from the corner of the upper frame to a quarter of the way along the outside of the bedroom windowsill. Mrs Webster has woven the first support of a new web. It's shining in the light, a strong thread to anchor her firmly back into my life. I can't resist taking and posting a photo.

It takes a spider around an hour to build a new web. Mrs Webster don't often have to start completely from scratch though. When her web has been damaged by heavy rain or a bumblebee tearing itself free from the sticky threads she just kind of patches it up. You can always see the joins. Make do and mend. Better to repair it in minutes and be ready to catch the next fly than start over.

While I was stuck in Brighton General, the weather had been getting steadily colder. Garden Cross Spiders don't tend to survive the winter. If I'd been able to stay at home, the plan was I'd bring her inside if frost was expected, and put her back out if it was warmer the next day. Jonas, one of her followers, reckoned I could keep her indoors during the winter months, by 'culturing fruit flies'. Why the fuck does a fruit fly need culture? Even in arty old Brighton that sounded unlikely. Jonas explained that all he meant was if I left a banana to rot, after a couple of days loads of tiny flies would hatch out and Mrs Webster could eat them. I didn't really need telling about rotting food and little flies – it happened in my old flat on a regular basis. What I hadn't known was it was called 'culturing'. Fortunately, we haven't had a hard frost yet this year, so Mrs Webster survived on Mrs Latimer's unheated window while I was away. Now there's the convector on the inside wall below her web, and fuck the expense, if it gets nippy I'll open the window a crack and give her a bit of warmth.

"Yay!" says Abby in response to the web-in-progress photo. She includes three thumbs up emojis and a face I think is crying with joy.

"Good on you, Mrs W!" says Davy. Davy is studying molecular biology, at Loughborough or Leeds or somewhere else beginning with 'L'. He has cerebral palsy and makes youtube videos explaining things like how every snowflake is different, and no, by snowflake, he's not referring to Abby. He's got me reading 'New Scientist' regularly. We both have this app where you can download loads of magazines for free from our libraries' websites.

Paige is also pleased to see the old team of two is still together. She says Mrs Webster is Scooby Doo to my Shaggy. Oddly, Paige was one of my first trolls, and she remains the only one of that toxic army to go over to the light side. I first met Paige, when Mrs Webster still had less followers than legs, I tweeted a photo of myself looking out through my misted window with Mrs Webster on the outside. I took it with my first selfie stick, dangling it out the window and hoping it wouldn't send my phone plunging down onto the concrete below. I was quite proud of that image. Anyway Paige photoshopped it rather badly, so the web had the words 'Some Pig' written in it. She obviously thought this was a great laugh cos of my weight.

Another early follower, Lavender Lady, tweeted to defend me and that's how I learnt of 'Charlotte's Web' which went on to be my favourite book. I loved it so much I ended up thanking Paige for the recommendation of sorts. To say she was gob smacked didn't come close. She replied saying she'd read the book in her exclusion unit. I told her I hadn't liked school much either, mainly cos of bullies like her. I wasn't even that fat in those days but insults and violence had still been a daily occurrence. Paige too had been bullied she said, but her answer had been to become a bully herself. She saw herself like Mrs Webster, but lurking in the worldwide web waiting for the next victim to eat alive. She used to think she might even be a psychopath, but she's definitely mellowing of late. The virtual card she sent on my birthday could almost be described as soppy. Mind you she does still send the odd bitchy comment, usually in the early hours of a Sunday morning after a few too many vodka jellies. She tends to follow up a few hours later with a more friendly comment. It's never an outright apology but it's the best she can do.

*****

"Fixput!!!"

"Err hello, are you okay?"

"Ah, hello. You are with John?"

"John – err no. I think he's moved out. I've just moved in."

"I break my fucking shoe. This fucking shoe is shit."

"I might have some glue. We could try to fix it. I'm Maisie by the way."

"Adelina."

*****

In her stretchy grey jersey mini-dress Adelina perched elegantly on the edge of my sofa. She must be over six foot tall. Her hair is bleached and she wears it in a bun like a ballerina's. Her eyelashes remind me of the giraffe pyjama case I had when I was seven. They can't be real. I unpacked my craft things onto the kitchen counter looking for a tube of superglue. "I paint the bottom red." She was showing me the soles of her shoes. "So they look like Louboutin yes?" It was no good asking me. My trainers come from a catalogue that specialises in wide fittings. "Maybe the glue do not like the paint, so it breaks." I lifted out my card-making papers, inkpads, stampers and stencils. Adelina was rather taken with the packets of stick-on fake jewels for brightening up cards and scrapbooks. She mimed sticking them against herself where beneath her dress her knickers might well be. It cracked me up.

"Course they're not to v-jazzle my fanny! There ain't much point when I can't even see down there. But we could stick a few on your shoes if you like?"

She considered it for a moment then perhaps wisely shook her head. Superglue isn't much good for mending slippers or trainers and I tend not to wear much else in the way of footwear. For sticking a hard plastic heel back on a stiletto though it worked a treat. While we waited for it to harden completely, I asked Adelina if she could hang my pictures up. It would be easy for her I figured. She could reach the picture rails without the aid of a barstool.

Adelina didn't wanna hang my pictures, until she'd had a close look at them all. "You paint this? It's good." She nodded approvingly. Art was always my favourite subject at school, even though the school itself was shit. I really enjoyed drawing animals. Give me a book with photos of anything with fur or feathers and I'd be off, scribbling away for hours. More recently, when I could go into town on my scooter I'd stop outside an art gallery that sold lots of animal paintings. On one occasion it was all bright coloured acrylics painted from life in Kenya. The reds, yellows and oranges were so strong I could still see them in my head when I returned home. There was this one picture, of a lioness and her two cubs. It was drawn with lines as free and wild as the big cats themselves. If I'd had a hundred and fifty quid that painting would've come home with me, but instead I went to the library. I got out every book with photos of lions in it, and used them to do my own version. I'm not saying it's anything like the original. I couldn't quite get the loving look in the mother's eyes or the sheer energy of the cubs. My first attempts were pretty shite actually, but finally after a couple of weeks I managed a version I could live with. And that one now has a charity shop frame and is about to be hung on one of my new walls.

Trouble is, I went and let my love of painting go to my head. I started thinking I was the real deal. There was a time last year, when I convinced myself I could become a pet portrait artist. It was when my Personal Independence Payment had been stopped, cos the health assistant assessing me had decided I wasn't disabled enough for her liking. So for eight months I had no income while waiting for an appeal date. How I kept myself sane, while surviving on the few quid I borrowed from Mum, was by drawing cats and dogs from more library books. I posted the paintings across my accounts and when they received lots of likes, persuaded myself it wouldn't be long before the commissions rolled in.

My life would change; I'd have money, work, and a lifestyle to envy. Daft? Yeah – totally. I didn't realise, mug that I am, that there're so many pet painters out there. Millions of them. Living in Brighton where every second person is an artist you'd have thought I'd have fucking twigged, wouldn't you? I ended up throwing my paints in the bin. No more acrylics and watercolours for me and I'd never lift another pencil. Fortunately Mum saw my art things sticking out of the rubbish and gave them back to me. I'd never have afforded to replace them. Now though they mostly sit there unused and unloved.

Adelina cooed over my cat paintings. I'd even given my imaginary moggies names, writing them on their food bowls or collar tags. She was surprised I don't actually own a cat. I told her Mum had lined up a kitten for me, but then I'd had my accident and bariatric rescue, and it had all been forgotten for a week or two. When Mum finally rang the breeder they said they'd now sold the kitten despite her reserving it. They even called her a time-waster. I was gutted. I'd made that little grey ball of fluff my phone wallpaper, as soon as Mum had sent me his photo. Now he'd never be mine. He's still there on my phone, peering out from between my apps and making me feel guilty. Adelina used to have a ginger cat back home in Gorki. She would like to get a cat here too. "But I travel sometimes, so it is not so easy." Perhaps in the future we can cat-sit for each other. She nodded, this is a possibility. "And Rube used to feed one – a street cat. But one night a car killed it."

"Ah you know Reuben?" Of course she does. After all they're both attractive people.

When her shoe was fit to walk on, Adelina went back upstairs and returned with a bottle of wine to thank me for the repair, despite the fact that hanging my paintings was, as I explained, payment in full. After checking her phone, she said she didn't have to go to work for nearly an hour, so I unpacked my wine glasses and we opened the bottle. After the second glass she took a little bag of white powder from her bag and suggested we shared it too.

"Not for me thanks. I'm asthmatic." I pointed to my inhaler.

"Maybe for you then it's not so good. But for me, it help me breathe." She said it with a faraway sadness in her pale blue eyes. I think Adelina may be homesick.

To cheer her up, I suggested a game of 'Hungry Hippos'. It's my favourite of my boxed games, although I only have one other. That is 'Guess Who', and the plastic flaps holding the characters are getting a bit brittle now, so the hippos were a safer bet. I tried to explain the rules. Usually I play it with Mum, on days when we've nothing much to say to each other.

"You shout gobble, gobble gobble."

"I shout what? You mean you hear me from down here?"

"No. Err God no. Err I don't know what you're talking about. It's just how you play the game see? You shout gobble and gobble up the balls. – Shit."

"Gobble the balls – ah that is so funny!" I let Adelina have my favourite hippo – the green one. This was very generous as I'm sure its neck stretches a bit further than any of the others. It gives it the advantage when it comes to scoffing marbles. We both gripped our hippos' levers tightly, ready to let battle commence. She turned out to be very competitive, fuelled by the plonk and the line of what I think was cocaine, which, while I was getting the board set up, she sniffed up her diamond-studded nose. I'm not sure living here's gonna be exactly like 'Friends' but somehow I think it'll be alright.

CHAPTER 3

"Smells like a whore's boudoir in here!" said Mum, sniffing like a bloodhound with sinusitis. "New air freshener is it?" She'd brought my washing round; tumble-dried and ironed, and a few bits and pieces I'd asked for from Wilkinson's. I got some flower seeds to grow in the window box below Mrs Webster's new web. I'd picked yellow and red Snap Dragons and something called Shoo Flies in the hopes they lure a few juicy bluebottles in for Mrs W.

"Ooh, cor..." Mum said admiringly, looking out the back window. This was something of a turn around. She usually shudders if she sees Mrs Webster and wants to knock her web down with a feather duster. As I pondered Mum's miraculous conversion to arachnid admirer, I noticed she was actually staring at something in the little garden below, despite the superstar spider doing her best to look all cute and cuddly. Mum was ogling Reuben, who happened to be doing press-ups on the paving below. The little square garden has a bench and a table and chairs, plus a string of coloured bulbs attached to the surrounding flint walls. "He's very fit, isn't he?" Indeed he is. On the TV, I've seen members of the SAS struggle to manage as many dips. "Muscles like that eh?"

"Yeah why don't you film him on your phone, Mum. Give you something to wank over later." Mum laughed her dirty laugh and sashayed over to the kitchenette. She'd thankfully remembered to bring refills for the biscuit tin. The malted milks looked suspiciously counterfeit though. As previously mentioned, only one cow on the biscuit isn't a promising sign. The border round the edge was also uneven in places. They should give me a TV show, a cross between 'Fake Or Fortune' and 'The Factory' where my skills as a biscuit connoisseur could be put to good use. Meanwhile Mum was wittering on about some couple Shaun knows from work. They own an eighth of a villa near Marbella she was saying, though this turned out to be a share in the property, not say just owning half the roof. The time-share duo had just had to cancel a holiday there as the man's kidney stone has him in "absolute agony". Instead Mum and Shaun will be jetting off to Marbs next week, well as long as they can find cheap enough flights at short notice. "What? Another fucking holiday! Deserting me again!"

"Oh Maisie don't start." Believe me, I had every reason to 'start'. Leaving me to fend for myself while she and the waste-of-space sun themselves is way beyond callous. She said she knows I'll cope "now you're on your feet again." My feet and the rest of me suddenly felt very tried indeed. I slumped into the sagging sofa. Mum was going on about how I've got my care team to meet all my daily needs. I couldn't even be arsed to tell her that it's now a team of one, visiting just once a day for a few minutes of eye rolling. I didn't mention it because I knew it wouldn't make no difference. Don't get me wrong, I'm not saying she's a bad mother or anything. I do know it's not fair to rely on her as much as I do. I'm thirty-one, not eleven after all. By now I should be looking after her and even given her grandkids. That's what's probably happened if parallel universes exist. It's bad enough that my sister has moved to Australia, and I suspect a lot of that is about not allowing me to become in any way dependent on her. Mia has never understood my eating problems. Why should she? For her Dad's death was still awful, but it didn't crash her world, like it crashed mine. For Mia life's still exciting, still an adventure, still almost as good as it was when he was here. For me it isn't. It never will be.

When Mum comes round to see me sometimes we have a right old laugh, playing board games, singing rude words to songs on the radio, or trying to fart a tune. Other times like today, she just stirs up feelings, whether about all the holidays I've missed out on, Dad dying, or being left alone to fend for myself. Today I just wished she'd go home.

"Have your carers been in this morning?" I nodded. "And they're coming back to make your dinner and help you with your shower later?" I nodded again, lying. She looked relieved at that, as she had to be getting back. Shaun had invited her to the pub on the corner to watch the football with him. Mum hates football. Dad never used to make her watch it, but she always makes this big pretence for Shaun. He's one of those men who like to wear a Brighton shirt whatever the occasion. It's probably his idea of formal attire. Even if an event was White Tie; Shaun would wear the bow tie over his favourite away kit shirt guaranteed.

****

As soon as Mum had gone I rang Masoud for a pizza. I wanted to show him the photos I've been taking as Mrs Webster has built her new web. I need his advice about whether to post them as they are or do a bit of photoshopping in terms of jazzing up the backgrounds. The phone was answered straight away, but it was Masoud's day off. Hadi's going to bring my pizza. Hadi is fine, but it's not like he'll stop and chat while I eat it. I mean I've never asked him to, but if I did he'd probably look at me like I was bonkers. We don't have that relationship. At least I've saved up a voucher for days like today. It lets me have a free dipping bar with my order. A dipping bar, in case you've not had one, has four little pots; two of saucy stuff, one spicy, one garlic, and two containing some crunchy bits of fried onion and peppers which you can dip your pizza slice into, once it's all coated in sauce.

'Kin 'ell! I've just noticed the bleeding voucher's out of date. I don't have enough cash to pay for the dips and Pizza On The Pier isn't accepting cards at the moment. Bollocks! Shit! Bollocks! ...Hang on, if I screw the voucher up a bit, hopefully Hadi won't notice the date on it. Having gone to all the trouble of bringing my dipping bar up here he wouldn't take it away again would he?

****

The Great Dipping Bar Con worked. Mum says I always look guilty if I'm doing anything wrong, but I reckon I've got a poker face to beat Lady Gaga's. The sun's shining and I'm tempted to walk down to the beach. I might just about make it, but if I slip over, or one of my knees gives way, once I'm on the ground I can't get up again. I'm as helpless as a tortoise on its back. If I had someone to come for a walk with me then that would be fine. I need to make some friends locally now I'm modestly mobile. There's a pub at the end of the road, but pubs rarely have anything I can sit on, and beer does tend to bring out the fat-hater in some people. On my own, I'm not sure it's a good idea.

****

Soon after I'd licked the last morsels from the dipping bar pots, I heard voices shouting outside. Nosy cow that I am I lifted the heavy curtain from the bay window to peer towards from the seafront. It was just two student-types joking around. One had a bike and purple hair. Typical Brighton. Then I noticed something had been written on the windowpane in front of me, by a finger dipped in the grimy condensation. It wasn't freshly done, the letters were old but the slightly greasy smear of their outline meant they remained readable. 'H E L P'. It was probably a joke. Probably meant nothing at all, but it made me feel a little uneasy all the same.

At the bottom of the stairs is a door opening onto the back garden. If all four flats in the house can access it then hopefully I'm allowed to use it. It probably tells me if this is the case in one of the documents in the folder with the electricity safety certificate – the one that doesn't explain you can short a circuit by switching on the light in the bog. If the garden is Reuben or the basement dweller's private patch and they want me to piss off then at least I'll know where I stand. I've taken my tablet down here with me to try to take a photo of Mrs Webster high on the window above. As it turns out my wi-fi still works down here, so I've been giving Abby a little tour. She thinks the space needs 'greening' and has recommended some guerrilla gardening websites. Gardening, I told her, unless it involves a window box, is a tad ambitious for me at the moment. She explained the guerrilla gardeners would come and do the gardening. They volunteer their services for both public spaces and private ones where the owner is housebound or disabled. They built a little waterfall in Abby's mum's garden so Abby can watch the birds bathing. She's always posting shots of blurred sparrows splashing water about. "That one's not a sparrow, Mais, it's a female chaffinch." The blurred grey smudge could have been Daffy Duck for all I could see of it. Masoud has tried to talk to her about shutter speeds and resolution but to no avail. If Masoud takes a shot of a pigeon bathing in a puddle, the water droplets will be frozen in mid-air, sparkling like a shattered chandelier.

****

Whoaaaa! What? I must have drowsed off in the sun, perched on the generously proportioned bench. Now I've jerked awake and there's a tall, skinny guy with blond dreads studying me from across the garden. He's now probably wondering what I'm onscreen typing, dear reader. A grey Staffie is taking a squat in the corner. She's not a dog that looks like her owner, having a neck like the Honey Monster and a barrel for a tummy. Meanwhile Blondie's on the phone, "Your first's not now 'til eight, so you've got time to do some shopping, have a splurge." The Staffie's showing the whites of her eyes and so would I be, if had a turd that long hanging in mid air from my butt. It seems to be taking forever to drop, coiling like a cobra towards the paving. Blondie has finished the first call now, and answered another, on a second phone. "No, no, no, man. Ain' happening blud." He's ended that call and the same phone is ringing again immediately. He answers, mentions a time, a number and place and rings off. I'm wondering if he usually sits here to make his calls rather than pacing like a cheetah, as he's doing now. Perhaps I should offer to move, but my swollen feet aren't willing.

****

When Blondie finally had a pause in his calls, he started to come over. I quickly switched the screen to my favourite TikTok of kittens playing, so he didn't realise he was featuring in my blog. "I'm Tom." He offered his hand. It had long fingers like E.T. There was something scrawled across the knuckles. The word was faded but it didn't look like 'LOVE or 'HATE'. Or even 'RIGHT', as it was his right hand. I wondered for a moment what I'd have tattooed across my own hands if I were ever to consider it. 'STOP STUFFING' and 'YOUR FACE'? I'm not sure that even one of my dinner plate sized mitts could manage that instruction. "EAT" and "LESS" would fit, but knowing me I'd just end up looking at the 'EAT' one and doing as it said.

As I'd brought my sugar-free toffee selection down to the garden, it seemed only polite to offer one to Tom. He took it and chewed slowly. For a young bloke he doesn't have many teeth. I don't know if that's down to fighting or a rogue dentist.

With a squeak of rusty hinges, Reuben opened one of the French doors that lead into his flat. "Rube, my man." Reuben looked towards the canine shit snake. His eyes narrowed. Tom quickly rummaged in the pocket of his skinniest of skinny jeans, pulling out a pile of Rizla papers that fluttered to the ground and finally a black poop bag. I laughed; I couldn't help myself. It was the tension of Reuben eyeballing him and the sudden appearance of the little poo sack, arriving with a flourish like a particularly under-whelming magic trick. Reuben grinned and plonked himself down beside me, as Tom cleared up after the dog.

"I'm more of a cat man, myself. At least they have the decency to shit in someone else's yard." I offered him a toffee for the sake of diplomacy, but he declined. Perhaps that's why he seems to have all his teeth. "Adi tells me you're an artist." He leant back on the seat. His boots were the kind motorcyclists often wear, with lots of buckles on them.

"Adelina from upstairs? I showed her some sketches. They're nothing special."

"She was impressed. And she went to art school. I'd like to see your pictures, if that's alright with you?"

"Well okay. I'm going back inside now, so I could get them?"

"No hurry. I'll come up a bit later." He walked over to Tom and dropped his voice, the way teachers do when talking to each other, so I couldn't earwig on their private conversation. The dog sneezed loudly making me jump. I don't know why I'm so tense around these people when they've been nothing but neighbourly. Am I right to be distrusting, or have the many hours I've spent watching 'Killer In My Village' made me paranoid? This is just normal life. This is Brighton, the sun is shining and my neighbours are not from hell.

****

Reuben's just come up. He handed me a mug of coffee and took my sketchpads before departing back downstairs. This coffee tastes amazing! It's definitely proper coffee. I've no idea if he made it with a machine, a percolator, or simply stirred granules into a cup, but it's a miracle whatever. There are lots of artisan coffee houses in Brighton, or 'Arty Sand' as Mum calls them. I used to pass one when I had Bessie my mobility scooter. The customers all looked a bit on the extreme side of hipster, so I never actually went in. Also there weren't any cakes on display, as far as I could see from the pavement. A towering cake plate or shelf of handmade bakery delights would've lured me straight inside, beardies or not.

I've taken another sip and truly I'm in heaven. But should I really be accepting beverages from strangers? Especially one who may or may not still have a gun in his possession? What if the coffee is drugged? I'm feeling slightly light-headed. A few crushed sleeping pills in my latte and it could well be burgle Sleeping Fatty time. I'm not going to drink any more of this. ...No damn it, I can't let it go to waste. That would be a crime in itself. The thing is I'm definitely feeling sleepy. What if the plan is to kidnap me and turn me into some kind of sex slave for perverts who are into larger women? One Internet advert and the chubby chasers would be queuing up. This is Brighton after all. Anything and everything happens here. Have you read the Evening Argus online? Fortunately my door's got more locks than Fort Knox and you're keeping watch, aren't you Mrs Webster?

****

I'm in the bathroom looking at my shocking pink nose and cheeks in the mirror. It appears I've caught the late autumn sun from sitting in the garden. It must be over a year since I last sat outdoors and I could never cope with warm weather. It's not just the prickly heat and rivers of sweat chafing my many nooks and crannies. I get headaches and feel sick if I sit outside without a hat for too long. I now realise my dizziness was caused by the sunshine, not a drug-laced coffee. It's kind of how I am with alcohol too. If it's been a while since I've had a beer or two, I forget it gives me wind and sets off my cystitis. And chips - chips are ace until you've eaten too many and then even the word 'chip' has you reaching for the vomit tub. The next day however, low and behold, your love of chips has been magically restored. Wish I knew how that works.

I'll wash up Reuben's cup and take it down to him, as I am rather keen to have my sketchpads returned now he's had a chance to have a gander at them. My drawings are part of me. I don't often post them on my Instagram, like I do my photos and the occasional homemade card, made with my stampers or stencils. They feel a bit too personal for that. I mean I'm not pretending to be a proper artist or anything. Apart from Reuben, the only other person I've shared them with in recent years is Abby. I sent her a drawing of a chicken once, in the actual post to make it special. It was when she first started knitting those jumpers for ex-battery hens. Abby loves chickens. She's still trying to persuade her mum to get some, a bit like me trying to get mine to buy me a kitten.

It was Dad who encouraged me to draw. He'd sit one of my toys up in front of us and we'd both try to draw it. "Look, really look. Look hard," he'd say. He'd sketch fast, with lines zigzagging in all directions and then he'd stop and you'd realise he'd caught it, the teddy or Hot Wheels car or whatever, he'd completely caught it in a maze of whirling lines. Me, I'd still be struggling, and reaching for the eraser. "Never rub anything out, Mais," he'd tell me, "mistakes are how you learn." To my mind, Dad was an artist, the best artist in the world. When I've flicked through art books there are a few famous paintings that remind me of Dad's drawing style. There's a hare by Durer, and a woodland by Van Gogh. By rights Dad's paintings should be hanging in a gallery. That's if many of them still exist. I keep asking Mum, but all she says is there might be one or two in the loft. She threw most of his things out when he died, and I wasn't thinking straight enough to stop her. Getting rid of his things might've helped Mum cope, but it's made it worse for me. Not everyone grieves in the same way do they? The few things I have left of Dad's or that remind me of him are my most precious possessions. Among them is a piece of card from a box of tea bags. We were on holiday at Mudeford and drawing shells. There's a long conical one that he's copied to the tiniest detail, shading it with grey and pink pencils. I often wonder where Dad and me got our urge to draw from. None of his family were artistic as far as I know.

Dad would've liked me to go to art college. He was a plumber, which is a skill in itself, but had to go out to work at sixteen to put food on the table as my granddad had suffered a stroke. I guess I should've at least applied to the college. The thing was though after being bullied at school, I was so glad to escape, I didn't feel able to face entering another place full of people my own age. It didn't help that girls who went to art school were all impossibly slim. Plus they had rainbow hair, faultlessly winged eye make-up and lip rings. They wore artfully torn clothes and leggings or the tightest of tight jeans. They were the kind of people who had been too cool and self-absorbed to pick on me, but for them I hadn't existed. In my school art class I can't remember even one of the soon-to-be art students glancing at my work, let alone speaking to me. If I'd looked like them, I might've have given art college a shot. The thought of me waddling up the steps or wrestling with an easel put me off. Now when I see some of what passes as art, I'm half glad I didn't go. Tracy Emin I'm looking at you. My old flat was a shit tip too, but I wouldn't make an exhibition of it. Mind you it wouldn't take much work to create a tent embroidered with the names of everyone I've ever slept with. Me I'd just be able to buy a tent from Mountain Warehouse and stick it straight up, with no sewing necessary.

****

When I knocked on his door, Reuben invited me in. He has a pool table and a full-sized bar crammed into the living room, which is still bigger than my entire flat. There's an old leather sofa and armchair, like something from one of those London clubs where posh blokes hide from their wives. He gestured to the sofa. I sat. It was miles more comfy than mine. There's a chrome desk with a computer and several phones and other gadgetry on top of it. On the wall, he has a framed film poster from something called 'The Night Of The Hunter'. There's a bloke on it in a black hat who looks a bit like an older version of Reuben. He has 'love' and 'hate' tattooed across his knuckles. I glanced at Reuben's knuckles at that point. He wears a silver ring on almost every finger but no tattoos on his hands. The flat smelt of the impressive coffee, though I didn't see the machine that creates it. The bookcase has a pile of glossy tattoo magazines on its top, and contains mostly art books. There are also guides to The Louvre and other galleries. He noticed me looking and said if I wanted to borrow any of the books I could. "Came from a skip up the road, along with the Ercol lamp." He gestured towards the angled light on his desk.

"So you've not been to The Louvre either?"

"I have been actually. And the Uffizi in Florence." He laughed, stretching out like a cat in the armchair. "Got the books for nothing and then paid an arm and a leg to see the real pictures."

"Do you paint?"

"Nah." He got up and headed into another room, possibly his bedroom, and returned with my sketchbooks. They were all opened on my attempts to make quick drawings of the pigeons that thronged round the café next-door's bins. That was at my old flat, the one over a closed down takeaway. The café would throw out its old pastries at the same time each day and me and the pigeons got to know when. It's also how I learnt the meaning of 'anticipation'. Before I became completely bed-bound I'd know to get down there around four pm and see if I could bag a few free cream cheese bagels, almond croissants or pain au chocolates before they went in the bin. In fact I'm sure I was a bit of a pain au something to the poor café owner. She always had a certain look on her face when on the dot of four, I'd rock up, eyeballing the last of that day's pastries. After I lost my mobility, no doubt in part due to the four o'clock ritual, all I could do was draw the pigeons as they enjoyed the delicious spoils that were now beyond my reach.

It was the pigeons in flight, taking off or landing that interested Reuben. He liked the moving wings and the way I'd drawn the feathers. I get the feeling he's a man who says what he means. There's no bullshit or bollocks. He genuinely likes my pictures.

"Maisie, are you busy tomorrow?" I think he already knew the answer to that one. "Only maybe we could go on an outing, you and me? You see, I'd like you to do some drawings for me. I'd pay you of course." I was gob smacked, but had to tell him that although I'd be free, I'm not much of a walker and can't currently use public transport or get in a car or cab. "How did you get here? If you don't mind me asking?" I explained about hospital transport having a specialised vehicle. Now I'm slightly more mobile again, there is also a community transport mini-bus I could manage, but I'd have to be the only passenger, as I hog all the space. Reuben was keen to ring and book this vehicle immediately, but I shook my head.

"It's not that simple. You have to book it weeks in advance, even for something like a doctor's appointment." He asked me for the number anyway.

"I might still give them a call if that's alright with you? See what they say, eh?"

****

When I went back upstairs, I decided to make a few sketches from the front window of the flat. There was a small flock of pigeons gathered in the square, pecking at both the remains of a packet sandwich and something that looked suspiciously like vomit. I drew the pigeons until they flew away and it started to get dark outside and then before I went to bed, I copied a Yellowhammer and a Kingfisher from one of my books. I've never seen either in real life, but who has these days?

This morning I've had breakfast from a can, cooked on the one ring of the cooker that gets hot enough for rice pudding. It's made such a mess of the pan though I wished I'd shoved it in the microwave instead. I'm only cooking properly to give Elaine a chance to tick a box on her 'enabling' form, and I don't really know why I'm bothering, when she's so bone fucking idle, but there it is.

Around lunchtime, Adelina tapped on my door. "Reuben says the bus will be here for you at two." How many times can a gob be smacked in one week? She was wearing jeans and a little cropped flying jacket with a furry collar. She had a case on wheels and matching handbag, both covered in logos from some French designer whose name I've forgotten. "Going on holiday?"

"No just come back. Work trip." She smiled, "and shopping." Her heels and case clickety clicked up the rest of the stairs.

****

Towelling my hair dry from the shower, I remembered I've a sachet that came free in one of mum's magazines. I usually rub the perfume samples on my wrists and they smell expensive for all of ten minutes, but this is a 'hair tamer' for those who experience uncontrollable frizz. Apparently it turns a bird's nest into curls. I rub it in, but on reflection I'm not sure whether there's any difference between frizz and curls, at least where my hair is concerned. It looks exactly the same as it did before it came in contact with the recommended hen's egg sized blob of gunk. Still the great thing about a free anything is when is turns out to be a reeking pile, you don't have to turn the place upside down for the receipt. The times I've given Mum some product to return, reminded her of where she bought it and insisted she takes no shit from them. Then back she's come, with an exchange item instead of the money. Honestly, if one of their stretchy thermal vests, tin openers or sweat stain removers didn't work, why would I want to try another?

My special occasions outfit came from a rather pricey high street store that caters for larger women, but I purchased it from Joey. Back in my old neighbourhood, if you wanted something you couldn't afford, you'd give Joey a bell, tell him how much you could afford and he'd go get something. When it was clothes, he'd insist he'd bought it from a charity shop, but I've seen his name in the court section of the paper too many times to believe that. Plus new clothes and charity shop items don't smell anything like the same. The outfit is a pair of black trousers and a long emerald green tunic. Now I've lost a little weight I can get into them both again.

When Joey first brought the top and trousers round for my

inspection the security tag was still on the tunic. I suspect he uses the old baking foil lined bag trick to stop the shop's alarms going off. I saw that on one of those police programmes. You'd have thought Joey would've been able to jack a tag remover too though wouldn't you? Don't get me wrong, I don't approve of shoplifting, I really don't. It's just that it's hard to get anything other than joggers and t-shirts in my size at an affordable price. Plus Joey has a little girl, and his wife's forever threatening to kick him out if he can't provide for them by selling stuff round the doors. Well that's what he's told me anyway.

****

The Community Transport vehicle pulled up outside at ten past two. These buses never arrive on time. I did wonder if I should wait for Reuben to escort me down, but it takes me so long to manage the stairs that in the end I didn't. I'd put my drawing things in my bag and they were light enough to manage. "All set?" the driver asked once I was safely onboard.

"Yes, but we're waiting for my neighbour."

"He's meeting you there." I realised then that I didn't even know where we were going. The driver wasn't one I recognised either, though it's been well over a year since I last used community transport. Before I could enquire about our destination, he'd put Radio Two on, very loud. That's unusual for a Community Transport driver, the loudness, not the station. Because I wanted to create a professional impression, I'd put the better one of my two coats on. That's the one without greasy cheese marks from eating pizza in bed when the heating failed at Mrs Latimer's. For two whole weeks I lived in that coat 24/7 and sadly it shows. I didn't realise it was dry clean only. I'd have sent it straight back if I'd known, even if it had come from Joey, which it didn't incidentally. What use is a dry clean only coat when life is so dirty? Anyway I wasn't wearing the greasy coat, I'd my wool one on, which is more sophisticated. It does however have the disadvantage of fake pockets; they're just a flap and nothing else. That meant I'd forgotten to bring my phone. I hadn't told anyone I was going out and if the mini-bus was only booked one way, I was going to be stranded at fuck knows where. When you've my issues, that's a problem believe me.

As we headed up through the shopping streets, I noticed many of the shops I used to visit on Bessie are gone, replaced by cafés, estate agents or inexplicably, eyebrow shapers. I mean why would anyone get his or her eyebrows shaped? Mind you, you do see some elaborately sculpted ones these days. Everything from the Fiona Bruce arch, to the very hairy caterpillar, to the painted black sperm.

On the radio they were playing 'Build Me Up Buttercup'. It's a song I know only too well from the hospital radio station. The evening DJ seemed to be a big Foundations fan. There's another one called something like 'Now That I've Found You' that used to crop up nearly every night. Helen The Snore used to sing to it and tended to continue with her own tone death rendition long after even The Foundations had tired of it. Made me almost long for her to start snoring. Almost but not quite.

We turned into Dyke Road. "Not going to The Devil's Dyke' are we?"

"Pardon?" He wasn't deaf, it was just 'Build Me Up Fuckercup' stopping him hearing me. Devil's Dyke is where Mia and me used to go kite flying with Dad. It's miles out of town and there've been a few murders there. If you were a sex trafficker kidnapping a larger lady to order, there's a car park made for transferring your hapless captive into a van. From there she'd be whisked away to a grubby little room somewhere, where she'd be forced to perform the kind of degrading acts that could only worsen her lumbago. Why did I forget my phone? Why did I wear my best sparkly emerald tunic? I even put my earrings in for fuck's sake.

The mini-bus pulled up, but we weren't at Devil's Dyke. We were somewhere halfway up Dyke Road. The driver got out and helped me disembark. We were outside The Booth Museum of Natural History. I remembered it from when I was a kid. It had terrified the life out of me when I was six. A memorable birthday treat it had certainly been, but for all the wrong reasons.

What had freaked out my mini-self were the hundreds of glass eyes staring at me accusingly, as if I was personally responsible for the mass slaughter on display. I dreamt about them for nights after and didn't eat chicken drumsticks again for at least a fortnight. Nowadays I can cope with a few stuffed birds – well actually there's a hell of a lot of stuffed birds. In fact there're so many it makes you marvel that there're still a few flying about in the world.

The driver had another transport to make, so left me to walk in. The museum was echoey and quiet. Fortunately it's free to visit, so I got straight on with revisiting the glass cases that are stacked from floor to ceiling. In the first row were some pretty impressive eagles and ospreys, arranged so it looked like they were about to soar into flight. There was some blurb about the collection's Victorian creator, explaining, how he'd shot pretty much anything that moved. The information seemed too bloody obvious though I almost expected to find him, blunderbuss in hand, posed in a cabinet among his victims. I mean if I'd been his wife that's what would've happened. I'd have caught him once too often slicing up a bittern on my kitchen surface, fed him a dodgy toadstool quiche, and stuffed him. I'd have quite liked to have been a Victorian poisoner. It's a shame in a way that it's fallen out of fashion as an occupation. A bird called a Crowned Crane stood uncased, its pale yellow eyes giving me a stare as if I was the thing on display. I found myself raising a finger – giving the bird the bird.

"The moral of this place seems to be that a wing can't protect you from a bullet." Reuben was behind me.

"It's like a temple to death."

"Or the worship of flight. That's why I thought we'd meet here. I want to get a tattoo of wings. Life-size wings on my back. Like a fallen angel." I stared at him. He wasn't joking. "Thought if you could do a few colour sketches, it might give me some inspiration. I've taken in some photos, but as yet I haven't come up with anything I've liked enough to have inked you know? Your pigeon drawings, they looked somehow real – alive. They had movement and light, and you could get a sense of their power from that." We were both reflected in a case containing a pair of barn owls.

"I saw on a wildlife programme that owls have fringes on their feathers so they fly silently. Would you hear an angel swoop down, do you think?" I was thinking aloud more than anything, but Reuben took the question seriously.

"Probably not. I can't imagine one making a racket like a swan taking off. Have you ever heard that?" I had. Dad had a friend who used to take us out on his boat up the river Adur at Shoreham. There were lots of 'no speeding' signs but Dad's mate used to rev it up full throttle. Poor swans, they'd take one look and kind of stampede into the air, little feet running across the top of the water as their huge wings struggled to lift them.

Reuben took a photo of the owls with his phone "in case you need it for your homework."

"Homework?"

"This is a job, Maisie. If I like it, you get paid, love it, you get more." A job! This would be my first job ever! It will be the first time I've earned money from anything, well apart from the trickle that comes in from Mrs Webster being an influencer and me flogging my few belongings on ebay last time my Personal Independence Payment was stopped. I've never been able to replace my alligator toothbrush holder or my Wade Whimsies.

The next cabinet contained a mallard duck that looked as though it had a green head, but when you looked from a different angle the colour turned to blue, mauve and pink, a bit like the neck feathers on a pigeon. "See the iridescence, Maisie? Could you capture that? I think an angel's wings might be like that... shining..."

"There's a painting by Durer." I'd seen it long ago in a book I'd borrowed from the school library loads of times, cos I loved it so much. "Not 'The Hare' which is his famous one, it's called 'Roller's Wing'." He took out his phone and typed the title in, then held up the image. I hadn't seen it for so long it almost made me well up. "Magnify it and you can see how the blues and greens alter down each feather." With his finger and thumb he enlarged the detail.

"Yeah, I'd like something like that, and maybe the creams and gold of the barn owl too." Ripping a page from my sketchbook, I offered him my box of pastels.

"Nah, I can't draw," Reuben protested.

"It's just to try out how the colour's mix. You can crayon thickly with two or three colours, then rub them into each other..." I used my fingers to show him. "It's a bit messy, but you can wash your hands after." He tried it, leaning against a wall, merging red into blue to create a purplish shade. He grinned, delighted.

"It's like being back in art class at school, only back then all I did was throw the clay at the ceiling." I nodded. They boys had done that at my school too, hoping when it dried out, it would drop off onto somebody's head.

"Can you draw me a sea eagle and an osprey – the one that looks like it's swooping down? And maybe the raven too?" I made a start, using a charcoal pencil.

"Would you like to fly away?" I don't really know why I said that. Just trying to get my head around the whole wing tattoo thing I suppose.

"If only it was that easy..." he said, giving me the impression there might well be something that he'd like to escape from. His mobile rang and he answered, snappily, as if annoyed our afternoon had been interrupted. "Yeah? Alright. On my way." He ended the call with an angry jab. "You might as well stay here and draw. The mini bus'll collect you when they close. If you get fed up with the birds, there are butterflies in the middle gallery." I promised to check out the insect section and returned to my sketching.

I must've spent hours drawing. Luckily there were seats in the butterfly gallery, or I'd probably have been dead in a glass case myself by closing time. Still, no aching feet or repetitive strain injury was going to stop me. I was gonna produce something amazing. I had to impress Reuben, cos I don't think I've ever really impressed anyone before.

For a few years, when I was younger, I'd hoped I'd manage to lose weight and be a famous slimmer- of-the-year, in a figure-skimming outfit and blonde highlights. Then I saw some photos of people who have slimmed down from my size, but they'd got left with loads of folds of skin. These trap sweat and get itchy and chapped, as if I didn't have enough of that stuff going on already. People have them surgically removed but I couldn't face that. I mean I was relieved to discover my asthma ruled me out for gastric band surgery. I've seen people on Youtube talking about how they were fully conscious on the operating table. For them it was no better than in those costume dramas where just as you're thinking you'd love to live in the past, they decide to saw somebody's leg off. As soon as they do that – and trust me they always do, just to show you it's olden times – you start to think thank fuck I live in the twenty first century. This is of course deliberate on the part of the TV programme makers, because it's what the government wants us to think. They couldn't cope if we all wanted to be Victorians or Romans or something. We'd all be riding about on horses, dancing or fighting with swords all day, and nothing useful would get done. That's why every historical programme has an amputation or two.

I was pretty pleased with my osprey drawing, and a couple of the others. I did the raven's wing in close up showing the feathering, and a couple of blue butterflies with tiny, mirrored scales on their wings. I was the last person to leave the museum and my driver had dozed off waiting. He didn't tell me off about it though, which is a first for community transport. On the way home I asked him if he could stop at the café on the corner, pop in and get me a cappuccino and a muffin. I was pushing my luck I know, and he did scowl a bit, but he went and did it all the same. I think I might be getting a taste for posh coffee, but as I've a job now, what the fuck eh?

CHAPTER 4

"Abbs, I'm fucking scared!"

"Are they still there?"

"I...I don't know."

"Call the police! Like now."

"Shhh!"

"I'm still whispering. Turn your volume down more."

"What?"

"What did you hear?"

"Eh?"

"You shushed me cos like you heard something?"

"Maybe. Gonna check the rest of the room."

"Be careful."

"I'll hold the phone out in front of me. Can you see round the door, Abbs?"

"No one there."

"Okay... Okay."

"Breathe, Mais. Breathe slowly."

"Okay."

"Can you still smell the smell?"

"Yeah."

"What's it like?"

"Sweet, slightly vom-making... Just a smell that wasn't here when I went out."

"Or you didn't notice it."

"It wasn't here! For definite!"

"But it's not like um damp, or something burning?"

"It's a person smell. Someone's definitely been in my flat."

"But you locked the door?"

"Course I did! But now there's a smell and my scarf's on the floor, like it's been trod on."

"Is there a footprint?"

"No. But my kitten cushion's upside down and I always leave it paws down."

"Someone else must have a key."

"– Oh my God! Oh fuck!"

"What? What's happened?"

"Fuck..."

"Maisie, you're scaring me..."

"The toilet seat is up! It's up, Abbs! ...There. Can you see?"

"The seat's up, but um like so what?"

"There's been a man in here! A man. While I've been at the museum!"

"Um it couldn't be someone from the housing association? They might have a key."

"No, no, they don't let themselves in unannounced. They're not allowed. Shit! Fuck! What's that! ... Oh it's someone coming in downstairs."

*****

Adelina was with two friends. I was really glad to see her. I mean Abby is great, but I was shitting myself, and needed actual, in the room, company, rather than someone on a screen. I'd tried to ring Mum, but her machine went to answer. Hopefully when she gets in and hears my shouty message, she'll get back and tell me what to do. Nothing like this ever happened at Mrs Latimer's. I mean it was a rancid dump and all, but I always felt safe there. Completely safe.

Adelina saw instantly how upset and breathy I was. She made me sit down. She didn't introduce her friends, but as we talked, I discovered they were Karla and Grace. Karla is probably in her late teens, thin with hollow eyes and a monotonous voice. She has an attitude – 'chippy' Mum would call it. Grace is maybe around the same age, and seemed very sleepy. Almost as soon as she sat down on the sofa, she nodded off, her head sagging right down onto her lap. Her long, lank fringe covered her face completely but I'm sure beneath it, her eyes were shut. Adelina said something about Grace having worked a nightshift and Karla sniggered like she knew something we didn't.

Right away Karla snatched up my kitten cushion, shouting, "My nana's got that exact one!" Lobbing it at me she asked "are you a fat cat lady too?"

"I think the phrase is mad cat lady."

"Mad cat lady. That's my nana. Mad *and* fat. When she makes you fish fingers they're always coated in fur. One of the cats is blind and all. No deaf. It's actually deaf."

"Poor cat," murmured Adelina, my fellow animal lover.

"Poor cat? Vicious bastard innit."

Whatever I said to Karla, she either repeated part of it back or sniggered, especially if it wasn't funny. She wasn't only like that with me though. When Adelina asked her if she liked the new charm on one of her bracelets, Karla said "No." Her eyes are hard, narrow and were glued up with false eyelashes that looked more obviously fake than Adelina's. She had at some point dyed her hair blue, but the brown roots are now very obvious. She probably thinks it's trendy, but to be honest it looks a bit skanky. Not that I'd say anything. There's nothing more fragile than a teenager's esteem, even one who appears to be part hyena.

"So who was it? This person who let 'emself into my flat?"

"Maybe John?" Adelina shrugged. I'd hoped for some advice, but instead got a glug of something throat burning from a flask in her bag. It was probably vodka, and by the way she laughed, as I asked about 'John', she and her friends were already a little bit pissed.

"So what was he like?" Karla sniggered. Grace didn't move.

"He was okay. Quiet but not when he was drinking. Then he was so crazy."

"How'd you mean crazy?"

"Oh you know, singing, shouting, throwing things out the window."

"Right... How old was he?"

"Old, old," said Karla.

"Maybe forty?" guessed Adelina. She didn't know what the weird new smell was, or whether it had any connection to him. Karla though seemed about to say something on the subject, before Adelina gave her a look.

"It's an odd smoky smell, but it's not cannabis is it?" Adelina took out a little snap bag of something dried and moss green for me to sniff. That ponged but it wasn't the smell in my room. Well not until Adelina rolled and lit a joint and started passing it around. That got rid of the first smell, but didn't exactly replace it with something better. Course I said no when the roll-up came my way, due to my asthma. Adelina wafted her own smoke away from me, wrist jangling with charm bracelets. Karla inhaled deeply and started coughing hard. When it was her turn, Grace let the joint drop through her fingers, before it had even reached her mouth. I had to bend and grab it before it burnt the rug. No one else noticed. At my request, Adelina went to open a window. "The front one, not the back. You gotta mind Mrs Webster. I don't want her getting squashed or stoned." The cold, fresh blast of evening air made me shiver and reach for my fleece. Adelina spotted someone across the street and started a shouty conversation, in something that might have been Russian, and didn't sound at all friendly. There were lots of hand gestures on her side, which seemed to be telling someone to fuck off, but that's only a guess.

At this point I realised Karla had wandered into my kitchenette. She had the fridge door open and was, for some reason, stacking the contents on the floor.

"Looking for anything in particular?"

"Uh, bread?"

"Bread bin, on top of the bench."

"Fresh is it?" She sniffed the half loaf suspiciously. I didn't answer. Bloody nerve. Since she'd helped herself without asking, it was a case of eater-beware. Karla went ahead and made herself a jam sandwich, like this was actually her flat rather than mine. She slathered the jam on thicker than cement on a brick and didn't think to ask anyone else if they wanted anything. "Young people today" Mum would've said, but I let her get on with it. To be honest, after the fright I'd just had, I'd have been happy for even a tiger to come to be tea.

I told Adelina, about the trip to the museum with Reuben.

"So it wasn't him?"

"Sorry? So what wasn't him?"

"Rube. He was not the man in your flat."

"Why would Reuben let himself into my flat?" She exhaled, remembering again to fan the smoke away from me.

"I don't know." It had recently crossed my mind that the trip to the museum might've been an excuse to get me out of here long enough for someone to rake about for whatever it was they'd been looking for. But Reuben's interest in the bird paintings had struck me as too genuine for this to be the case. Also, if there was something in my flat that he wanted, then surely he would've asked me. He doesn't strike me as a man who's backward in coming forward.

Among the few items of crap furniture and random kitchen utensils left by John, there don't seem much worth pinching. I could of course be wrong on that account. A blue sink tidy, or a mug with a not-so-witty sexist slogan might be the latest must-haves on ebay, but I doubt it. Also as far as I can see, none of my own stuff seems to be missing. Of course the person or people who were here could've been looking for something I hadn't noticed, and took that. Or maybe there was something they were hoping to find, but didn't. I hope it's not the last option, cos if so they'll be back.

"Urgh, dry," said Karla, fingering the crusts of her sarnie.

"Well thanks for your feedback, Masterchef," I said, giving her a taste of her own snarkiness. She snorted through a mouthful of crumbs in reply, something that might have been "fuck off", but as it wasn't clear enough to be sure, I charitably gave her the benefit of the doubt.

Grace woke, scratched her shoulder like a dog with fleas, and grunted something, but her eyes were still heavy and she didn't look up. She'd make a great double act with Helen The Snore. If any bed salesrooms out there need a couple of promotion women, you can get in touch via this blog. Mum's friend Patti works nights in Morrison's shelf stacking so perhaps that's the kind of work Grace does, if it ain't night shifts at the hotel that gets the odd mention from Adelina and Karla.

When the joint was finished, Adelina showed me some photos on her phone. They were all of her standing in various model poses in shop changing rooms, mostly taken through the mirrors. Often she had a shop assistant standing behind her holding another outfit, just, I suspected, to make her feel important. I'd probably do the same thing myself if I had loads to spend. The assistants didn't look very happy about being human clothes rails in Adelina's pictures, probably dreading being spotted by their friends on her Instagram or whatever. Adelina has been on this buying spree in Winchester where apparently there're loads of designer shops. She'd bought a dress by Chloe someone, in royal blue, but now wished she'd got the red one instead. She'd also had to buy a new handbag because for spring/summer next year the must-have shape has changed. Considering we're still a couple of months away from Christmas, I asked if she wasn't worried the fashion in bags might change again by the time we actually reached next year.

"It might. Who knows? But today I am ahead of fashion. I am making the style." Cue a hyena cackle from Karla.

"I think you are a little bit jealous, Karla." Karla 's own sportswear had seen better days, and she hadn't noticed the spilt jam from the sarnie down the front of her top.

"What? Jealous of your old, old man?"

"At least my old man does not leave me bruises." Karla fell silent at that. It sounds as though she has a violent boyfriend, and I thought Adelina as her friend should be privately advising her to ditch him rather than mentioning it in front of me. There's no point in making Karla feel worse about it than she already does.

Karla got up and I thought for a minute she was going to leave, but instead she headed to the kitchenette again, opening cupboards and peering inside. It was a bit of a cheek really, even if Adelina had upset her. In the days when I could still visit other people, I never rummaged in their drawers. You don't do that at anyone's apart from your mum's do you? Instead of moaning though, I told her to stick the kettle on, which she did.

"You not got any foil, Mais?" It sounded funny, Karla using

my name like we knew each other well. I wonder if Adelina has mentioned us playing Hungry Hippos. I hope she enjoyed the game as much as I did. I'm not sure I'd want to play it with Karla though, as I get the feeling she'd be a bad loser, and Grace, well she's the dormouse from that 'Alice In Wonderland' film, basically. I told Karla I didn't have any tin foil, apart from the little bit wrapping a block of Red Leicester Mum had shared with me. As soon as I'd said that, Karla opened the fridge again, took out the cheese, unwrapped it and pocketed the foil. Then she came and sat down again as if unwrapping someone else's cheese and leaving it on their work surface is a completely normal thing to do. When I was at primary school we collected foil for retired greyhounds – raising money, not giving the dogs the silver paper, obviously. I confess I did go a bit mad, even unwrapping toffees and adding that to my ball of the shiny stuff to make sure it was the biggest, but this was something else. If it had been a whole roll of foil I'd have suspected she was making a shoplifting bag like Joey's, but it was only a small square. I got up and made the tea, as Karla clearly wasn't going to do it. Adelina and me were the only ones who drank ours. Karla looked at hers as if I'd offered her a mug of piss and Grace didn't even notice she had been supplied with a beverage.

By this time, it was dark outside, and I was still in desperate need of sensible advice on dealing with the home invasion. By now the housing association office would be shut. Even if it hadn't been however, I could hardly call out someone from there or indeed inform the police, now my flat reeked of marijuana. My chest was tightening from the smoke, despite the open window, and I took a couple of quick puffs from my inhaler. When I looked round, Karla was flicking her lighter, trying to set light to Grace's fringe. Worryingly, Grace's hair looked greasy enough to sizzle like fish shop chips.

"Pack it in!" I hollered, and Karla stopped, sulkily shoving the lighter back in her pocket. I looked across at Adelina, hoping she would say something, but she had a far away look in her eyes. I hate bullying and cruelty. I've suffered enough of it not to let something like the hair burning go unchecked. If Karla hadn't stopped, I would've stepped in and stopped her. It's a long time since I got in any kind of physical fight, but I think my size might be enough to make anyone think twice.

I gave a few hints then about needing to get on and make my dinner etc, but Adelina had made herself comfortable and Karla was not one to take or maybe even understand subtle hints. "So when's your party, Maisie?" Adelina purred. I'd actually forgotten I'd invited her. Now I'd have to let the other two come along too, despite their less than perfect behaviour. It was going to be a snug fit with Masoud and Hadi from the pizza place, Donal, the hospital driver, Donal's wife, Reuben, maybe Tom and these three, plus Abby on my laptop and Davy or Paige taking turns on my tablet screen.

"Saturday night." I decided there and then. It would give me time to make and send invitations – posted under the doors of those in the building, scanned and emailed to everyone else. Mum and Shaun would be away by then, but since Mum was deserting me for Marbella, I didn't feel exactly guilty at making her miss out.

"We'll bring balloons!" offered Adelina, becoming animated again. "Lots of balloons eh?" Karla mimed blowing one up. This did seem like a good idea and Adelina could help me climb up and decorate the flat beforehand if she's time. I suggested we hang a flat warming banner up too. This idea was met with a snigger from Karla, but I'm sure it's normal to have banners at flat warning parties. I could swear I've seen them for sale in 'Clintons'. "If we push back the furniture we could dance." Adelina got up and demonstrated some moves I've definitely seen on 'Strictly'. A rumba? Samba? It was slinky and even without music had a rhythm to it.

"Are you inviting any men?" said Adelina.

"Cha cha cha" added Karla, for no good reason.

"Yes, some you know. Some you don't."

"Ah, we know some nice guys too."

"We need to be careful about numbers, Adelina. It's not the biggest of flats."

At that moment Grace jerked awake and stared at me, eyes wild with fear. "No! No please. No, no please.... Give me... give me..." She shut her mouth abruptly and her head fell forward again.

"Is she okay?" The other two barely glanced in her direction.

"Look, maybe you could take her outside or something? For a bit of fresh air?" As nobody seemed to have any intention of moving, I hauled myself to my feet and took out my phone. "Ah, oh dear, I've just received a text from my care team. They're on their way round now to help me get ready for bed," I lied.

That finally did the trick and Adelina picked up her handbag and made to leave and Karla got up to follow. She yanked Grace's arm and she stood and walked or sleepwalked to the door. On the landing Adelina stopped, and for no reason I can think of, gave me a little hug, touching her cool cheek against mine. The affection of it took me by surprise.

"Goodnight, Maisie."

I phoned Mum the moment they'd gone. My heart sunk when Shaun answered. He said she'd already gone to bed. I looked at the clock. It was that late. Then Mum picked up the cordless receiver on the bedside table. The phone rings in the bedroom too, so it would've woken her up. I said I was sorry to wake her, and she said she wasn't even in bed yet. It had been Shaun trying to make me feel guilty. That's one of the reasons he gets on my nerves so much. Anyway, I told her all about the person being in my flat while I was out and she agreed with me that it was extremely worrying. Oddly, she didn't sound surprised to hear I'd been out or ask where I'd been. I'd have thought she'd have taken more of an interest, but she was probably too wrapped up in her holiday plans.

Mum insisted I change the lock. It would be quicker she thought for me to call someone myself in the morning, rather than wait around for the housing association to put it on their 'repair list'. "Patti did that with her leaky water pipe and had mushrooms on her ceiling before it was fixed!" Mum called to Shaun to fetch her address book. There was a locksmith in there who she insisted was 'very reasonable'. She meant in terms of money, not that he always saw both sides of an argument. Over the phone I could hear her turning the pages. Mum tends to ignore the fact that an address book is alphabetical. Either that or she files people in her own way – so the locksmith might be under 'l' for locksmith, or his firm's name, his surname, his dog's middle name or whatever. Finally the pages stopped turning and I heard her sigh heavily.

"Mr Morton. Nice man, but I remember now, he passed away back in June." I don't remember Mum ever using this locksmith, but she sounded genuinely upset by his demise. "He cut keys and re-heeled shoes too," she added almost wistfully. I didn't really need to hear the entire life story of the late lamented Mr Morton. I was still trying to air my flat of dope smoke before I went to bed. Fuck knows what kind of dreams I'd have if that fug was still hanging about. I told Mum not to worry. I'd find a still living locksmith on the internet.

"You be careful with The Online!" she warned. I explained I'd choose someone with loads of good reviews and the top star rating.

"It'll be fine, Mum." Before I went to bed, I made sure all of John's multitude of bolts were slid across the front door.

****

'Lady locksmith. Half hour response. No call out charge. All locks supplied and fitted.' She even has a free to call phone number. I'll make that call right away. The sooner that lock is changed the safer I'll feel.

****

In the kitchenette I retrieved the now sweaty foil-less cheese and reluctantly binned it.

That's when I noticed it. There'd been two rusty biscuit tins on top of the kitchen cupboards, too high for me to reach. Now they were stacked in the store cupboard sitting alongside my cornflakes and teabags. I opened them up but both were empty of anything but rust. The mystery had deepened.

*****

The female locksmith took exactly thirty-seven minutes to arrive, but who am I to quibble? I was relieved that she thought I was being sensible rather than paranoid. She said she'd change the door's main lock right away for one she had in the van. I could then keep one key myself, give one to my current carer and one to Mum. At the old place I used to leave a key under a plastic frog outside when I became bed-bound, but being able to answer my own door means here, thankfully, I can be more security conscious.

The locksmith's name was Belle and she had teamed a biker jacket with a pixie crop that made me think of Tinkerbelle from Peter Pan. She declined a cup of tea and immediately set to work. I was fascinated by the pieces of the old lock when it had been taken out of the door. She showed me how the key made the little gears of the mechanism work. It was all reassuringly old school. Proper locks haven't changed much since the middle ages she said. Those awful electronic ones where you have to swipe a card or remember a pass code are no substitute.

I used to have this card thing that enabled me to use a disabled toilet at the community hall where I attended a dieting club. I used to spend most of the time swiping the card up and down the ruddy card reader on the door, while crossing my legs and trying not to think of anything involving water. It was one of the things that stopped me going to the weight losing sessions eventually. That and the fact that the hall where it was held was on a hill and Bessie my disability scooter burnt her motor out twice getting me up there.

I'd like to be a locksmith. When I've lost a little more weight and got a bit more mobility back, perhaps I can teach myself from Youtube tutorials. It's a thought isn't it? Having a trade that could earn me a decent living would motivate me to keep improving my fitness. I'd definitely rather work for myself than have a boss and colleagues. For anyone who's been bullied, self-employment is an attractive option.

Changing a lock isn't a quiet job unfortunately. It seemed to involve a lot of banging, chiselling and prising. After a couple of minutes, Reuben's door opened and he glowered up the stairs at us.

"Lovely smell of filter coffee," cooed Belle.

"Is that a not so subtle hint you'd like one?"

"You know me only too well, Rube." I went cold, realising I'd hired a locksmith who's on first name terms with someone who might have been involved in my home invasion. Shit! I've wasted my money and my place is no safer than before.

Reuben brought us both coffees on a tray, with a little bowl with lumps of brown and white sugar. "Ooh, lovely. He don't half make a nice coffee."

"I know."

"Lock break?" Reuben asked me.

"Yeah, yeah it did." I didn't look at him or Belle as I lied. Seemingly satisfied, he headed back downstairs. "So do you know Reuben well?" I asked Belle, when his door had closed behind him.

"Well I've done a few jobs for him."

"Locksmith jobs?"

"Locksmith jobs" she repeated mechanically. I could've said something like "small world" but I didn't really see the point.

CHAPTER 5

I spent half the night on my artwork. I didn't notice the time passing as I drew and shaded feathers, and tried out various wing shapes. I used the sketches I'd made at the Booth Museum as a starting point, then started to search out images of angels online. 'The Toilet Of Venus' by Velazquez features a cherub with what looks like actual birds' wings on his back. They're realistic as wings, but look like they're super-glued on. I'm trying to draw angel wings that you can believe in. They need to be large, strong and looking like they'd fix to the muscles of a human body. Caravaggio's 'Victorious Cupid' is a good example to work from. The feathers are detailed, but not too perfect and you can almost feel the long ones that bend and brush the figure's leg. When I first saw that painting I thought it was painted from a photo, but there weren't cameras in 1602. I didn't know my old friend Durer had painted an angel too, but I googled it and he had, getting the shape of the tips of the red and blue wings exactly right. It's funny though how some of the best-drawn angels have the worst wings and some of the most believable wings are on the least realistic angels. I started to wish I'd been able to get an art book from the library rather than doing my research online, because a book has a final page – an actual end. With the internet you can just keep searching and searching, instead of grafting. Eventually, I had to force myself to let the screen dim, and pick up my pencils, or I'd still be gawking at angels.

The door buzzer buzzed at nine am. Now I don't do early mornings, and if that's not early for you I apologise, but after the hours I'd spent drawing, it's still virtually last night for me. I growled something into the intercom; to be told I need to sign for delivery of a crackle, burrrrr, crackle.

"It's a what?" The man, though I didn't even know at that point it was a man, repeated that I needed to sign for the something or other. I hesitated as I wasn't sure I really wanted to be seen in my brushed-cotton teddy bear jammies. Also, since I haven't yet ordered anything since I moved here, I wasn't entirely convinced the delivery was for me. The suspense got to me though. Fuck it; I wanted to know what had just turned up.

When I got to the bottom of the stairs, the man had got bored of waiting and pissed off. Typical. I looked around but there was no parcel either. The front door was still open, welcoming in a chilly sea breeze, which made me suddenly grateful for the brushed cotton, if not the grinning rows of navy blue teds.

A removal type van was parked outside and a man in a high visibility jacket was wheeling a mobility scooter down its ramp. It was a beauty, with metallic red paintwork, four wheels for extra stability and a roomy basket on the front. This was my delivery – a far better surprise than any parcel.

The booklet telling me everything I needed to know was, the man said, in the front basket. He was from a charity that supplies reconditioned mobility vehicles. My social wonder had worked her magic once again. Close up I couldn't help but notice a few scratches on the paintwork, and when I thumbed the instruction manual, page two had been ripped out. Still all the important information was on page one, and most of it was in English. The vehicle should withstand my weight, well almost at any rate, and its top speed, though possibly with a lighter jockey, is twenty-five miles an hour.

As I signed a squiggly signature with a stylus on the man's signing-gadget, I wondered aloud what I should call her. Mobility vehicles, like ships, tanks and interplanetary cruisers are always a 'she'. In these gender-neutral times, I'm not sure why, but there you are. I suppose I could break with convention and sit with my thighs astride a male, but while I was pondering the pros and cons of that, the delivery man said, "Delores. You could call her Delores. After my wife's granny." So Delores she is.

There's no way I can get my trusty steed up the stairs to my flat, and I'm not having her left to rust in the back yard, so I've parked her in the recess beneath the stairs. There was only a cobwebby bicycle and an old Henry vacuum cleaner with paint or pigeon spatter on his hat, already in the alcove, so I can't see anyone objecting. I just wish there was something I could lock her onto. I mean I could attach her to the bike or Henry, but a lot of good that'll do if one of my housemates decides to flog her to the scrap man, or ebays her. In case of accidental misunderstandings, I've left a note on her seat. 'Maisie's – please leave.'

I went back upstairs and looked over last night's artwork. I was reasonably pleased with three of my attempts at wings, all designed to look as if they are in some way folded behind a human back. These all look big enough for a man to get airborne with, but my God they'd involve a serious lot of tattooing. I know I should've knocked on Reuben's door to show him my paintings, but I lost my nerve at the last minute. Suppose he hates them? Luckily I'd put the pictures in a thin plastic file and instead I slid that under his door. At least this way if he doesn't like them, it'll be slightly less awkward. We can never mention it again. I wouldn't expect to be paid if the customer wasn't entirely satisfied.

Looking again at Delores, stabled cosily in the alcove, I started feeling excited about the day's possibilities. Normally I'd ring Mum to see if she'd like to come for a walk, but I've not forgiven her over the holiday. I'd feel more confident onboard Delores for the first time if someone was with me though. With that in mind, I heaved myself up to the top of the stairs and knocked on the attic room door. There was no answer from Adelina, so there was nothing for it, I'd have to incur some serious data charges on my phone and take Abbs with me.

Abby was keen on the idea of an outing. She loves any opportunity to escape from her four walls. I've a small beanbag neck cushion that you're meant to microwave and use like a hot water bottle. Uncooked, it sits cosily in the basket on the front of Delores, holding my phone upright. Now Abby just needed to decide if she wanted to face me, or the view. The view won over my ugly mug, no contest. She begged me not to drive too fast, as she'd find taking it all in via her home computer screen a sensory overload. I also knew from the virtual tour of my flat that stability could be an issue. If the scooter wobbled, I'd make my bestie seasick.

In the event, the ride down to the prom was a smooth one, despite Dolores wanting to now and again veer wildly to the right. In the event I somehow managed to keep her on the pavement. Although not exactly balmy on the seafront, the sun was out and the nearest kiosk selling teas and ice creams was open. I'd wrapped up in my cheese stained coat and a jumper and was by then feeling a little too toasty, so a soft cone was the ideal remedy. Abby's mum got her a choc-ice from their freezer, so we sat there together, looking at the sea and eating them. Handily, the kiosk had customer wi-fi, so I was able to switch from burning up all of my data, to hanging out with Abby for free. Bliss.

Abby has a book she uses to identify the birds in her garden and using the seagull section she was able to tell me that I had both a Lesser Black Backed Gull and a Herring Gull eyeing up my cornet. When a third gull made a fiendishly daring aerial swoop, I managed to bat it away with the other hand, calling it a few choice names in the process. Abby insisted the bird was only following its natural instincts, but natural my arse, I'm sure the feathered thieves evolved long before ice creams. I suggested the gull might like to remember the old ways of its kind, and eat a flipping fish instead. Mind you, a bit later I did see a gull, possibly the same one; grab a mouthful of cod from someone's fish and chips as they walked along the prom, so perhaps it had heeded my advice.

It was nearly a year since I'd been able to take myself anywhere, and it made me feel more optimistic about the way my life's going. I no longer cared about Mum being about to jet off to Spain. I had a much quieter beach here almost to myself, plus a reasonably priced ice cream, and good company too, in the form of onscreen Abbs. I didn't envy the passing joggers, slaves to their Fitbits, or the dog walkers with their bulging shit bags swinging in the breeze. I was happy to sit there in the sunshine and simply gawk at the kids on scooters, students on skateboards and spice-addicted zombies passing by. If Abby saw a particular gull she'd like to Instagram, I took the photo for her. When I'd finished my icey I got out my pencil and pad and made a few quick sketches in case Reuben ever felt the need for a seagull tattoo. I don't even know if he's an Albion fan or not.

A homeless guy, skinny as a macrobiotic whippet, asked me for change, but I have to budget far too carefully to be charitable. Abby offered to google the nearest soup kitchen for him and he nearly jumped out of his skin when he heard her voice, having clearly assumed I was sitting there all on my own-some chatting to myself. When he spotted her onscreen presence I worried for a moment that he might steal my phone, but it's an old battered thing covered in glitter and stickers. It probably wouldn't raise much dosh at 'Stolen Gear Exchange'. Instead he smiled toothlessly and waved a grubby hand and she waved back.

"You have a nice day, Sweetness."

"You too." When he'd gone, Abby said she couldn't remember when she'd last met a new person face to face, outside in the real world. I know it was actually more face to screen but I'm not one to quibble. I decided to try and find her someone else to have a virtual natter with.

An elderly woman came into the café area and sat alone with a cup of tea, so I drove over, and struck up a conversation about the weather. Not the most original opener granted, but I'm not really sure what her age group are into these days. Since Max Bygraves kicked the bucket it could be anything. All I know is that you never under any circumstances mention Brexit. The woman's name was Muriel and she regularly Skypes her son who lives in Stirling, so Abby being an onscreen acquaintance didn't faze her. She was delighted to talk to both of us. It turned out that Muriel's a regular on the 'chatty bus' – a special bus service where passengers are encouraged to talk to each other. Apparently several octogenarian men had used the opportunity to try to pick her up, but as she insisted quite firmly, she's "all done with men." Conversation turned to our favourite presenters on the crafting channel, and the card-making techniques we'd all tried and failed at. Quilling in my case, 'tea bags' in Muriel's. We talked stampers, die-cuts and glue dots until it started we getting a bit chilly – well me and Muriel at any rate, Abby, obviously not so much.

As I was out and about I decided to motor on along the prom to the pier, which apart from a psycho three-year-old on a shocking pink scooter attempting a dangerous overtaking manoeuvre on my left hand side, was uneventful. I even risked driving up onto the wooden deck, to pay a surprise visit to Pizza On The Pier. Masoud was shocked to see me, but in a good way of course. He came out from behind the counter and folded up the seats so I could park. Hadi had just returned with a margarita that couldn't be delivered, to an address that didn't seem to exist. The guys offered to re-warm it for me and add the toppings of my choice, all for free, being as I'd actually managed to visit them for the first time ever. With peppers, pineapple and chorizo pieces cascading over a sea of melted cheese, I was in seventh heaven. Even when I'd finished it, I still savoured the aromas of the freshly cooking pizzas as customers came and went with their takeaways. Masoud sang along to the radio, and if there was a rap or hip hop number he and Hadi prowled around doing all the 'gangsta' hand gestures and bendy leg strutting, while trying to avoid bumping into each other on the narrow strip of floor between the counter and the ovens. Masoud added lots of 'yeah, yeah, uh' and the occasional 'Yo!' to the songs, even where, strictly speaking, they didn't require it. If I could've permanently rented a spot there in the corner of Pizza On The Pier, listening to Masoud singing and watching Hadi balance a stack of boxes on one hand, while doing a badd-ass swagger walk, I'd honestly still be sitting there now. After a while, a Chinese guy came in, wanting some change, and it turned out that he runs a fish and chip shop nearby. He tried to offer me a business card, before Masoud chased him outside with the broom.

"Don't you dare try to steal our favourite customer!" They were both larking about of course, but it's still nice to be valued.

My only criticism of Masoud's establishment, of which I'd heard so much, was the walls are rather bare, apart from a few faded laminated photos of pizzas. I asked him why he didn't display some of his photos there. He shrugged and said he wasn't sure company policy allowed it. "Oh come on, who's to know?"

"The area manager visits sometimes." By the way he pursed his lips when mentioning this person, I gained the impression Masoud wasn't too impressed. I told him how I was now working as an artist, and he said that maybe we should hold a joint exhibition somewhere. Now I'm able to get out and about I might start asking around. Perhaps the library or one of the arty looking cafés could offer us a space to hang a few pictures. Masoud showed me the latest photos on his camera. There was one of three aliens – proper little green men with angular black eyes, sitting side by side at a bus stop in Churchill Square.

"Aliens!"

"I know. Maybe people from a Comic Con or something. You'll like the next one.

"Not sure how you're going to top three aliens unless the Loch Ness Monster drops by or something." He showed me the next photo. An elderly man with a white beard had arrived at the bus stop, and was staring with bug-eyed surprise at the green men. It looked like Father Christmas meets 'Starship Troopers'. In the one after, a woman on the opposite side of the street was gawking across at the space people, while colliding with a hipster carrying a coffee cup.

"If I send them through to you, will you put them up on the site and try to get some interest?"

"As soon as I'm home. Trust me, Masoud, if you don't sell one of these I'm Kim Kardashian."

Masoud and Hadi's party invitations were the only ones I had so far got around to making. Delivering them in person was my real reason for dropping by. I thought the guys would be thrilled to come to my party, but Masoud looked a little unsure and said it was on their busiest night of the week.

"Then I'll just have to order the pizza during the party rather than before. Twice during the party so you both can take it in turns and come." I decided to make up a few VIP goodie bags for those who could only pop in to take away with them. Now I just need to find out what a posh goodie bag contains and then see how much of that stuff you can actually get at the pound shop.

It was starting to get dark outside, and I wanted to get home before the streets became a bit challenging, if you know what I mean. It's too easy to mug a mobility scooter rider and I can't risk Delores being hijacked. The person or persons who threw Bessie into the Marina are, after all, probably still at large.

I was at the bottom of my street when the soddin' engine cut out. By now I was stiff and aching from Delores attempting inappropriate right turns all the way home. Having to get off and push her towards my front door was something of a tall order. I tried, but she is so much heavier than Bessie. She just wouldn't budge. The cold night air was starting to make me breathy and light headed. I could've done with one of my neighbours coming by and giving Delores a push for me. No one seemed to be about however and I didn't have a number for any of my housemates. The only number in my phone that looked like being any use at all was Mum's. I really didn't want to call her, but there was no other way.

Shaun arrived, moaning that there was nowhere to park around here that didn't cost an arm and a leg. Eventually he decided to risk leaving his car in a meter bay where he could at least see if a traffic warden was approaching. Huffing and puffing he managed to get Delores up the slight hill and into my hall. I reluctantly offered to make him a cuppa but he shrugged off my thanks.

"You need to start managing your own life, Mais. You can't keep on calling us every time some little thing goes wrong. What'll you do when we're not around to sort you out eh? We won't be here forever you know." This was a bit rich as I'd actually rang Mum rather than him. He'd answered her mobile, which considering it's her personal phone, I think is a bit iffy. Isn't it frankly a bit controlling, like reading someone else's diary or emails? Anyway, Mum doesn't mind helping me because we're family, and she knows Dad would've done anything for me. Shaun's not a relation and clearly doesn't want to be. He's just a guy who likes his washing done and his dinners cooked. I'm sure he'd prefer it if Mum wasn't a widow with daughters. He always has a grumble about what she spends on us at Christmas and birthdays, simply because he'd rather the money was spent on him. Yet he's got a half-decent job and now he's about to head off on a luxury holiday. He could certainly afford to be a little bit more generous to those of us who didn't ask for him to invade their family.

I'm glad Shaun and Mum aren't coming to my party. It'll be a lot more fun without them. I'm getting on well with the planning now. Delores might be out of action for a while though. Getting repairs done to a disability scooter is a tricky process. It's not like you can just walk into your local garage. Most of them won't touch them like a barge pole for some reason. It also usually involves ordering specialist parts and they don't come cheap. I don't know how I'm gonna afford it.

Luckily though I've found a cheap site online that sells cheap party goods and promises speedy delivery. I should have everything I need by Friday. I wonder how you get a job as a party planner? It might be something I could do from home to earn a few pennies. I know most of the pitfalls, like don't get a chocolate fountain if you've got nylon carpets. Also nobody really likes fondue. Themes and fancy dress can put a lot of people off. Your friends are your guests after all, you shouldn't ask them to bring anything but themselves, and maybe a little something edible or drinkable.

Later, as I was multi-tasking; emailing the social wonder about Delores' breakdown and watching a wildlife programme about seals, someone started murdering my doorbell. I heaved myself up to answer the intercom and couldn't make head nor tail of what the caller was saying, apart from "emergency". I thought he'd probably have been let in by someone else in the building by the time I had negotiated the stairs, but no, as I peered around the door chain, he was still there. He said he was looking for Reuben or Tom, neither of whom was answering their phones or doorbells. He had only tried buzzing 'John' as it was an emergency. He was young, fifteen or sixteen probably, with a bit of acne, neatly gelled hair, dressed in black jeans, designer trainers and puffer jacket. Readers and followers, I decided to let him in.

It's alright Shaun moaning about me relying on him and Mum, but actually I've been doing a pretty good job of looking after myself, and I'm always willing and able to help anyone in distress. The teenager gratefully accepted a cuppa and rather shakily lit a cigarette, which he thoughtfully smoked out of the front window. He wouldn't tell me what was wrong, but whatever it was it was serious. He needed Reuben to "sort it" but seemed rather nervous about what his reaction would be when he heard about it. He kept trying both Reuben and Tom's phones, with no success. From the messages he was leaving, I learnt his name was Avery. Presumably that's how you spell it rather than Aviary, which is what we used to keep our budgies in. I asked if he knew Adelina upstairs, but he assured me he'd just rung all the buzzers, so I wasn't entirely sure if that was a yes or a no. When I enquired, with some concern, if his situation was a medical emergency, he gaze me a look that said yes, but simply muttered something that sounded like "not yet". He didn't seem threatening in any way. Just scared.

At least here was someone who might shed some light on the mystery that was 'John'.

"You didn't know John had moved out?"

"Has he now? Yeah, if you're here now, I suppose he must have."

"What was he like?"

"Alright." On cop dramas, people always say interesting stuff in interviews don't they? Maybe they're better at asking the right questions. I tried again.

"Did you used to visit John?"

"Maybe. Sometimes."

"So you knew him well then?"

"Not 'well' well. I mean I don't know nothing about him. He liked a drink. And there was always a party happening innit. Think the council put him in this place, or the socials."

"Put him here?"

"Gave him this flat. That's right..." He nodded, remembering.

"When his Mum died and he need somewheres."

To distract Avery from his troubles I told him about Mrs Webster, who was just visible, tucked up under the back window ledge. "Have you ever thought about getting a proper one? Like a tarantula or something?"

"That's an idea. I've never really thought about that. I do like spiders, though what I'd really like is a cat."

"A tarantula is way, way cooler. There's this one on Insta called GrimMonster – you should check him out." I told him about Mrs Webster's career as an influencer and showed him her site. He was rather impressed by all her followers and likes. Pleasingly he hadn't heard of Tracey and George, Mrs Webster's two closest rivals in the popularity stakes, though when he showed me GrimMonster's profile and pics, I had to admit that though a relative newcomer, being shot in a graffiti-covered crate, furnished like some drill rapper's 'crib' was going to make him a contender. In one photo he had his furry legs inside a human knuckle-duster, and in another he was lazily dangling a furry limb in his own swimming pool. We both had a snigger when we found he lived not in downtown Compton or New Jersey but Reigate.

Avery's phone lit up. "Tom my man, all my days! Things have gone mental! He just came round, yeah, in a merc, with these other two dudes. Yeah, yeah, I know that, but I was panicking blud. For real. The size of the shank, and he was chopping at the door. It's the war – it's started. I thought I was done. Seriously. Yeah? What's he say? Is he? Okay? Okay. Stay away? Yeah, yeah no worries. No way I'd go back there now after that. I thought I'd go and stay with me dad in Littlehampton. Lie low yeah? I'll need some cheds though. Thanks, man. Station. Hove? Yeah will do." I couldn't write down his actual words as he was speaking so quickly, and he was using that kind of street accent that even posh kids all put on when they're speaking to someone who isn't old and not remotely 'down' with them. He hadn't used all that 'Yo, blud' type stuff with me, but as soon as he was on the blower with Tom, he was speaking his best middle-class gangster.

Avery ended the call and prepared to leave. By now I had an inkling what had happened. This teenager had obviously got into some trouble with a gang, maybe over being in the wrong place, or perhaps it was a cannabis debt or something. He was lucky not to have been stabbed by the sound of it. It was fortunate the gang hadn't followed him to this address either. He said he'd lost them in Brunswick Street West, which is near, but not that near, if you know what I mean. I wondered if I should suggest he called the police or "the feds" as the youngsters seem to call them these days, but I kind of knew what the answer to that would be. Instead, I just told him to be very careful if he was venturing back out into the night.

"Yeah, no worries. Thanks, Maisie for the tea and that."

"Any time."

"Hey Maisie, you okay? I mean you don't usually post this late. Can't sleep either? I was going to call you and then I thought, well it's four am, she'll probably have ended up like dropping off, and you'll end up waking her. Anyway, the thing I was going to say, is this – what were you thinking, letting someone you didn't know into your flat at night! He could've been some murderer or anything! He could've been part of the gang himself and let them all in to rob you. You just can't help people these days Mais, even if they're in trouble and you want to. You just have to let the police deal with it. You should've called 999. Promise me you won't do anything like this again. Like Ever."

I agree with Abby, that calling the police would've been the most sensible option, but when you've a scared kid standing on your doorstep, and you suspect the forces of law and order may not turn up and even if they do, you'll just get given a crime number, well you can see why I decided to do something. You hear so much about young people being stabbed now. There are cases in the news every single day. I wouldn't like to think something like that had happened on my actual doorstep, all because I wouldn't get involved.

Late the next morning, I was struggling out to the communal street bin with the rubbish, when I met Reuben coming in, all suited and booted.

"Hi. I was a bit worried about your friend last night. Is he okay?" He looked wary.

"What?"

"Your friend Avery. He came here looking for you. He told me what had happened." That last bit was a bit of a fib, as I'd actually eavesdropped on Avery's call to Tom, but you can't really blame me for trying to find out what was going on. Reuben sighed.

"Oh right. He's like... like my sister's cousin's kid... sounds like someone was giving him a bit of grief."

"A large knife was mentioned. Chopping through his front door."

"That doesn't sound good. Goes awol a lot, he does, so fuck knows where he was hanging out."

"Did Tom help him get safely to his Dad's?" He gave me a slightly irritated look, as if he resented my prying.

"Yeah, yeah. All sorted."

"My friend doesn't think I should've let him in, but since you know him..."

"Yeah, thanks, Maisie. But your friend's right, you don't want to be opening the door to anyone you don't know personally. Where the main door to the house is concerned, even if they say they know me or Tom or whatever. Don't let them in."

"Oh. Okay."

"Whatever their story, okay? Don't do it. Look, I'll give you my number right? And Tom's. From now on just call one of us if anything happens okay? Don't think you're the one who has to deal with anything." I let him enter the numbers into my phone. I noticed later he's put Tom as 'Tom' but himself just as 'R'. "So you just call one of us, yeah?" He smiled. "I'm the guy everyone calls when they've got a problem."

"Same here. People always expect me to solve their problems too. Err you don't happen to know anyone who can mend disability vehicles – quickly and cheaply?"

"I'll ask around for you." I gave him his party invitation. I'd drawn an angel on it.

"It's Saturday night, if you're free." He studied the card carefully.

"Mais, I've just started getting the bird wings you drew tattooed on my back."

"Oh. Oh right." Obviously he liked them. I hadn't dared ask.

"It's covered in cling-film at the moment, but you can have a look if you like?"

"Um okay, later, maybe." He told me to wait while he popped into his flat, returning with an envelope stuffed with cash.

"Your fee for the drawings." It looked like a lot of money. I was, for once, pretty much lost for words.

CHAPTER 6

This morning I was chuffed to receive an RSVP from Donal, even if his wife is bringing a bottle of homemade perry to the party. The navy blue sparkly tunic I'd been the only bidder for, arrived in the post around midday. It's a slightly scratchy material, but a generous fit, so I can forgive it that. It's also better than having to buy something off Joey the tealeaf, though I did wonder if, as he's an acquaintance, I should invite him to my flat-warming anyway. Or perhaps I'd better not. I once bought a pair of polka-dot woolly socks off him, after my own pair had vanished, I'd thought into the black hole that is Mum's tumble drier. When I wore the new pair for the first time however, I noticed the left one had a pulled thread above my little toenail, in an identical place to the same fault on my original pair. He couldn't have pinched them off my clean washing pile on his last visit and sold them back to me surely? Could anyone really stoop that low and be that devious for a poxy quid?

A possibly unjust suspicion over polka-dot socks might not be a good reason for not inviting someone, but the thing is, if he had pinched my socks, then he might just take something else the next time the opportunity arrived. I'd feel terrible if that something belonged to one of my guests. For one thing, they might suspect it was me who was on the rob. Me, I don't have a dishonest bone in my body, well apart from purchasing the occasional shoplifted item, but then who hasn't?

Tom was out in the back garden earlier. His dog was sniffing what looked from my window like a snail, but could've been another curled up dog turd. They do, do those sometimes I've noticed – a spiral cone of shit that looks like its been piped from an icing bag on 'Bake Off'. Tom was striding up and down, on his phone as per usual, nose ring glinting in the sunlight and dreads looking like they badly needed conditioner. Breakages and frizz seem to be Tom's twin issues. I decided to go downstairs and speak to him, though not about his hair care issues.

"I meant to ask Reuben, but do you think it'll be okay for my party guests to use the garden?"

"Yeah, man." He took another call, which seemed to involve someone needing to collect pre-booked railway tickets from the station.

"And you don't happen to know where the outdoor fairy lights switch on?" The dog was staring at me, all grin but no tail wag. That made me slightly uneasy. I'm definitely a cat person. Tom reached behind the bench, flicked a switch and even in the sunshine, I could see the bulbs glowing. He switched them off again. "You did get your party invitation, Tom? I put it under your door."

"Yeah, man." He took another call in which he was going to meet someone and everything was "sweet as". I waited for him to finish before asking if he'd more any news on Avery. Hopefully, he'd be slightly more helpful than Reuben had been.
Tom frowned.

"Do I know him?"

"He's a teenager. Came round here a couple of nights ago. Someone had tried to shank him." The word 'shank' got a reaction.

"Oh, yeah, he's cool yeah. Just kids messing about, y'know."

"He seemed very worried, Tom. Talked about a 'war'."

"Yeah? Wouldn't wanna be that age again huh? Fighting over girls, weed, whatever, y'know."

"Did he mean like a postcode war or something to you reckon?"

"No idea, man. You'd have to ask him." A phone rang in his pocket. He took it out, looked at the number, muttered something that sounded like 'fucking hell' and put it back, only for it to ring again. Not wanting to intrude any further when he was clearly a busy guy, I went back upstairs.

"Hi Maisie, it's totally like a soap opera, where you're living. Like 'Eastenders', which I'm still not watching FYI, because they're still not giving proper trigger warnings when people shout at each other. They do if there's like serious violence, but hearing people shouting can be very stressful too. My mum's emailed the Radio Times about it. Anyway, I've been trying to look up everybody in your house, to see what I can find out, as they're all so mysterious. Is that like really weird and stalkery of me?

And, I think I've found Adelina – see link below. Having an usual name helped. It's a dating profile and she's looking for a very rich man to pamper and spoil her. I found that a teeny bit shallow if you know what I mean. Like I'm not being judgy, but it's slightly gold-diggery isn't it? A less well off person can make a really good partner too. Just saying.

I can't find anything about Tom, but in an online Brighton lifestyle magazine there's this charity casino night in the social diary section and Adelina is named, see link. No surname though, but by the photo she fits your description. OMD – she is so glamorous! There's a guy in a suit in another of the photos. He's not looking at the camera, but you can see several women are looking at him. He's got a glass in his hand, and he has a silver ring on every finger. Might he be Reuben?"

I checked the links and Abby was correct with her identification of Adelina. The guy that might be Reuben is in shadow, though there certainly is some resemblance. Clearly the photographer didn't take his or her own lighting, but then it is only a free magazine, so that was a bit of an ask I suppose. I think I need to up my game with regards to preparing for this party though. It appears several of my guests may well mix in glamorous circles, and may even be high rollers, what ever that means.

Reuben paid me two hundred quid for the wing artwork! I'm almost a high roller myself all of a sudden. I could scarcely believe it. I'm sticking a bit of it away for a rainy day. I've never really had savings, unless you count the few loose coppers in my piggy bank, and they tend not to be left alone for long. I mean would you rather have 76p or a bar of Dairy Milk? Well exactly.

The other day I discovered a radio show where you can win three grand for noticing how many times they played songs by the same singer or group in the space of an hour. Last time I only started listening in time to hear some woman win. She was gonna spend the money on a handbag and shoes, so didn't really deserve it either. Three grand though would sort me out for months. I don't reckon the Department Of Work and Pensions have the radio on in their office, so its not like they'll be able to sign me off for earning money if I win. This morning, I've been jotting down the singers and bands and so far only Rihanna and Rudimental have been played more than once. I'm multi-tasking, as I'm also looking through my old photos to see if there's one I can send in to BBC Weather-Watchers today. I know that's cheating cos you're supposed to go out and take one of that day's weather, but with Delores currently in the pits, I could only take it out of the window. It's sunny, but the sun over rooftops, or even a partial sea view doesn't often cut it. Sunset would have a better chance but in all honesty I can't be arsed to wait that long. Shortly before I went into hospital I got one of my pictures after the main news, not just on the South East part, which is where I occasionally strike lucky. They don't pay you, but I title mine "Mrs Webster, Brighton" and get her followers to send me screenshots of them gawking at it. It's useful for keeping people interested. A lot of my photos are shot through her web and sometimes she features, but again, unless it's a sunset or sparkling raindrops on the threads, we struggle to get those ones chosen. A comical seagull, if I could get down to the seafront again, might make the grade. I did suggest to Masoud he sends in his aliens at the bus stop, but he's a bit sniffy about non-paying markets. Shit! That's the beginning of 'We Found Love (In A Hopeless Place)'. Time to ring the radio station, and then keep pressing redial if they don't answer. I'm gonna get a serious repetitive strain injury for sure.

*****

"Congratulations, Maisie, you have just won..." Nope, dream on, girl. Couldn't get through – 'kin 'ell, how many phone-lines does that radio station have? One? I've probably spent enough dosh on calling them to buy them another. The guy that actually got through didn't need the money. You could tell that by the way he talked. Typical. He certainly hadn't had to find love in a hopeless place. Probably bought it in Harrods. Bastard.

I'd muted the Brighton Biscuiteers on What's App a month ago after Allegra from Rottingdean suggested semi-jokingly I think, that Balzen shouldn't be sold to anyone who voted Brexit, and the ensuing storm kept my phone pinging all night. When at two in the morning, I was finally and unwisely tempted into entering the fray myself, I suggested that by her logic no one living outside Lincoln should eat Lincoln Creams. Unfortunately my spelling was a bit ropey at that hour and no less than three people got back to 'helpfully' correct my typos. If that wasn't bad enough, Nigel then lamented that the 'BB' had once 'been the preserve of postgrads and professionals, but lately standards have been very sadly slipping.' A bit rich when he was the one who'd invited me to join, after liking my arty Insta photo of a malted milk Stonehenge, atmospheric shadows and all. Well I called him a fucking nob. You would wouldn't you? Actually I meant 'snob' but this typo made sense so I left it. I then muted the group for a month. Hopefully by the time thirty-one days had passed, I reasoned, the Nigels and Allegras would've taken their petty-minded middle management pretentious wanking somewhere else.

A jaunty ping from my phone has just heralded the Biscuiteers return, and they don't seem to have learned any new social skills or gained even a gram of charm in their month of exile from my socials. 'It is widely considered to be common to gnaw the custard off Custard Creams' says Lotus-loving Allegra, discussing a thread started by Sainsbury's-own brand-Rich-Tea fan Lacey. 'Why do digestives make me cough?" worries Jill. 'Is there something wrong with me?' 'Only the usual hypochondria love – just saying' and a winking emoji from Paul. 'Paul, must you be so passive aggressive?' 'Shut up, Nige, you gluten-free asshole'. 'Asshole? Oh for Fuck's sake, you're not American, you're from fucking Newhaven, Paul'. 'Fat reduced cocoa powder anyone? Me neither.' It's Jill again with her magnifying glass looking for new things to be allergic to. I decide to mute them without joining the conversation, and for a year this time. What a shame it doesn't give the option of silencing them for a millennia. The Hove Cat Loving Group are all busy consoling Monica after the sad demise of Madame Pompadour from kidney failure. Saying something tactful in these circumstances is never my forte, so I just offer a single tear emoji. I hope it brings her comfort. After I've sent it I start to worry that I should have used the two tear one. Fearing a backlash for being insufficiently grief stricken I mute them too, though only for a month. Hopefully when I've got my kitten, I'll be able to contribute in a more sincere and constructive manner. Pretending to this group that I've three cats – a Burmese, a Turkish Van Cat and a Maine Coon, and remembering what name I'd given each has at times been, I admit, something of a struggle. The group were sometimes rather too good at making my deception feel real, especially when they reminded me I'd failed to take Washington (the Maine Coon of course) for his boosters, and chiding me for using the wrong flea treatment on Taj (the Burmese).

"Hello, Coastal Landscaper Gardeners."

"Oh hello. Err it says on your website 'no job too large or too small'. Is that factually correct?"

"Yes, we'll tackle any horticultural job, no matter how difficult or time-consuming for a very reasonable price."

"Right, good, cos I've got this weed in my window-box."

"Your window box is full of weeds?"

"No. Just one weed. I'm a bit worried it might be Japanese Rope Plant."

"Knot weed."

"What? It's not a weed?"

"The plant I think you're talking about is Japanese Knotweed. But that's most unlikely to be found in a window box."

"It could happen though?"

"It is possible I suppose. Can you describe it?"

"Err yeah. It's green, a shoot and then there's a leaf just started."

"How big is it?"

"'bout the size of my thumbnail."

"Right. Nothing to worry about."

"No? I mean it says you come out for free to give quotes and that. You don't wanna come out and take a look? Just in case it's something poisonous or spider-eating?"

"Ah, sorry, we're currently really short staffed. And you don't really need a gardener, not for one weed. You've got a kettle?"

"I have yeah."

"Okay, well you go and boil it up, love, Make yourself a nice cup of tea and then pour the rest of the water on the weed. That'll probably deal with it."

"Sorry no can do. My basement neighbour and his dog are down below. I might scald them. Could be very nasty."

"Well maybe pour the boiling water on the weed when they've gone back inside. Sorry not to be anymore helpful. Bye now."

"Okay, but can I just... hello? Hello?"

****

Damn I've still got that bloody Rihanna earworm on the brain and it didn't even win me anything. Shit. Bollocks. Shit. I just sent it to Donal. 'We Found Hove (in a hopeless place)' but he pinged back almost immediately with "Have moved on to films now. For example 'From Russia With Hove'." I wasn't impressed. All I could think of was 'Hove Actually' when 'Love Actually' was actually named after that expression, which for your information locals don't use anyway, so it hardly counts. A look online gave me 'Enduring Hove' which is a little harsh, but I honestly couldn't do much better than that. Donal did say he'll take a look at Delores when he comes to the party and see if he can fix her. I said that he could leave it to another time if he liked, but he said it's no bother to bring his tools and have a quick tinker with her motor. I got the feeling he'd prefer doing something practical than sitting making small talk with the other guests. Either that or it's a desperate measure to avoid the perry. He must be sick of the stuff after all. I think they've made a vat-load.

****

A courier has just delivered the package of bunting, balloons and house-warming banners. It's all great stuff and I can't wait to see it all festooning the ceiling. I've some paper tablecloths too, which will co-ordinate with the blue and silver colour scheme. I've bought a balloon pump, as my asthma doesn't leave me with enough breath to fill even one balloon. The pump though is also surprisingly hard going. My elbow is soon aching from pressing one cardboard tube inside the other. You'd have thought they could've made it electric or battery powered. I could have ordered helium to fill the balloons with, but I'm not too sure about that indoors. I mean it's supposed to be a harmless gas right, but where does it go if a balloon bursts? As it doesn't smell, there's no way of knowing if it's hanging around the way a fart can linger. Besides I'd get tempted to inhale some to make my voice all squeaky, just to entertain people if the atmosphere goes a bit flat. That is supposed to be a bit dangerous, especially if you're breathy to start with.

Adelina has a boyfriend round at the moment. I think she has more than one, as the last one had hair and this one doesn't. I assume that's the problem with placing dating adverts, not that you attract baldies, but that you get too many men answering at once or none at all. Like buses – either loads of 5bs come or it's all 5as. I know you'll only understand that if you live in Brighton, Hove or Hangleton but it's a fact.

****

I wanted Adelina to help me put up the decorations, so I was glad when I heard her new fella heading back down the stairs. It had only been a short visit. I hadn't heard much in the way of noises while he was here, but I still decided to give her a good half hour before knocking on her door. I mean if they had been enthusiastically making love then she might like time to have a little rest, make herself a cuppa or smoke a cigarette. I know I'm talking about an experience I've not had personally, but I imagine sex is a bit like gardening, or hoovering – a little sit down afterwards doesn't go amiss.

Adelina was almost as excited about the party decorations as me. She loved the bunting, though she didn't know the word, and burst out laughing, thinking I'd said something rude. "Ah little flags on a string!" she said spinning round and wrapping herself up in it. When she'd untangled herself, she busied herself blowing up balloons, by mouth, not pump, which she also found funny. She pulled all kinds of saucy faces, while getting lippy on the necks before tying them off. She thought we should keep a few balloons not blown up in case guests wanted to use them for gas. I said I hadn't ordered any helium, but weirdly she seemed sure people would bring their own.

Adelina was still hanging up the balloons, with me cutting the sticky tape to stick them to the ceiling, when the doorbell rang. I remembered what Reuben had said about not letting anyone I didn't know in, but I was still going to answer my buzzer. I wondered for a second if it was Avery. Despite Reuben and Tom reassuring me that everything was now alright with him, I still had a nagging feeling that the kid had been in more trouble than he had let on. If he was having bother with a gang, well those people are like bullies, they don't suddenly melt away and leave you alone. Sooner or later, often just when you start to think things are getting better, they catch up with you again. That's when things usually get worse.

It wasn't Avery. It was Mum. My stomach lurched. I know I should've made an excuse not to let her up, like I was starting a cold or something. "Sorry Mum," I should've said, "but I can't have you catching this for your holiday." But I didn't think of it in time. Instead I pressed the button to let her in, knowing that as soon as she set foot in here, she'd know the hurtful truth. I was throwing a party on the evening she was flying out to Marbella. For the first time I was holding a celebration that I hadn't invited Mum too. I knew she'd be gutted, utterly gutted.

"Hi there. I'm Adelina. You are Maisie's mother?"

"Shel. My name's Shel. Shelley actually."

"You don't look old enough to be her mum."

"Well I feel it, believe me love. So what's going on then? I know it's not Maisie's birthday."

"Do you wanna cuppa, Mum?"

"Yeah, ta Mais. So what you celebrating?

"Err it's my flat-warming."

"Tonight?"

"Tomorra night. Just thought I'd get it all ready."

"You never told me. Didn't think to invite your poor old Mum."

"Well I knew you'd be in Marbs."

"You could've made it another night. Any day this week."

"Yeah. I didn't think. But hey, you're going to Spain, where life's one big party eh?"

"Is it?"

"Oh Mum..."

"So who's coming to this party then?"

"Just a few friends."

"Friends? Since when have you had friends? You don't know no-one." I knew she was only saying that because she was upset about not being invited, so I let it go.

"I'll post the photos. So you can see everyone here."

"I won't be looking at the online while I'm away." She was doing her disappointed face, one I remembered from when I was a kid from when I tried to run away and when I told her I hated her. It was different than her angry face – the one caused by my younger self felt-tipping the TV screen and feeding the goldfish on custard. Mum's disappointed face still affects me more than her angry one. It's because after Dad died, we promised each other we'd be best friends, come what may. We'd always be there for one another. We were too. Until she met Shaun – the deal breaker.

Mum had sat down and left me to unpack her bag. She looked really tired, probably from needing to remember all that pre-holiday stuff like checking how out-of-date her sun block is and cancelling the milk. Mum still has a milkman, even though they're an endangered species now. Well actually it's a milk woman, milk person, but traditional in every other sense, apart from the fact she doesn't accept money, you have to pay by direct debit. That seems a bit weird for milk, but there you are.

Anyway Mum had turned up with a few things she thought I might find useful when she was away and a contact number for the place in Marbella "in case my phone doesn't work on their roaming thingummy". She'd left Shaun doing the last of the packing, thankfully, and later they were going to get the train to Gatwick to avoid "the parking cowboys". Last time she and Shaun went abroad they left their car with some private firm at Gatwick, which promised secure, luxury, valeted parking but actually dumped it in a field of cows. The company then forgot where they'd left it, and when Shaun finally tracked it down, he had to get someone with a tractor to drag it out of turd lake.

I offered mum a biscuit and when she turned that down I tried the delights of the non sugar-free 'occasional' sweet tin. She didn't even want a blackcurrant gobstopper so I must've really, seriously offended her by holding my party while she's away. Not that there's anything I can do now. The invitations are sent and some are even RSVPed. Perhaps I can hold another bash when she's back. I've had my birthday for this year, but maybe I could have a modest Christmas do. I always go round Mum's on Christmas Day, cos I can't cook for more than myself, and then it's pretty basic. Mum does the whole roast and though on occasion it's been seriously under cooked and given us the trots, she does put the effort in. She still sets fire to the pud, even in these days of health and safety, plus we always have crackers with proper gifts in them, rather than little bits of plastic rubbish. If I do a party here, it'll have to be before the 25th. Maybe a 'start of advent' one. I think advent is supposed to be something a bit religious, but to me it's just when you open the first door of your chocolate calendar. If I need to start a new tradition of having an advent party, just to stop my mum having the hump for the rest of the year then so be it.

Shaun rang Mum to ask her if she wanted him to pack up her medicines and toiletries but she told him she'd do it herself when she got back. She was quite snappy with him actually which surprised me. She's usually all over that waster like prickly heat. They then got into an argument about whether she should take her bikini. She insisted she didn't want to, as she hadn't been able to have a fake tan, and wasn't going to be sitting in the sun anyway. Mum loves the sun, so I imagine she was only being difficult because she was in a mood. Maybe Shaun had done something to offend her, but I had a nagging suspicion it was still due to me and my party scheduling.

Normally I'd be pleased if Mum and Shaun were fighting, but I wouldn't want them breaking up abroad or anything. I don't think Mum could find her way back to the airport on her own, let alone ask for assistance in Spanish. It's not like she even knows how to use google translate. Can you imagine what I'd do if my Mum was marooned in Spain or some other country? It's not like I could get on a plane and go get her. I don't even have a passport, and then I'd probably have to travel first class, to have anywhere near enough leg room or space generally. I'd probably have to set up some online funding appeal instead, to get her found and flown back, co-ordinating it all from here, like International Rescue. "He's such a tosser," Mum said, putting the phone down without even saying 'bye'. Normally I'd have congratulated her on finally coming to her senses but instead I reminded her that if she really didn't want to go to Marbella, she didn't have to. She turned to look at me, seemed about to say something but stopped. Then she got up and headed for the door.

"Don't expect a postcard, love. I don't know if I can faff about with Spanish stamps." I watched her walk away, down towards the bus stop. No postcard. Even though she didn't mean it and would still send one – that's the moment I knew I'd really, seriously upset her.

CHAPTER 7

Miracles do happen, it's true. Donal and his wife Sarah arrived bearing two bottles of actual wine. When they'd gone to check on the latest batch of perry, which was 'maturing', two of the bottles had bits of something Sarah didn't like the look of floating in them and the third had recently exploded. It seems you can make bombs out of pears. I suppose I shouldn't really be putting facts like that in my blog in case any of my followers are terrorists of some sort but there you go. There's one of Mrs Webster's followers who I strongly suspect works for MI5 or MI6. It's the random questions she'd ask about our old neighbourhood, and the fact her profile picture has a Venetian blind hiding her face. Very fishy if you ask me. Why would a spy be keeping an eye on a spider though? My original theory was it was surveillance on the flat in the street behind, which you could often see on Mrs Webster's live webcam stream. If so, I wonder why she hasn't stopped following, now Mrs Webster has a new address.

Anyway, Donal and Sarah were the first guests to arrive, which they apologised for, completely unnecessarily. I don't know why the earliest people at a party always say they're sorry. It seems to be a 'thing'. Personally I think it's the latecomers who should feel guilty. They don't give anyone a hand with laying out the nibbles or uncorking the wine do they? They just swan in when everyone's done all the setting out, with a bottle of wine nobody now needs cos there's a table full of open bottles, and they still expect to find somewhere comfy to sit down. Sorry latecomers – only the hard chairs will be left.

Donal asked if my mum was coming to the party as she'd sounded like a laugh when I'd told him about her in my emails. He doesn't do social media and although I'd told him about my blog he still hasn't checked it out. I suspect he's about as keen about 'the online' as Mum. Fortunately he'd remembered to bring his toolkit and was happy to go downstairs and look at Delores. Sarah was surprised to discover a few of my party guests were going to be joining us virtually. I propped up my tablet and dialled Abby. I'd posted her a couple of balloons and a party hat in advance, and when she answered, I could see they'd arrived safely. Her Mum had even blown up the balloons for her. As Abby was wearing her party hat, Sarah and I put ours on.

"Can she hear us?"

"You need to get closer to the mic."

"Hello Abby, I'm Sarah."

"Pleased to meet you, Sarah."

"Is that a guinea-pig I can see behind you?"

"Her name's Marmite, she helps me when I get stressed."

"You're not feeling stressed now are you?"

"Oh no, I just got Mum to bring her in so she could join the party."

"Abby, sorry to cut in but could I ask a massive favour?"

"Course, Mais. Sorry, I mean like if it's something I can do."

"I'm gonna try ato live stream the party. I got Adelina to stick the detachable webcam on the top shelf in the kitchenette and point it in this direction. It should be on my channel, will you have a look for me?"

"It's working, though you both look really far away."

"We're on the internet, Maisie?"

"You don't mind do you?"

"No... not at all."

"You're not supposed to wave at the camera or keep looking at it. It's just a kind of fly-on-the-wall look at the party. So my followers and Mrs Webster's can see what a good time we're all having."

Tom was next to arrive, staggering under the weight of an enormous mixing desk and two speakers. He said he could work from my playlists from my phone, play some old vinyl or a bit of grime. I decided to start with some of my stuff, as eighties and nineties pop is probably an easier listen for Donal and Sarah. At first even then it was a bit loud, and when I asked him to turn it down a bit so me and Sarah could natter, he gave me a look like I was his gran or something. He then plugged in these two long bars of rainbow lights that changed colour at random and seemed to flash along to the beat of the music. As it started to get dark, they created patterns across the walls and ceiling. I'll have to ask him where he got them, and buy my own if they're not too pricey. The party already looked the business and hardly anyone had even arrived yet. I was glad I'd taken a chance and invited my new friends and neighbours.

Sarah got a call from Donal and beckoned me to go to the front window with her. There was her husband zipping up the hill on Delores. He looked up at us and waved as he came zooming back down at all of thirty miles an hour.

Donal explained that Delores' problem had simply been a loose connection. He did explain all the where's and how's, but if you're expecting a tutorial on mobility scooter repair and maintenance, you've come to the wrong place. Grace had arrived by that time, looking almost awake, and carrying an icebox full of cans of beer. She looked surprised to be thanked, muttering that she was just the one who'd carried them up the stairs. Close behind her were Avery and two other young lads. Both grabbed handfuls of nibbles, without so much as a 'hello'. They all started playing about with Avery's phone and suddenly the music changed to some horrible din, with a beat that made my bowels throb. The words 'yeah' and 'mother-fucker' featured rather too heavily for a civilised party, but with a grin, Tom changed the music back to mine. Avery started doing something else on his phone, fingers working like fury, but whatever it was didn't sabotage my play list.

"Jonas, you on the way, mate?" Tom perched on the counter, a knobbly knee appearing through a rip in his jeans. "Can't be too careful eh?" I had no idea who Jonas was. Certainly not someone I'd invited. In a way though, having a couple of extra people was quite exciting. My previous parties had all been on a smaller scale than this one – well with four guests tops.

About an hour later, Adelina and Karla turned up together. Adelina had a tiny leopard print skirt and a PVC bra top on with some killer jewellery. Someone should probably tell Karla that trackie bottoms don't really cut it as party-wear though even if they are pink, but it ain't gonna be me. The girls had brought more balloons that they and the teenagers then filled with something from little silver bottles. Whatever it was made a shrill hiss, as it escaped the pressurised containers. I thought it might be helium, but the bottles were too small, and when the young people inhaled from the balloons their voices didn't change. Seeing Sarah and Donal exchange nervous glances at the goings on with the tiny gas bottles, I topped up the bowls of crisps and twiglets. The broadband had gone a bit iffy so Abby had started buffering and Paige and Davey were unable to join us.

Masoud arrived on his moped, with a free dipping bar as a gift, which makes me feel a bit guilty about the Great Dipping Bar con. He doesn't drink alcohol but I'd got that covered with plenty of alternatives, and as Donal's wife Sarah was a member of the U3A photography club, we started comparing photos on our phones, as you do. Sarah had some shots of street performers in Paris which even Masoud was envious of, though I swear I've seen both the stripy t-shirt wearing mime artist and the South American Pan Pipers outside Western Road, Waitrose. Perhaps street acts have a tour circuit that includes Brighton, Paris and other touristy destinations. I'll enquire next time I see one. It's always good to know things.

It was dark now and Grace and the lads had gone out into what they called the 'yarden'. I think that either means a backyard that's used as a garden or a space that's a cross between the two. They were laughing very loudly and smoking something that ponged, so I closed the back window. Mrs Webster had already gone to bed under the top ledge and I hope she could sleep with all the noise and nasty niffs.

A mountain of a man turned up with a wild-haired woman in her sixties who had heavily winged eye make up and a nasty cough. The man mountain looked exactly like a life-sized version of one of those wrestling action figures that come with a ring to fight in. He was dressed in black trousers and shirt fortunately, not tiny wrestling shorts, otherwise he'd have been a bit of a distraction. As it was I managed to take a quick photo of him on my phone to send to Mum. As you know, she is partial to a bit of muscle, and I want her see what she's missing, while she's lying by the pool.

Tom handed Mountain Man a beer and I was a bit disappointed when he didn't rip it open with his teeth. "If I look like I've escaped from somewhere, it's cos I have – ha ha, ha!" drawled the older woman with hair like Einstein. Mr Muscle turned out to be Jonas and he was supposed to be minding Carol, who is the escapee. She said she got out "when they weren't looking" and isn't going back, dead or alive. When we heard a distant police siren she yelled "Hide me!" and got down on her knees behind the sofa, coughing wildly. The siren faded away up the coast road and Carol emerged to grab a just opened bottle of wine and start necking it. "My son knows how to throw a party eh!" she cackled. I pointed out that it was actually my party. It sounded as though she'd come to the wrong place.

"Who are ya?"

"Maisie."

"So you're the birthday girl!" she croaked before singing 'Happy Birthday.' Even Karla joined in, though she appeared to need to look up the words to the song on her phone. When it got to the 'dear Maisie' bit, Carol sung her own name as she's already forgotten mine. I didn't immediately tell her she wasn't even at a birthday party, not after she'd made all the effort to sing the song and all. Then she started telling Karla about her escape, but Karla as ever was deeply unimpressed:

"It was just an unlocked door. Grace has got out of there like a zillion times. And you told me you'd gone there begging them to let you in, in the first place?"

"Changed my mind. Cos they don't help you. Trust me, Karlie, they don't help."

"Karla. It's Karla. Nobody calls me Karlie, got that?"

"Where's the birthday cake? Why's there no birthday cake, Fatty?"

"Nobody calls me Fatty okay?"

"Ha, ha, ha!"

"And this is a flat warming, not my birthday." Taking no notice, Carol lurched off down the stairs singing "There must be a cake shop," as "There Must Be An Angel" was playing. "My son'll get me a cake. He's an angel. A real angel." Tom indicated to Jonas to go after her.

Masoud had been called to make a delivery before I could ask him to dance, as I'd planned. That was a bit disappointing as judging by his gangsta moves at the pizza place that would've been a laugh. Luckily Donal decided to have a little boogie so I joined him. Sarah didn't mind, but insisted she had two left feet. I've two swollen feet, a hammertoe and a stick but it didn't stop me giving it my best Hot Slipper Shuffle. Surprisingly Avery and his friends, who had reappeared to raid the beers, decided to dance too. They asked politely if we could have some Madonna because "we love that era". Bless 'em, they can't have been born. We all started trying to 'Vogue' with the boys clearly knowing how poses could be confidently struck. I ended up aggravating my rotor cuff injury by lifting the arm not holding my stick above my head. Madge might have been purring that there was nothing to it, but I beg to differ. Adelina joined in, and with her icy elegance, all eyes were on her.

Jonas and Carol came back up, arguing, but once she saw the dancing she was happy to join in, even if she did immediately tread on the tail of Tom's staffie which understandably let out a loud yelp. Tom suggested she sit down and was told in words of four letters where he should go and what he should do when he got there.

I used 'La Isla Bonita' as the excuse to persuade Karla to dance with me. Her stomping moves may well have been an attempt to mock me but at least she was dancing, rather than cackling. Grace wanted to stay in her "happy place" and started pestering everyone for more "laughing gas" which must've been what those tiny silver bottles had contained. Perhaps it explained Karla's almost constant hyena-like sniggers too. She laughs a lot for someone with angry, unhappy eyes.

'La Isla Bonita' is hard to dance to unless you can do that slinky, Spanish thing, and I couldn't, particularly with Karla playing at mini-me. The music changed to Shakira's 'My Hips Don't Lie', apparently on one of the vogue-ing boys requests. I managed a bit of bump and grind, much to Karla and Grace's amusement. Sod the laughing gas, my pelvic thrusts had taken her to her happy place and beyond. For a minute there I was the centre of attention, the belle of the ball. Then Reuben strolled in, fashionably late of course.

Reuben had the Latin American moves down to a 't'. He was mesmerising. If he'd been on 'Strictly' everyone would've given him a ten for some seriously sexy samba-ing, or was it rumba-ing? You're not getting the words of an expert here, clearly. The music changed to INXS's 'Need You Tonight' and we were dancing opposite each other. In my head I was dancing at any rate. The reality might have been something entirely different. The Vogue boys started to whoop and clap their appreciation. I was glad I was live streaming rather than recording, and hope no one else records my efforts and posts it. You wouldn't do that to me now would you? I want to imagine, that just for a moment, I was graceful. Reuben's moves were wild and as the song put it 'raw'. He's one of my kind. Definitely.

While we were dancing, another six younger people who I didn't know arrived in a huddle. Tom clearly was acquainted with them though, by the way they all fist bumped etc with him as they came in. Now they were sitting around drinking and smoking, with their multi-coloured hair and 'curated' ears of jewellery. I wondered if I should ask Tom to play some more youth oriented tunes next. As well as Rag 'n' Bone Man, I'm quite partial to a little bit of Dua Lipa, Sigma and Stormzy from time to time.

Suddenly I couldn't get my breath. I coughed and wheezed, and did my best not to hoik up phlegm which trust me, is never a good dance-floor look. On seeing my face turning purple Reuben went over to the front window to let some fresh air in. As he reached it and looked out, his expression changed to one of horror and he beckoned Tom who straightaway left the decks to join him. They exchanged panicky glances, Reuben rushed over to Jonas and muttered something in his ear. Then all three rushed out of my flat towards the stairs.

Reaching the window, I saw a mob of forty to fifty people, some carrying cans of beers, others dressed for a festival or rave, thronging to the front door. Then they were banging on it and shouting out to me to 'open the fucking door!'. At the bottom of the stairs, Reuben, Tom and Jonas had locked and bolted it however. Loud bangs and crashes suggested those outside weren't going to let that put them off getting in. I heard a window smash and a cheer went up.

"They're round the back," cried Adelina from the flat. I followed her to the back window and watched as the yard filled with people. The backdoor has glass panels in it and Reuben, Tom and Jonas were unable to prevent a hand shattering one and fumbling for the catch on the inside. A struggle ensued with the three guys trying to brace themselves behind the door, but more panes of glass broke and then the door itself gave way, crashing in on them. Adelina ran screaming upstairs to her attic room. Sarah and Donal followed her, shouting to me to follow. Unfortunately I hesitated a moment too long, as Reuben and his friends were engulfed by a tide of bodies, with punches being thrown and parts of the back door being used as weapons.

The horde of gatecrashers rushed upstairs and into my flat. The sheer force of the stampede forced me back into the kitchenette. Cans, bottles and food were being trampled and broken underfoot in the confusion. The gatecrashers were mainly teenage, some of the girls wore glittery face paint as if they'd decamped here from a previous event or party. There was a loud bang and a flash as the mixing desk went over and both groans and cheers from the crowd as the music died. I couldn't see across the mass of bodies that all seemed to be pushing and shoving each other for no reason. A wild-eyed girl was propelled into me and screamed loudly right in my face. I was being crushed in the kitchenette, so I pushed back and pushed hard. I let out a bellow and somehow propelled myself through the sea of interlopers. Then my foot turned on something, probably a beer bottle and I lost my footing

I don't know how long it went on for. It felt like forever but it was probably only half an hour or so. I couldn't get up, so I could no longer see everything that was happening. Fortunately I'd landed on the sofa, my bulk forcibly ejecting those already lounging there. Once I had landed, there was no way I was going to be able to get up again, even if there had been floor-space to put my feet. The crowd were throwing food, drink, chairs and everything else at each other. As twiglets rained down on my head like shrapnel, all I could do was wait for it to end.

Then it did end. With what sounded like a gunshot. With screams. With a stampede back down the stairs. I kept my hand over my eyes. I didn't want to see the devastation. Everything ached or throbbed. The sweat started to go cold on me and my teeth chattered violently.

"Can you get up?" I tried, my swelling leg wouldn't even bend properly let alone bear weight.

"Uh no."

"Are you hurt?" Reuben wiped the blood from his own split lip with the back of his hand as he peered down at me.

"Has everyone gone?"

"Yep."

"What about Donal and Sarah?"

"I don't know them, do I?"

"Can you hand me the landline?" My mobile had probably been nicked or smashed, along with everything else I'd valued or cherished. Naturally I hadn't been able to afford to insure anything. The horror was starting to sink in.

Donal picked up straight away. He and Sarah had left via the fire escape. He apologised for deserting me.

"I didn't know where you were and I just needed to get the wife out of there. Are you okay?"

"Yeah. Pretty much. But it was a good party wasn't it? Good until the gatecrashers."

"It was a great party, Maisie. You sure you're okay though?"

"Don't worry about me." At least my guests had enjoyed the party. It sounded as if Donal and Sarah would stay in touch and still be my friends. The last thing I wanted was for anyone to get the idea I'm not a good host.

Jonas came in and Reuben, having noticed I was shivering, sent him down to his flat to get a clean blanket. Tom arrived, with the beginnings of a black eye and his nose ring partly ripped out. Reuben winced.

"Err you need to get that looked at mate." Tom though was more intent on showing him something on his phone. "Fucking hell!"

"It was Grace... she shared Maisie's party with fuck knows who. Made out it was her party actually."

"Well she'll pay. However much it costs. And she and her friends can clear all this shit up." He grinned. "I'd thought it was just gonna be a little tea party or something."

There was the sound of sirens approaching.

"Great." said Tom flatly.

"Fan-fucking-tastic." scowled Reuben as the sirens grew loud and stopped outside. He looked out the window. "Suppose I better go out to them." He wiped the blood from his still bleeding lip and headed off down the stairs. I dialled my mobile. It started ringing. Tom picked it up and brought it over to me. Fortunately it was still in one piece.

"I don't suppose my laptop and tablet are still here?" Jonas went to look and returned with both. Pizza cheese and ketchup was smeared across the laptop but it has in the past suffered worse indignities at my hands.

Reuben walked in with four police officers. Two looked pumped and had their hands on their tasers. They were clearly expecting to find a riot in full swing, but upon only seeing Tom and me they relaxed a little. Their beady eyes surveyed my trashed flat. One let out a whistle.

"Armageddon eh?" said Reuben.

"And you say you weren't involved? Only came upstairs when you heard the racket?"

"Yep." he lied. The policeman turned to me.

"Your neighbour tells me, you said that you didn't know or invite any of these people?"

"That's right. They just smashed their way in."

"Broke down the door. As you can see," said Reuben.

"And they were mostly teenagers you said?" He directed that at Reuben.

"Yeah. Looked like it."

"Someone who'd been invited probably put it on their socials. You'd be surprised how often it happens," a policewoman advised me, rather unnecessarily, considering. Mind you, at that particular moment, if they'd dragged us all off in handcuffs it wouldn't have surprised me. I don't think anything would've. One of the policeman trailed a finger in some white powder on the tabletop. Reuben noticed. "Probably only icing sugar – from Maisie's flat-warming cake, which now seems to be mostly trod into the rug. Though they could've brought anything with them – the gate-crashers." Reuben picked up one of the little gas canisters and shrugged. I hoped, as no doubt did he, that with the home invasion reported, presumably by the occupants of a neighbouring house, any drugs on the premises couldn't be easily blamed on any of us.

"We had reports of a loud bang sounding like a gunshot."

"A firework – someone threw it and it caused a stampede back out into the street. I can show you where it scorched the wall over the stairs." Tom left at this point and went downstairs. He returned with the long stick of a rocket with part of the wrapper still attached. The policewoman took it and made a face.

"Could've been very nasty eh?" said Reuben. He was very cool and confident with the police. One of them in particular gave the impression that they were previously acquainted. Perhaps Reuben had, after all, dropped the gun from the fuse-box cupboard into the police station. That might explain their familiarity.

One of the police cars headed off to see if they could round up any of the gatecrashers in case they were still in the vicinity. They could apparently be charged with criminal damage, though unless we could identify individuals who had committed a particular offence then it was unlikely anyone would be. Reuben's lip was bleeding again and he was asked if he would recognise the person who had assaulted him if he saw them again. He thought it unlikely. There'd been a scrum of bodies as he'd rushed up the stairs to check if I was alright. Tom from the basement flat had only arrived for the same reason. They were asked if they had themselves assaulted anyone, even in self-defence and both insisted they had not. Of course I knew there had been a live stream of the whole event and someone, somewhere might also have recorded it, but I didn't tell the police about the webcam, still sitting on the top shelf of the kitchenette. It had, had a full view of all the action, bar that on the stairs. I hadn't told any of my housemates the party was being streamed, and with all the smoking of dubious tobacco, balloon sniffing etc it was probably better not to let the old bill know.

I was advised by the police not to have any more parties in the near future as they didn't want the problems to start up in this building again. I said I was unaware of any previous problems in the building as I'd only just moved in. I gestured to my half torn down housewarming banner, still dangling forlornly from the ceiling. The policeman who had brought the subject up looked at Reuben, as if expecting him to comment. Reuben though said nothing.

"Only in the past we've been called to a number of incidents, at this address. I believe it's a housing association flat, yes? You don't want to get yourself reported to them for anti-social behaviour."

I couldn't believe it. My home had been wrecked and now the police were suggesting I could be in trouble over it. That's when I lost it.

"I'll have you know this was a quiet, well organised soiree – for a few friends. We were eating pizzas and twiglets while listening to eighties pop! If it turned into a riot, it's cos you lot are letting gangs of teenage hoodlums roam the streets, to rampage into people's properties and trash them. Why don't you know who they are? Why weren't any of you around to stop them!"

"Oh we do know who most of the local troublemakers are," came the reply, "But we have to catch them in the act before we can do anything. And we will. We will." He repeated that last part, with a sideways glance at Reuben.

"Glad to hear it officer," he said.

****

I spent the remains of the night under the blanket on a beer sodden, crumb-covered sofa, still dressed in my party clothes. The leg I'd twisted as I fell throbbed constantly and I was glad that when the police had finally left us in peace, there was not much of the night left to endure.

This morning my leg is more multi-coloured than a packet of M&Ms and the ankle is the size of a giant marrow. Although I made a real effort to stand, bracing myself against the sofa arm and heaving with my arms, it didn't happen. I realised I wouldn't be back on my feet for a while. Probably a long while. That's when I started blubbing again. I couldn't help myself. The first blub, by the way, had been caused by seeing my kitten cushion had been completely stained with red wine. I loved that cushion. It's probably as near as I'll ever get to owning a real cat. At least Mrs Webster is okay. I can see her swaying serenely in a gentle breeze.

I couldn't believe Grace's naivety and recklessness over tweeting and whats-apping my party, but then I started to wonder. Was it really all her fault? Or could my live stream of events have been at least part of the problem. It couldn't be you, my dear followers, laying waste to my life? Could you be so cruel and callous after all I've shared with you, as to do that to poor old Maisie? Or did you just want to be part of my party, and share being there with your own followers? Was it just that Mrs Webster and I are so popular that I've kind of been crushed by my own popularity? I'm not going to be judgy, as Abby would say, but any tips on getting red wine out of cushions, ketchup from a rug, and cannabis stink from your curtains, do send those helpful hints my way. Oh and if you were here, and you broke or pinched something, well you know the address. Maybe stick a couple of tenners in an envelope with my name on and pop it through the door. I'm not setting up a funding page to beg for donations. That would be so humiliating. But if you can help, even if you weren't responsible, well it would be appreciated.

****

Reuben sent Tom to the chemist to buy some surgical spirit "before the end of your nose rots off" as he charmingly put it, so I asked for some paracetamol and a packet of peas from the corner shop for my swollen leg. I really need prescription only painkillers, but I'm not likely to get a doctor to come out until Monday at the soonest. I could try NHS Direct but with them it's always been such a huge palaver of questions and more questions, over and over. Then someone will call me back, usually in the middle of the night. I've done this kind of shit to my legs before and they do recover. I don't need to go back into hospital, and have all the hassle over my PIPS and housing that would cause. I mean if Mum was here to sort it out I wouldn't need to worry, but as it is, I think my best option is to stay put.

Tom got the paracetamol and also a packet of frozen sweetcorn from the corner shop. They were out of peas but sweetcorn, wrapped in towel should work as well for the swelling. Grace and Karla have made themselves scarce, but I was able to get Adelina to bundle up all my soft furnishings including the cat cushion and take it all down the launderette. It will cost a fortune, but it'll be worth it if the stains come out of the kitten cushion cover. I gave Adelina a wodge of the notes Reuben had given me for my artwork and told her to get some cleaning stuff. I'd meant bottles of stuff that I could try to scrub the floors and surfaces with when I'm back mobile, but she returned with one of those nifty general-purpose floor washers and a furniture steamer. I was surprised to be handed change, but she explained that I had in fact hired them, rather than bought them. This worried me a bit as I'd be responsible for seeing they were returned. I remember what happened when I was a kid and we lost a video of 'Cutthroat Island' from Blockbuster. The fine would've actually bought the film ten times over. The joke is I don't think we'd even got around to watching it.

As Adelina mopped up, she told me she had once had a cleaning job in an office block belonging to an oil company. It had been a rubbish job and she'd been treated in her words "worse than a small dog" but things had looked up when of the executives had taken a shine to her and invited her to the opera. Back in the present, her new boyfriend is taking her for a meal at the Grand Hotel later. She said she liked him a lot but that Reuben wasn't happy, as he didn't think he was rich enough for her. It seemed quite a shallow attitude and frankly I would've expected better of him. Perhaps he's jealous. I don't know if he's seeing anyone. I did put 'plus one' on his party invitation, as I did on Tom's, just in case.

By the time Elaine arrived on Monday morning, there was no sign that a party had even happened, though she did give my new, multitude of multi-shaped air fresheners a slightly quizzical look. Upon discovering I couldn't actually get up, she didn't enquire how I had managed to have my shee-wee, biscuit barrel and water bottle to hand. Perhaps she thought Mum was looking after me and that she still needn't really bother. I did persuade her to give me a wash down, as I was absolutely reeking by that point, and she did help me into my best pair of pyjamas.

"You'll need a hoist if you want to go to bed." I've broken several in the past and I feared a collapsing hoist would end up with me on the floor and the whole bariatric rescue thing starting over. I'd nagged about my physio team but now I could do with seeing Justin or one of his fellow torture merchants. Elaine said I'd have to ring them myself. My 'care', if you can really call it that, has never really had a joined up approach. When she'd gone I rang the rehabilitation unit and was told my needs would have to be reassessed. They'd send someone out to do that as soon as they could but they had a backlog of cases and I might be waiting for a fortnight for that. I told the receptionist that she should look at my file and see that I had only just been released from hospital, and should actually still be under the physio department from that. Apparently I still needed to be reassessed because my needs might have changed.

"Of course they've changed – they've got more urgent!" She wasn't having any of it – typical.

At lunchtime it was back to the old dial-a-pizza routine. Hadi delivered it and having not been able to come to the party, wanted to hear all about it. On reflection, it had been quite a successful evening, even if like most things concerning my life, it had later all gone tits. Masoud had left before the gatecrashers arrived, and it seems he'd told Hadi, who was stuck at the takeaway cooking and boxing the pizzas, that my party was "the business". So I gave it a bit of PR spin, glossing over the ugly bit, and talking up the music and dancing. I even told him how good the other food was, even though I'd barely had a chance to sample it before it got trampled on. Hadi insisted that next time I have a party it'll be his turn to attend. I didn't have the heart to tell him that there won't be any more parties, at this address at least, probably ever.

I expected Mum to text me from Spain this morning asking how the party had gone. I thought she'd be itching to know, but I think she's still pissed off about not being invited. Eventually I texted her, "Crocked my leg at party, now stuck on sofa." No reply as yet.

CHAPTER 8

My kitten cushion cover has survived. True the background is now pink rather than white, but the little ginger kitten looks okay, all clean and fluffy after his wash. I've had visitors popping in and out all day, so although I still can't get up, there are people about. Reuben suggested I left the flat door open so I can holler if I need anything desperately. The most difficult thing is using the shee-wee or the pot. It's not only a struggle to lift my arse high enough to do the business, I don't like having to ask someone to empty the ruddy things either. I have what they call sluggish transit. It would be a great name for a rock band, but it just means I don't poop that often, and when I do it involves a lot of effort. Never the less, if this sofa-bound situation goes on much longer, someone is going to have to deal with some serious Maisie sausages. I'll have to ask one of the women to flush them. I can't ask one of the blokes. I know that's discrimination but that's how it is.

My printer is wireless so I've printed a couple of 'no smoking' signs and got Elaine to put them up with blu-tack, though my guests, who've been popping in and out, tend to ignore them. At the moment Karla, Grace and a teenage boy I don't know are here, sitting on my bed, drinking and smoking weed. If I need anything I've only to ask though, and they've made me a gin and orange which is quite warming. They're nice enough I suppose, though they're not exactly what you'd call company for me. I mean they rarely actually make an effort to talk to me and when they do there's something a bit patronising about it. "Alright, Maisie?", "Enjoying that are yer?" It's always in that singsong voice people use to talk to a goldfish or someone they think's thick. That's a little unfair where I'm concerned as if it came to a GCSE count, I bet I've loads more than Karla. Better grades too. Well unless you're counting sporty type stuff where she might have had a slight advantage, but we're not. I've been trying to earwig and write down their conversations but street slang has changed since I was at school. Their chief interests seem to be smoking weed and waiting for calls from Tom, who occasionally sends one of other of them running errands to this place or that. I wonder if it involves drug dealing, and I've heard of county lines, but if that is what the young people are doing then they're fairly discreet about it. Things are so different than my day. We used to spend all our spare time watching TV, raiding Mum's drink cabinet and buying blue or cola flavoured ice pops in the newsagents. Oh and reading magazines like Cosmopolitan, though anything with a problem page would do. Even though we all knew they make the problems up.

****

I've still heard nothing from Mum, which is odd. I mean I let her know I've injured myself and everything. My leg is still huge and purple so I sent her a photo of it. It's not that I want to worry her or make her feel guilty. I certainly don't expect her to rush back on my behalf – in fact I know she won't do that, but I would like to hear from her. Spain isn't far away if you're a normal able-bodied person but from where I'm sitting, she might as well be in another galaxy.

I wouldn't like a beach holiday. I get sunburnt ears just walking down the street in the summer, never mind the sweating and the prickly heat. If you can't sit in the sun it's pointless going to Spain as you'd have to rent some enormous umbrella and sit underneath that reading some book you bought at the airport. I've got a pile of Mum's old magazines here and one has a double page spread on beach reading. Some years it's all stuff about having kinky sex with billionaires, which I don't find terribly easy to relate to, but this year's thing seems to be people disappearing, or being murdered, and the person who is investigating doesn't know what is going on cos they're either bladdered, got dementia or they're just not really cut out for the murder solving business. I wonder if Mum's bought one of those books at the airport. She does like a whodunit, as long as it's not too long and there are no dead children or gore. "Oooh, that's another one full of severed limbs. I'll have to drop it down the

Co-op bookstall when I next go out." She only buys her books from fetes and jumbles anyway usually so it's easy come easy go. Anyway, Mum doesn't read this blog. She says it doesn't interest her, so if I happen to find a severed limb or a murdered kid and then try to get to the bottom of it all after one too many helpings of tiramisu, I can tell you all the gruesome details without her going "oooh!", and screwing up her face at me..

I texted Mia to find out if she'd heard from Mum at all and got a reply straight away saying that Mum had rung her from the villa as soon as they'd arrived, as arranged. Now I don't know if Mum usually lets Mia know when she gets to a holiday destination, but she always, without fail, calls me. I suppose the fact that her arrival time would've been during my party might've put her off ringing. She might have felt it would be inconvenient with me having a flat full of guests and all, but in that case why didn't she text at least? I know texting isn't her really thing; she manages a typo in every word and hasn't found how to turn off the predictive text, so I often have to try to decode what she saying. Even M15 would have trouble understanding Mum's texts. I probably shouldn't have taken the piss so much though. It might be what's stopping her texting me now. There's also her fixation with roaming charges. I know it's pricey using a mobile abroad but the way Mum talks about it, you'd imagine she was running up a several grand bill just for saying "Hi love, we're here. Gotta go – the roaming charges." That's about the length of her average holiday call.

Mia is currently in Australia with her boyfriend Josh. What started as a gap year has ended up as just a gap, as the college has long since given up expecting her to turn up. I bet she can't even remember what she was going to study. I can't either come to that. Even when Mia comes back she plans to live in Sunderland. That's where Josh has a job to go back to. We were close as kids but she's turned into one of those people from the adverts – you know, "have passport, will travel wherever my spirit takes me". That kind of garbage. There's not much to talk about when it's all about this or that waterfall, surfing, kayaking or picking bloody olives. I mean I don't even eat olives, and while riding Delores could well qualify as an extreme sport, I don't really think she'll want to hear about it. When we talk on the phone or Skype she's always a bit fidgety like something more interesting is happening where she is. Fair dos it probably is – like a revolution, escaped tiger, attack of the killer mosquitoes or whatever, but you'd think once in a while she could make just a tiny bit more effort to listen to the exploits of her little sister. She sent me a necklace made of wooden beads last year, so I suppose I shouldn't moan, but it was too heavy to wear, and the paint rubbed off on my neck.

****

Teenagers have completely taken over the kitchenette. They do bring me food and make mugs of tea if I ask, but they spend a lot of time there, bunched up together talking in low voices, their ever present rucksacks dumped on the floor among the discarded crisp packets and dog ends. There's loads of to-ing and fro-ing and although I know a few of the regulars like Grace, Avery and the Vogue Boys from the party, there are others whose names I can't recall, or who've only been in once or twice. They all know my name though.

"Alright, Maisie!" or "Woss happening, Mais?" they call as they arrive, in all weathers, checking their phones, and sometimes laughing together over something on a tiny screen that is never shared with me. Perhaps I'm too old and uncool to get the joke. After I'd asked Avery to buy me some haribos though, the kids often now give me a bag and won't take any money for it.

The other thing that's quite sweet is they're all concerned about the environment. Avery sometimes wears a little mask when he's on his bike to block out the fumes and I've heard the Vogue Boys talking about the cutting down of the rain forest. The Vogue Boys went to one of those Greta Thunberg Friday protests, but then got in trouble with Tom over it, as he had been out looking for them for some reason. The taller one – Billy? Bailey? – I'm not sure - has Extinction Rebellion badges on his rucksack. He told the other one off for eating a sausage roll too, so I think he might be vegan.

Sometimes, when one of the teenagers gets a call and has to leave, someone else tells them to be careful or to watch out for themselves. Other times there's a bit of bragging and talk about murking and cheffing various people they have a 'beef' with or who are on their 'turf'. It's quite funny to hear Billy/Bailey talking about 'having some beef' with somebody or other, after he was so down on his mate over the sausage roll.

I never feel threatened by any of the tough talk though and everyone tends to be peculiarly polite around me. They always talk to me in normal English even when they're using that street way of chatting among themselves.

When Elaine comes in, the youngsters all head out, saying they were just visiting me to check I'm okay. Karla even got quite chatty with her the last time, giving her all this bullshit about how she's checking in on me as part of a community project where she's keeping an eye on the elderly and vulnerable. Well I wasn't going to stand, well lie down, for that.

"That's a loud of old bollocks! I'm not old or fucking vulnerable either for your information."

Karla shrugged and said, "Some of them are like so in denial." Elaine said Karla should register with her agency.

"Then you'd get paid for being so caring."

"I wouldn't have to like wash people's bums and stuff would I?"

Elaine said she'd be given proper training. When Elaine had gone

I told Karla I couldn't really see her making the grade as a carer, as she always forgets to put sugar in my tea, no matter how many times I ask. Karla said she had no intention of taking any kind of shite job for a few measly quid. "I'm like so in demand right now, I could make like two grand a week if I wanted."

"In demand doing what?" She shut up at that. It's all pure fantasy. I asked if she had got rid of the loser boyfriend.

"Him? Oh he won't show his face in this town again. I only had to say the word and he got what was coming. Big time." She snapped her fingers. "I got friends looking out for me see?"

None of my flat's guests seem to go to school, college or work or anything. I asked one of the younger boys, called Lucas I think, and he said he'd been excluded from school. I said that was like my friend Paige, but that he didn't strike me as the type of get in trouble. He laughed and said that's not how it is.

"Things aren't like in your day." Cheeky sod. How old does he actually think I am?

Lucas then explained that now you can get excluded because your attendance is bad due to a health problem, or you have trouble getting good grades. The school needs pupils with good grades and good attendance to get a good Ofsted rating, which it needs to keep going. They've all become businesses apparently. You're not a pupil but a customer, using their services. The lad said the school excluded loads of people but once it happened to you, you were fucked. He now went to the exclusion unit but it only held classes three days a week and there were nasty kids there who stopped you learning anything, so it wasn't worth bothering to turn up. Sometimes the unit was full and you got lessons streamed to you on your computer at home for couple of hours a week instead. The only thing to do, now he couldn't get on in the world by getting good grades, was to be an entrepreneur. I thought that meant going on something like 'The

Apprentice' with your little wheelie case or 'Dragon's Den' to get the piss taken out of you. He told me it actually involves "grafting 24/7". He said he ran errands, delivering packages. Someone would call and he'd collect from one person and deliver to another. When I asked what were in the packages he said "this and that".

"Are you actually drug dealing?" I asked. He said drug dealers dealt drugs, he just delivered packages, to and from people who might well be drug dealers but he knew better than to ask questions. He wouldn't say who he was working for, but that there was a 'firm' who gave him regular gigs. They ran the town apparently, like in that Rihanna/Kanye song.

If I could get up I would lock my door at night, but I can't. Instead I have to tell my visitors to leave cos I want some shuteye. Often I have to threaten to shout the place down before they take the hint and head out. "Piss off now will you! Don't you have homes to go to?" Yesterday morning, in the early hours I got the fright of my life when I heard a sneeze. "Who's there?" I called out in that quivery tone of voice people use in horror movies right before they get murdered. It was Avery. He'd smuggled a sleeping bag in and was trying to kip on the vinyl tiled floor of the kitchenette. I told him he could move to my bed, as I wasn't currently able to use it myself, but he said he was okay. I was woken at six am by his phone going and him whispering into it. I still have my suspicions that Tom is behind all the activity involving phones and travelling about and odd packages, though he rarely comes up here himself. Reuben is apparently out of the country, though due back at any time. Someone said he's in Spain, someone else Morocco, so he's probably catching some rays, like Mum.

****

I said the youngsters can watch the TV, but they rarely bother. Daytime they get everything on their phones. If they do watch the box, it's usually in the evening and always some reality shit about people with too much money and shiny, waxed bodies shagging each other or bickering, or both at once. More often it's still Youtube on their phones though. I must admit that I too have been watching it and TikTok a lot more lately. Normally I'm really bad at watching anyone but myself, but while I've been sofa-bound, I've been studying tutorials on practical things like electric guitar playing, or hen keeping, just in case I ever get the urge. Oh and kitten videos. Lots of kitten videos. I can do without the make-up tutorials though, and the shrill, shouty pranksters – I fell victim to enough of those when I was at school to quite happily never encounter another one of those self-important prats, even virtually. They still never seem to find it funny if someone pranks them back, so some things stay reassuringly the same.

"Hey Mais, can I come in?"

"I don't see why not. Everyone else is here. The room's starting to look like a doss house."

"You lot, time to go."

"I don't know how you do that?"

"Do what?"

"Just tell the sofa-surfers to bail, and they go. Me, I keep dropping hints, but they just ignore me. I bet they've emptied the fridge again too."

"Just write down what shopping you need and I'll get it sent up."

"I'm not sure I can really afford to replace everything that swarm of locusts has eaten."

"Don't worry about that. They'll pay for it and deliver it. Just write a list of what you need."

"How was Morocco?"

"Wha... I wasn't in Morocco. Who said that?"

"Karla."

"Karla – right. I imagine she failed geography. I was in Manchester, visiting friends."

"Oh, so no sunshine and souks?"

"Just the Arndale Centre."

"And that gallery in Salford with the Lowry paintings."

"The Lowry. Shit. I should've gone there, shouldn't I?"

"Oh well, next time."

"I was just going to make a coffee actually."

"Oooh yes please."

"Thought you might say that."

Reuben has gone back downstairs and I'm waiting expectantly for a cup of caffeine heaven. I now wish I hadn't asked him to evict all of the young 'uns. There'll be no one to empty my shee-wee until Elaine gets here, if indeed she turns up at all. Did I mention that things are sounding a bit iffy where the care company she works for is concerned? They haven't paid her for two months apparently. She thinks they're about to go under. I can't really understand why. You'd think looking after the elderly and disabled was a growth area. It doesn't make any sense to me. I do hope she turns up today. I could desperately do with a wash down. I'll have to tell Reuben not to sit too near me in case I'm a bit whiffy. Well, perhaps I can phrase that a bit more elegantly.

****

Reuben didn't come back with a coffee. Now don't get me wrong, I'm not having a moan about that. Completely the opposite in fact. Reuben returned with a battered looking cardboard box with air holes roughly punched in its sides. From inside came the sound I've longed for so long to hear.

Miaow.

The cat is called Arthur. He's black with a white bib on his chest and little white socks. I mean his markings look like footwear, not that he's actually wearing any. He belonged to someone who's recently died, Reuben said. Someone his mum knew, presumably here in Brighton. He's a house cat, so he'll be happy to stay in here with me and not go outside. In fact he has never been outdoors so I have to make sure he doesn't get out. He's already made himself at home, curled up on the seat in the front window. If Mrs Webster can see him from the back window she's not letting on. I don't know if spiders get jealous or not, and she's been my only animal companion for almost a year now. I've already spent so long taking photos of Arthur, even though he's a curled up round of fur at the moment that my phone and tablet are clean out of battery. Even in his sleep he has star quality, no kidding. Together Arthur and me, we're gonna break the internet, just watch us. Insta Webster followers you better ready yourselves for the next sensation. First photos will be exclusively revealed when I've set up his site at approximately ten pm tonight, or sooner if my bloody batteries hurry up and charge.

When Reuben opened the box, he had to tip Arthur out on the floor, very gently of course. Arthur explored the flat very slowly and cautiously as if he expected the furniture to be booby-trapped or the floor mined. Perhaps where he came from was a little more hazardous than Chez Maisie. He didn't look too impressed by his new surroundings either, but that could be just his normal expression. You never can tell with cats. Reuben had brought some little tins of posh cat food, but I think Arthur is going to have to get used to budget supermarket brands, if he's not going to eat me out of flat and home. Still I'm so thrilled to have him, you could almost say that I'm finally living my dream. Mum kept promising to get me a cat and then there was always this excuse or that why it didn't happen. The last kitten was all booked up and everything and I thought finally this is it. But then I fell on the floor and had to be winched out my window by crane. Course the people selling my kitty weren't prepared to wait for me to come out of hospital. They returned our deposit in an envelope with a note calling Mum and me time-wasters. That was just rude. Mum rang them up and didn't half have a go, or so she told me. I was still stuck in the General at the time.

Reuben says Arthur is a gift to thank me for my artwork. He showed me a photo of his back tattoo on his phone, and although it's still not quite completed yet, the wings are truly beautiful, if I do say so myself. The detail is all there from the way the feathers catch the light to the way they softly bend and lie against the unmarked skin. He says he's had so many great comments and his friends are queuing up for me to design inkings for them too. First though he wants another one himself, of a coiled snake which he can have tattooed around his lower right arm. It can look like it's dropping down from the jungle frieze sleeve art above. He says he doesn't care what kind of snake as long as it has fangs and is coiled ready to strike. I've already found some photos of Pit Vipers, Black Mambas and a King Snake which all look quite promising. It all depends on what colour scheme he'd like to go with. For me it would be the King Snake, with its yellow, black and red bands, but of course the customer is always right.

While we were sitting having coffee, and I can just about sit again now, I told Reuben about my worries over Elaine.

He said I don't need to fret about care visits and my Personal Independence Payment and all that stuff now that I'm working for him. "You're on the payroll. I'll take care of you." He also joked about how now he has his wings I should see him as my guardian angel. "That's what I do, Maisie. I take care of people." Well I say he joked about it, but he seemed serious as he said it. He really does seem to think his role in life is to look after others. I wonder if that's the case why he isn't working as a doctor, a social worker or something like that. He is certainly a good, sympathetic listener. I'm not sure I'd quite trust him if he was my doctor though. You don't really want your doctor to be a bit mysterious and have a slightly dangerous way about him or her do you? I wonder if his caring for people includes the various teenage waifs and strays who all now see my flat as their crash pad. Does it also involve Adelina, whose love life he seems to take more than a little interest in, and Tom and his multitude of phones? The person to ask, I suspect, is Karla, when she's been smoking skunk, as she seems to do most days.

****

Elaine hasn't been round today, and she's not answering her phone. It's getting late now. I'm just going to have to sleep on the couch, unwashed, surrounded by dirty dishes and with a full shee-wee. I hope I don't dream of waterfalls or anything.

****

It's eight am. I've tipped some of the shee-wee contents into my empty coffee mug – gross I know, but at least that's allowed me to empty my bladder again. I've managed to put on some of my skin cream, which has stopped some of the itching, if not made me feel a lot cleaner, but I really do need to go to the toilet properly. I daren't eat until I do. Elaine's phone still isn't connecting, and I've heard the care company's out of office message so many times I could recite it word perfect. I can't live like this. I can't.

I'm on my feet – just. By levering myself on one of the sofa arms and forcing my knees to straighten, I'm standing. Trouble is, if I let go of the sofa arm I'm sure to topple over. I have however discovered and called a shop that supplies walking aids. It's only a few streets away. The guy answered in one ring, and he could bring me a second-hand walking frame right away. Of course I said yes. I hope right away means in minutes, not hours. My only other option is to call 999 and hope an ambulance crew will come and sort me out. It's not really their job I know, but there's only so long the sausages can remain in the grill if you know what I'm saying?

****

I used to have a walking frame with a shopping bag on it, but it disappeared from Mrs Latimer's. I think the NHS guy taking away a wheelchair I no longer needed took my walking frame too, thinking it was theirs. I can't see any other way it could've vanished. Getting a new one today, albeit without the bag has been a lifesaver. I'm now in the bathroom – and it feels like heaven. I'm all refreshed, washed, and revitalised, well pretty much anyway. The funny thing was Arthur joining me in there and trying to drink from the toilet. Clearly his previous home was no 'Downtown Abbey' or he'd have more refined manners. Now I can reach my grabber, I can walk to the kitchenette, put some food in his bowl and lower it to the ground without bending.

I might jazz the walking frame up with some stickers or wrap some of my crafting papers round it. I got quite into papier-mache a few years back. I made loads and loads of bowls for mum. I thought she would find them useful but she kept forgetting what they were made of and leaving them in the sink to go soggy. Well that's what she said anyway. My hunch is that it was Shaun who was vandalising my creations, out of some kind of twisted, bitter spitefulness.

****

Coming out of the bathroom I had intended to sit back down on the couch, but Karla had arrived unannounced and taken my place, the cheeky mare. Then I noticed what she was doing. She had my dressing gown cord tied around her arm and she was injecting herself, just below the elbow. She looked up, saw me but carried on regardless. When she'd done, she leant back, relaxing, and patted the cushion next to her, inviting me to sit. Well you can bet I checked the whereabouts of that syringe before I sat, but sit I did.

"Karla? I was just wondering if you can tell me something?"

"Yeah?"

"Do you and everyone else work for Reuben?"

"Uh..."

"And what do you work doing exactly? I mean it doesn't involve drugs or something does it?"

"Uh..."

"Karla? Karla, are you okay? Karla! Karla wake up!"

"I am awake. Get off!"

"Karla? Karla you've fallen asleep again."

"No..."

"Not again. Karla!"

Miaow.

"Have you seem my phone, Arthur? It's an emergency!"

When I gave Karla another little shake to try to wake her, her eyes rolled up into her head. That cannot be good. Reuben wasn't answering so I called Tom. His is the only other number I had to hand and I had to do something. I mean I didn't know if she'd overdosed or just fallen asleep. Luckily he was in his flat and came straight up. He took Karla's pulse, then put his ear to her chest and said she was okay. He didn't seem surprised or worried about her at all. I just needed to look after her until she came to, he said. I felt like saying, what about me? I'm the one who needs care, and I didn't ask for someone to sit on my sofa, shoot themselves full of heroin or whatever and pass out, I really didn't. Still I stayed with Karla and eventually her eyelids flickered and she started mumbling about bees. I've no idea why. "Bees. No. The window. Let them out." Her hands moved as if trying to swat imaginary bees away from her face, but her eyes remained blank. "Let them out!" It was like she'd become a zombie. I'd hardly have been surprised if she'd ripped my head off and eaten it. Then she stood up, lurched forward and left without a backward glance or a thank you.

I watched the lunchtime news. There was a story from another part of the country where the police were shouting and smashing their way into people's homes. Some of those PVC doors are a pretty good deterrent to police with their red door smasher thingies. Some of them just wouldn't go in. Either that or the cops were a bit on the feeble side. They wear all that body armour so you can't tell. Anyway, the police were looking for young people involved in county lines drug dealing. Could this be something that Karla was caught up in, as well as some of the others? It did seem to involve teenagers a lot of the time, and the people with pixelated faces who were being dragged off in handcuffs did seem to have a similar dress sense as some of my young visitors. I can't go jumping to conclusions though. After all who doesn't wear a grey hoodie and baggy trackies occasionally at least? Also until Karla today, and leaving aside a bit of wacky baccy smoking, I haven't actually seen actual drug dealing going on, either in, or outside my flat. It's not like anyone's walking around waving wads of cash or weighing out pills and powder to the sound of drill music. I know the teenagers listen to music on their phones and I bet it's not Adele or Ed Sheeran, but they don't wear bling or bandanas or anything. The person who could put my mind at rest or not, is most likely Adelina, though I've not seen that much of her lately. A couple of days ago, I heard what sounded like her little wheelie case being heaved down the stairs, so she's probably been on one of her spa breaks with shopping. Earlier today though I think I heard her heels click, clicking back up the stairs. Hopefully she'll drop in on me soon. We're long overdue for a Hungry Hippos rematch.

I called Mum and she answered. First thing she said though was "do you know how much this is costing?" I told her to chill. I've a job now, I'm practically independent and can certainly afford to call my mother to see how the holiday is going. She sighed and said that it was very hot. I mean honestly. If she'd wanted to be cool and damp she could've stayed here in good old Brighton and saved herself the budget airfare. I didn't say that. I told her to get Shaun to treat her to the biggest ice cream they could find. She cheered up a bit at that. She said they sell ice creams with alcohol in them in Spain, even to kids, and they are seriously nice.

I started telling her all about Arthur. The fact he has a few odd clumps of white hairs where otherwise his fur is black, the fact he only seems to purr in his sleep, and his adorable habit of paddling his front paws in his water dish. I thought she understood and was entertained by the feline antics, but then she asked, "who's Arthur?" and I'd like made it really, really obvious he's a sodding cat.

"You've not got sunstroke have you, Mum?"

"No, no, I've stayed in all day."

"You're on holiday and you've just stayed in? You're no fun. Where's Shaun?"

"In the bar."

"You've had a row?"

"No, he's just watching some sport or other on the big screen. It's too noisy, too hot for me."

"Did you remember your HRT patches?"

"Yeah, it's just... it's just I'm feeling a bit tired, love."

"Hung over. Right."

"No. No not... I just thought I'd have a lie down. A little siesta."

"Fair enough I suppose. That's what holidays are for right? Taking it easy."

"Yeah, Mais."

"Don't forget my postcard will you?"

CHAPTER 9

I don't know if there's a problem with the Spanish post. Perhaps they just bin our postcards to punish us over Brexiting, I don't know. Anyway, Mum was due to fly back this morning, and I've still not received my card. Normally she would have at least texted by now to let me know the plane had landed. It made me wonder if there were any flight cancellations or other problems, but I've looked online and there seem to be no problems involving Gatwick airport at all today. I even went as far as installing a plane tracker app. It was free in my app store. I never like paying for apps especially as you still find they're stuffed full of adverts.

I had a rough idea of when Mum and Shaun's plane was leaving and from where so I followed quite a number jets across the English Channel. It wasn't the most riveting pastime and I started wondering what the most boring app you can download does. Half an hour into the tiny planes travelling across a map and I'd nodded off. Perhaps that's what it's really designed to do – counting planes rather than sheep. I woke with a start to the sound of Arthur sharpening his claws on the back of the sofa. Mum must be home by now. I could ring her again, but she's bound to be round later, showing off her tan, and hopefully bearing gifts of the edible kind.

My leg's less swollen and more moveable, so I spent last night in my own bed. I'd almost forgotten what stretching out feels like. I braved picking up Arthur from the couch and he let me cradle him in my arms. He seems quite a laid back character though he hasn't yet purred while awake. He still smells of his previous home, where his owner obviously used copious amounts of air freshener. I don't think that's because of Arthur though. So far he has proved himself completely house-trained, well apart from over enthusiastically excavating in the kitty litter, so that some of it has spilled onto the floor. At least he's done his business slap bang in the middle of the tray, and covered it up. Now I can't currently carry him over to the back window to get him and Mrs Webster properly introduced, but I held him up, and waved his paw at her. That's when an odd thing happened. I expect you think I'm going to say that Mrs Webster slowly lifted a leg and waved back. Wouldn't that have been perfect, if a little too 'Charlotte's Web' for you to believe me about? But no, that isn't what happened.

Taking one look, or should that be eight looks, considering how many eyes she has, Mrs Webster suddenly started jerking up and down, so quickly her body became a blur. I've only ever seen her do that once before, when a magpie sat on the guttering above her on her old window at Mrs Latimer's. I had banged on the glass and shouted to scare it off before it could think about making a snack of my eight-legged friend, but Mrs Webster had already begun that rapid jerking to and fro .She didn't immediately stop either, even though the bird was long gone. She'd kept it up for several minutes, then gradually slowed back down, like a runner beginning to jog, then walk, until once again she was hanging motionless in her web. Now I'm sure Mrs Webster's twerking is some kind of defensive measure, but if you ask me it's not a very sensible one, as the movement surely draws more attention to her? Anyway, it appears Mrs Webster is scared of or dislikes Arthur, which is a shame, but it's early days. Hopefully she'll get used to him being around before too long.

I've left Mum a text saying Arthur was looking forward to meeting her and included a cute picture of his face. She must be home by now. I finally got through to Elaine too. She said somewhat shortly that she was at the Job Centre Plus, waiting to see an advisor, and couldn't talk for long. The care firm had ceased to be, and although she suspected she could find another carers' role quite easily, she was thinking of going into something else, which didn't involve so much driving. She quite fancied working in a clothes shop. I said "don't we all" but most of them don't seem to last five minutes. Then I asked her about what I was supposed to do. Was a new company taking over the contract for my care, or did I need to notify the council or indeed the NHS? Elaine said she hadn't a clue, in a tone that meant she couldn't care less and added she was sure I'd get something sorted out, meaning 'sod off and bother someone else, you're not my responsibility any more'. I won't really miss her if truth be told. I wish there was some way of getting my old care team Orla and Tiffany back. They were reassigned when I went into hospital and that was the last I saw of them. Since it was the same care provider they're probably down the Job Centre Plus too. I wonder what the 'Plus' is for. Do they help you find something else apart from a job now? Like a date? A makeover? The mind boggles.

It's now four phone calls later and nothing is sorted out. Avery's here and made us both a Red Leicester cheese toastie, so I'm surviving. I keep reminding him that he said he needed to stay out of Brighton because of someone here who wants to kill him, but he thinks that "beef" is now "history". It has been "sorted".

"Avery, this has nothing to do with County Lines does it?"

"All my days, Mais! For real?"

"Well I had to ask. I mean you do hear all this stuff about gangs and drugs and stabbings, and you did seem pretty scared the first time you turned up here."

"Don't worry yourself right? That's over, I'm telling you. Brighter days, Maisie. Brighter days."

"Brighter days? You sound like an advert for soap powder. Which reminds me, if you're going out in a bit, could you take some washing down the launderette for me. later?"

"Maybe. Depends."

"Depends on what?"

"How busy I get yeah?"

"Busy? How busy can you get, Ave, you're a kid? I'll pay you. Sit and watch my washing and I'll give you a fiver."

"What? Five pounds? All at once?"

Followers, I think he was being sarcastic, but he did take my bag of washing when he went out, bless him. Normally Mum would've done the washing but there's still been no word from her. I'm getting quite cross to be honest with you.

I was still patiently waiting for my washing to reappear in a slightly cleaner if damper state when I heard raised voices, crashes and thumps from Adelina's room above me. She seemed to be having a mighty row with someone. There was a scream. Loud and scared. If I'd been able to get up the stairs I would've charged up there, or downstairs to get Reuben, but his phone was switched off, so I had to call Tom again. I admit I don't know if he has any relationship at all with Adelina, I didn't really see them acknowledge each other, let alone chat at the party, but she is his neighbour and she sounded like she was in trouble. The only alternative was to dial 999, and in the time it would take for the police to get here, Adelina might've been murdered, if she hadn't been already. Tom answered immediately. "Thanks, Maisie, I'll sort it." A few moments later there was the sound of voices on the stairs, and I could hear Tom knocking on Adelina's door. He knocked and called out to ask if she was alright, then knocked again. Suddenly Reuben burst into my room.

"You got anything I..." He trailed off as his eyes alighted on my newly customised walking frame. "Perfect" he said and carted it off. A few seconds later there was an almighty crash upstairs, then another and another.

"One, two, three!" shouted Reuben. Sounds of splintering wood, raised voices, thumps and crashes followed. I couldn't resist using my stick to limp to the door. Nervously I peered out. Adelina's door was open, and had a big, ragged hole in it. Reuben and Tom had hold of a thickset, balding man. Reuben was twisting the guy's arm up his back. The guy was shouting and yelling, nasty things about Adelina and women in general. I'm not gonna repeat them, you've all heard that kind of shit. As they came down the stairs, I quickly closed my door. I heard a car draw up outside and went to the front window. Jonas, the man mountain and a guy I didn't know got out of a car and buzzed to be let in, trying all the buzzers. I know Reuben had asked me not to let anyone in, but I knew Jonas was his friend so I pressed the button to unlock the door.

The next thing was Jonas and his companion were with Tom in the street, laying in to the man from Adelina's room. Reuben opened my door, beckoned me away from the window. I could hear them still kicking the guy outside, but I was relieved in a way, not to be watching it all. Reuben had returned my walking frame, but one of its legs now appeared slightly wonky when he put it on the ground.

"Is Adelina..."

"She's fine yeah.."

"That guy, he hasn't hurt her?"

"No, and he won't be round here again."

"Are you really sure she's okay, Reuben? I mean it sounded pretty bad from down here?" The shouting outside had stopped, car doors slammed and a car revved up and sped off. Reuben walked to my doorway.

"Adi – can you come down here a minute?"

Adelina walked in. She was wearing a tight leather mini-skirt and low cut top, but was barefoot in her black tights. She held a leather wallet in one hand. She walked slightly stiffly and possibly painfully but when she saw me she smiled.

"Thanks, Maisie – for calling the guys." Then she looked at Reuben, "I won't be seeing him again, right? Even if he does have a yacht?"

"He might not have a yacht much longer."

"Thanks, baby."

"You need to find yourself a new man, Adi." I thought at the time he was flirting with her, but now as I think about it I'm not so sure.

"Yes, but maybe not today, eh?"

"No, no, take a week... maybe longer..."

"I think maybe I'll change my profile, you know?"

"Ask Tom about it yeah?"

She walked over to Reuben and handed him the wallet. "What's this?" He looked surprised to have it handed to him. Curiosity got the better of him and he opened it. It was absolutely bulging with notes. Seeing my expression he threw it to me. I'd no idea how much money was there but it was all in fifties. I've never even owned one fifty-pound note. I threw it back to Reuben, who looked at it, unimpressed.

"He left it behind?"

"And his jacket."

"Bin the jacket."

"It's Armani, baby."

"Flog it then."

Reuben made as if to pocket the wallet, then grinned and tossed it to Adelina. Not expecting it, she failed to catch it and it landed at her feet.

"For me?"

"It's yours. Should keep you going until you can find another sorry sap to bankroll you. Hopefully a better tempered one." She picked up the wallet, but didn't seem particularly pleased with her windfall. She just looked tired. "How about we all go out tonight?"

"Okay." Again, she didn't sound terribly enthused.

"Great. I'll get Tom to book the VIP area." He turned to look at me. "Not quite sure how we'll get you there, Mais, but we will."

"Look, I expect you're going to a club or something, and after the party, I'm not really up for any more dancing yet..."

"Well you can just sit and sip champagne. It's really comfy where we're going. You'll love it, trust me."

"I dunno, do you think Arthur'll be alright on his own." Reuben glanced at Arthur, asleep in the window. He grinned. "He'll be just fine, Mais."

****

It's eight pm and I can see a stretch limo has pulled up downstairs. Adelina is sitting on my window seat, dressed in a sparkly silver dress. She has long earrings that are dripping with real or fake diamonds, matching the tiny stud in her nose. Her make up is like a model's – all sculpted cheekbones and wide eyes. I'm just wearing my best shiny green shirt and a pair of black slacks. Avery must've put my washing on at the wrong setting because although I've got my navy blue sparkly top back, Barbie would now have a job fitting into it. It reminds me of that thing we all did at school where you shrank crisp packets in the oven and turned them into little badges. I loved my Quavers one. Wore it for years.

Sadly the stretch limo's doors are ordinary sized and I know from experience that I can't get into a normal car. It was nice of my housemates to invite me to join them on their evening out, but I'm actually relieved not to be going. In a nightclub all eyes are always going to be on me, and sometimes I don't mind, but a lot of the time, like tonight, I do.

"Adelina, you need to go and get in the car. Reuben and Tom are waiting."

"I wait with you."

"I can't get in that car. Go on, go and enjoy yourself."

"We'll go soon." The limo is pulling away without either of us, but Adi doesn't seem too concerned. When she arrived, she had a bottle of wine with her, and now she is pouring us both a glass. "Always, always, pre-load."

"Pre-load?"

"Isn't that what you call getting a little pissed before you go out?"

"Or very pissed before you go out."

"Yes, very pissed! Shall we?"

****

We didn't actually have time to get bladdered. While Adelina was sipping her wine and cooing over Arthur, who seemed to for some reason, prefer her bony lap to mine, a mini-bus style taxi with sliding doors arrived below. "That's you and me," she declared. My walking frame is now not quite what it was, after being used as a battering ram, but with two glasses of wine inside me, it still seemed a safer bet than my stick, as I get ready to descend.

****

Adelina held onto my arm and helped me down the stairs like I was her elderly auntie. I was surprisingly easy to load into the taxi and there was still plenty of room for Adelina. "Let's have the radio." The driver obliged, with an admiring glance at Adelina. She screwed up her face. "Not this song. Is too hea-vy." It was only Bon Jovi, not the hardest rock in the galaxy. To me it's metal light. You should hear some of the stuff Shaun listens to. Death Metal I think they call it. All about Satan and jolly stuff like that. Perhaps though it's the lyrics Adelina doesn't like, as they deal with a broken relationship, and her love life has after all temporarily gone tits-up. Before I could analyse the words of the song, the radio had been switched onto another radio station and they were playing Rag 'n' Bone man. I do love Raggy and so it seemed did Adelina. We both sang along and the driver even joined in like a kind of 'Taxi Pool Karaoke'. I had a feeling it was going to be a really special night.

We headed along the coast road and there was enough light from the street lamps to see that the sea was looking angry, grey and very foamy. Every now and then a giant wave crashed right over the prom, speckling the windscreen with water. Then we were heading away from the bright lights of the city and down the long slope into Brighton Marina. There are clubs, there are bars, shops, bowling and a cinema, its neon sign shining out among the skyscrapers. Beyond the bars and shops are rows of super-yachts like the one that trawled Bessie my previous scooter from the briny, and a Walk Of Fame too. Mum and I did the Walk Of Fame once, but I can only remember Rizzle Kicks, out of all of the names of famous sons and daughters of Brighton. There has to have been a few people a bit more ritzy than them, but that's something you'll have to check out for yourself.

The marina is a cool destination for a night out, and has the added advantage of the random chance of meeting a zillionaire, straight off his or her yacht, or living in one of the luxury apartments and penthouses with sea views and concierges who go to the launderette for you. Though if you live in a posh gaff like that you must have a washing machine surely? Probably a tumble dryer too. My knowledge of these things only comes from those free property porn magazines that pop through the communal front door at regular intervals. The other residents don't seem particularly interested, but I've studied marina apartments large and small, and also read up the beachside residences of Hove Esplanade where Fatboy Slim lives. One day, when I'm out and about, I'll actually remember to buy a lottery ticket and not get seduced by the scratch cards instead. It's probably the only way I will ever live in a luxury marina apartment. I say that quite confidently.

The club was called 'the Chic Shark' which is hard to say without spitting on your neighbour, or saying 'shit' for 'chic'. You'd have thought the owner might've thought of that when he or she named it, wouldn't you? There was a cartoon shark over the doorway wearing a bow tie, which wasn't exactly my idea of chic either. I'd seen mention of this club in the free lifestyle magazines which are like the property ones but feature less houses. Apparently it is *the* happening place to go at the moment.

The noise, the heat and pulsating blue lights hit us as we walked in. Adelina gave her faux fur to the cloakroom attendant but I hadn't bothered to wear my coat, so it was from the Antarctic to Sahara-like conditions for me. I know I shouldn't be self-conscious about clothing adding a few centimetres or so to my girth but neither of my coats is very 'night-outish' if you know what I mean.

The bar stools looked perilous. Try to perch myself on one of those tiny red velvet cushions and it might've become a suppository. I opted instead to lounge as elegantly as I could at the side of the room where the light was more flattering – well actually it was seriously dark. Don't get me wrong, I wasn't feeling sad or wallflowery. As I literally don't get out much, watching this human throng was deeply interesting. I took few photos and shot as many video clips as my phone battery would allow. I'd be sharing those with Abby and other friends later. There was a couple tongue kissing like snakes mating. I got quite a sharp picture of that. It'll make Abby scream. She isn't keen on public displays of lust – PDLs. Then there was the guy dad dancing, though he couldn't have been out of his teens. If you move like Rick Astley when you're aged eighteen, then you'll probably be dancing like Russ Abbott by the time you're twenty-five. Shaun likes to sing one of Russ's. It's called 'What An Atmosphere'. He usually does it to tell Mum that I'm not speaking to him again. Otherwise she doesn't notice. I think she's used to people ignoring Shaun. It's not just me, it's most of the WI and the lady on the till in the Co-op who he always wants to tell one of his jokes to, while she's trying to read the number of a reduced item's barcode label that has failed to scan.

I'm not good with humidity and the place was simply heaving with bodies. I was sweating an ocean and could feel prickly heat beginning almost everywhere. I even get hives on the back of my neck where I'm allergic to my own sweat. It's like I'm allergic to myself – how is that even possible? I was wearing a new deodorant. It's one I ordered because it says it works for 48 hours. It might stop those under arm damp patches, but I'm sure it just makes you sweat elsewhere I mean it all has to go somewhere doesn't it? If you covered yourself from tip to toe in anti-perspirant you'd just drown on the inside where the water couldn't get out. Either that or you'd wee gallons and gallons. That's my theory anyway. Feel free to check it out with your GP if you want to annoy him or her.

Across the room I saw someone pushing through the crowd. I'd recognise those tatty white dreads and nose ring anywhere even with an ultra-violet strobe going bonkers. Tom spoke to Adelina and she gestured to me. He pointed to a spiral staircase at the side of the dance floor and beckoned to me before going up it. With the heat, the noise and a glass of two of vino inside me, I knew it was going to be a tall order getting myself and my walking frame onto even the first step. As I looked up it seemed to twist into infinity. Where's a team of expert mountaineers when you need them, with their crampons and fancy knots?

A bouncer with an earpiece loomed up in front of me. No joke, I swear he was almost my size, though much steadier on his feet. He bellowed in my ear, and I recognised the words 'escort' and 'lift'. I hoped that meant he was going to escort me to a lift rather than he thought I was some kind of escort and was about to try and lift me into the air, for reasons unknown. Fortunately, it did turn out to be an elevator he was taking me to, though a rather small one. There was just room for me and the frame to squeeze inside. He pushed a button, for floor one I think, and mercifully left me in there alone. If he'd joined me in the lift we'd have arrived resembling a cube-shaped meatball. The lift stopped, doors slid open and I was looking at a velvet rope with a 'no admittance' sign on it. I was standing there like the sweaty mug I was, wondering whether or not I was allowed to pass, when Adelina sashayed up from the other side, dress sparking like a movie star's at the Oscars, and unhooked it.

We walked through into a large room with another bar in it, but the music here was much softer and the lights were twinkling chandeliers. Mercifully there was also air-conditioning. Four large groups of people were sprawled on leather sofas with round shaped tables in the middle. On each table stood a metal ice bucket of what I assumed was champagne. Reuben and Tom were in one corner. Reuben was impressively dressed in a slim-fitting purple shirt and black trousers. His black curls were swept back and glossy, and I noticed more than one passing woman giving him an admiring glance. Several other women clearly knew him, one coming over to whisper something in his ear, which resulted in a slow, satisfied smile. Tom though had a suit on that looked like he'd hauled it from a charity shop reject pile, before the rag merchants had time to collect it. I joined them, reclining on a sofa that was the most comfortable thing I've ever sat on. It literally embraced my arse and I do mean in a good way. Tom poured me a glass of bubbles.

I started to thank Reuben and Tom for inviting me, but at that moment a small group of guys entered the VIP area and caught their attention. They wore suit jackets with jeans and gold jewellery. One had sunglasses perched on top of his head, despite it being night. Reuben excused himself from our group saying he had to go and talk business with the newcomers. I couldn't hear much about the business, but where the new guys were concerned, whenever they raised their voices, I could hear that their English was heavily accented. When one of them caught me gawking at him, he shot me a glance that was anything but friendly. I got a very bad vibe off them to be honest, and judging by the slightly apprehensive glances Adelina was also giving them, and the tense way Tom was now sitting, so did they. I checked my phone, just in case Mum had tried to ring while I was downstairs with the music banging, but there were no messages.

Tom was checking two of his phones simultaneously and Adelina had spotted a woman behind the bar who she obviously knew and after greeting her with two kisses and a huge hug, she sat on a bar stool talking to her animatedly, and by her gestures, the conversation was about men. Since there was good phone reception I called Abby. I knew it was past her bedtime but if she's not wanting to sleep she leaves it switched on but in silent mode, in case I want to call. She answered straight away. We'd agreed to hook up in hangouts, so we could have a natter. Abby got M.E in her early teens so she had never been in a club. She can't drink alcohol yet anyway, but when it's an onscreen night-out, who cares if you're under age?

"Your life has just got so glamorous, Maisie."

"Never imagined I'd be drinking champers in the VIP area."

"VIP – serious? Show me the room. I'm amazingly good at spotting celebs."

"Okay, moving round very slowly. Tell me to stop if I'm making you dizzy, Abbs."

"Oh my God! My God – him over there. On the table by the door?"

"Who is it?"

"Dunno his name but he plays for Arsenal."

"Are you sure? I mean this is Brighton. You sure he doesn't play for the Albion?"

"I don't know the Brighton team. Only really famous footballers."

"Ouch, don't let my Mum's fella hear you say that. But you can't remember his name anyway."

"I'd have to switch my computer on to google him, or close this screen down for a sec."

"Yeah, well it's not like I'm actually that interested. Look would you like to meet him?"

"What? Noooo!"

"It's okay, I'm just getting up. Give me a minute, I'll take you over."

"Oh my God! Oh my God. You so know what I'm like in like social situations."

"It'll be fine, Abbs."

"I'm in my pyjamas, Maisie!"

"Get closer to the camera then."

"You can't see them now can you?"

"No, but you need to back up a little bit, you look like a spoon-face."

The footballer turned out to be very nice and he got Adelina's friend to bring over her order pad, so he could rip off a bit of paper to give Abby his autograph on. It was quite a squiggly signature so I still don't know what his name was, until I remind Abby to give me all the details.

Across the room, things didn't appear to be going quite so well at Reuben's business meeting. Raised voices, threatening-looking gesticulations from the newcomers and Tom rushing to join him weren't to me good signs. Then one of the guys went to push Reuben and he squared up to him in return. With Reuben's back garden toned muscles, my money was on him if there was going to be a fight, but Tom got between them, and things calmed down a bit, though the discussion still appeared to be very heated. I glanced at Adelina, who was at the bar again, and she too looked anxious. Abby was oblivious, as the back of my phone was towards the bar, and she had eyes only for the footballer anyway. Finally the newcomers with the suits and jeans left their drinks unfinished on the bar and headed back down the stairs.

As they prepared to descend, one of the businessmen turned back and lifted his hand to make a very clear gun gesture at Reuben, before returning back to the club level. By the man's expression he was not joking either. Reuben looked about to go after him, but Tom laid his hand on his arm, eyes saying 'don't'. I'm guessing it would've been a rash thing to do because our geezers were outnumbered, and for all we knew, those guys were actually armed. I say this assuming Reuben and Tom don't or weren't carrying guns, though I don't know either of them well enough to be sure about this.

Abby's mum came into her bedroom and told her she should be in bed, so she had to end the call. Without her, I didn't really have much to say to the footballer, or he to me. His party consisted of a number of young women whose charms, if you get my meaning, were far more obvious than mine, and unlike Abby, I wasn't sufficiently interested in soccer to be able to make even slightly intelligent conversation about it. Abby watches sports on TV, but I don't. It takes me right back to cruel PE teachers and even crueller teammates in school games lessons. If he'd been a boggle champion, or even a tiddlywinks ace I could've seriously related to him, but as it was, I decided to return to my own table. It wasn't as if he was even that good looking, in my opinion.

Adelina, Tom and Reuben had all sat down again and were drinking champagne, but the fun had gone out of the evening. I felt for Reuben. I've had a fair few death threats made against me, even if most of them are virtual ones from trolls who wouldn't know one end of a gun from the other. No one spoke, as Tom refilled my glass. Unfortunately, the pre-loading was starting to affect me, and although I probably should've kept my thoughts to myself at this point, I didn't.

"Didn't look like the meeting went too well." Tom frowned to tell me to leave it, but Reuben regarded me levelly.

"People expect too much."

"Did that guy threaten you?"

"He wouldn't be the first." He stood up, and I thought I'd offended him. Reuben isn't all that easy to read, not to me at any rate. He beckoned me to follow him. I looked round at Adelina and Tom, imagining he was gathering us all to leave but it was only me he wanted.

I followed Reuben to the lift and he pressed a button, but my head was slightly woozy and I wasn't quite sure whether we were going up or down. To be honest, even when the lift jerked into life, I wasn't sure of our direction. The doors opened and we walked along a short corridor. I was aware I was painfully slow with my frame, but Reuben stayed alongside of me, and if he was irritated by my snail's pace, he didn't say so or show it.

Along the corridor was a fire door. He pushed the bar to open it and a blast of cold air hit me. We were outside, on some kind of flat roof, God knows how many storeys up. Reuben walked to the edge of the roof, where there was only a short wall of bricks preventing a fatal plummet. He stepped up onto the parapet. I wanted to scream then, to tell him to come down, to stop being stupid. I wondered how much he'd had to drink, although he still seemed completely steady on his feet. On one side of us were the chalk cliffs that led up to the coast road, far higher than the roof we were on. On the other side was the marina with the sea beyond. A bitingly cold wind passed through me like a knife. Why oh why had I come out without a coat? What's the point of being vain when you're me? It was a clear night and Reuben's earring sparkled in the light of the orange haloed moon.

"When you stand up here, you think of the city right?" He looked back at me and I nodded, not really understanding and more worried about him going over the edge than anything. "You think of Brighton and all the stuff going on in it. And you think about how do I fit into that? How you're gonna make your way? How you're gonna get by? And people don't make it easy. They don't want you to succeed. Either they want you to fail or they don't care." To my relief he turned away from the edge and sat down on the narrow brick wall. "And they don't leave you many choices, many chances to make something of yourself. So either you accept that, you take the crap job with its zero hours, you rent that rubbish room with the damp problem, or you start to look about you. What if you could do something else? Something others aren't doing or at least, aren't doing well? Now that thing is bound to have its downside, because that's why the others aren't doing it. It might be dirty, it might be dangerous, it might even be illegal, but if it's something you can do – you can choose to do it your way. Make it better, make it safer, and if you employ people, treat them right. They're going to do what they do, whether you're running the show or not, but if you pay them properly, provide them with security and better working conditions, then you're not doing a bad thing." He stopped and looked up at the stars. I did the same, it seemed only polite. "My life is always dangerous, Mais. And sometimes, like I said at the museum, I'd give anything to fly away from it. But that isn't an option. Not right now." He stood up again and held out his hand, as he stepped towards the edge again.

"Scared?" I was, I honestly was. I don't like heights at the best of times, and this well it was more like the weirdest of times. But I also didn't want him seeing me as weak – or as silly, fat Maisie. Did he see me like that? Was I the butt of his jokes behind my back? Had I been invited to the club tonight because he saw me as a friend and valued my company, or was I just some curiosity, some freak?

I took Reuben's hand. His rings were cold like ice. I joined him at the edge of the roof and looked into the abyss beyond, steeling myself to stop my teeth chattering as the wind bit hard into my sweat-damp face and ears. We can't have stood there like that for more than a minute or so, and I know this sounds really corny but time really did stand still. We could have been there for an hour or more. A week, a month, a year. Because as I walked back to the lift I had enough thoughts in my head to fill that length of time. The thing they all centred around was nothing to do with Reuben, the roof, the night or anything. The big thought was that I'm Maisie and my world is a big world. It's not one room, where I sit like Mrs Webster waiting for something to happen. My world is one where I go out, I have adventures, and I try new things with new people. I take risks, I flirt with danger, I know sexy people and I'm alive, as truly alive, as my globe-trotting sister, my holidaying mother, the people who have always written me off and seen me as not worth bothering with. My world is a big world and the doubters, the sniggerers, the pointers and the trolls can't make me feel small ever again.

****

Oh shit. Like... fuck! I just woke up and I've looked back over what I posted last night. I mean what was that? Did any of that really happen? I mean I know I went to that nightclub and I can see and smell spilt champagne on my shirt. But what on earth was I thinking, standing on the edge of a rooftop? Or did that not happen and I just dozed off on the comfy sofa in the VIP room? Why would Reuben have taken me up onto the roof, when he could have been impressing one of the beautiful girls who so clearly wanted to get to know him better? Why didn't he take Adelina up there? They would make such a beautiful couple. And what was he trying to tell me and why? I think it was a dream. It had to be a dream, didn't it?

Look, my first thought was to delete all that stuff. I mean I'm quite embarrassed by it actually, and that's saying something. You know me, we've shared my battles with thrush, under breast chafing and intermittent constipation over the years. But I don't make up stuff ever – and I honestly don't know whether I made that stuff about Reuben on the roof up. I might try to google that building in a minute and see if it even has a flat roof. I don't actually remember much about the journey home or going to bed, as I must've done, some time around four am. I suppose I could erase that post, but I'm not going to. I'll just say that I don't entirely know whether that's exactly what happened, or exactly what Reuben said to me. It felt clear when I wrote it before I went to sleep but I'm less sure of it now. Perhaps it'll make more sense to you guys than it does to me. Whether it does or not, I'd like to know your thoughts.

Maisie, I really thought you were going to tell us the guy suddenly unfolded his wings and flew off. How much champers did you have, love? @davyscientist

Get out of that house!!! Now!!!! @PaigeDunn456

On the roof, that was soooo romantic.... Like that scene in 'Titantic' @AbbyAtHome

Hi Maisie,

I've finally started reading your blog, because we wanted to check you're recovering after hurting your leg at the party. Please, please be careful. That Reuben sounds like a bad lot. Who knows what he's mixed up in? Do you think he was on drugs when he was standing on that roof? I saw him snorting what I think was cocaine at your party. You ought to see if your social worker, the housing department or whoever can find you somewhere else to live. I mean it's a nice enough flat, but I think you really do need to stay away from those people. After seeing them all at your party, I really wasn't that impressed.

Take care, your friend, Donal

CHAPTER 10

I know I'm a late riser. I know I can sleep through practically anything, especially when hung over, but it was still a bit of a shock when I reached the kitchenette. The bench was covered in cornflakes, some stuck in little pools of strawberry jam. There was a jammy trainer print on the floor too, which I'd already trod in, in my almost clean bed socks. Urgh! Clearly someone had made him or herself a breakfast at my expense again and in the messiest way possible. Probably Karla, though possibly Avery, Grace or persons unknown. I'm sure I'd locked the door when I came in, though as previously discussed, I'm not sure I'm the only one with a key. Clearly the breakfasting person or people had somewhere to head off to, quite early, and when I pulled out the toaster I found a couple of screwed up rail tickets behind it, dated for days last week. One is to Eastbourne, the other Ashford in Kent.

I'm less keen on Karla coming in here, now I know she uses hard drugs, but it's difficult to ban her, or indeed any of my visitors, even though some of them could almost now be described as lodgers. When I need a small amount of shopping, washing done, an undelivered parcel collected, they are, I admit, pretty useful. Now however with Mum being back, perhaps I can find a way of relying on my guests less. I'd like to have a bit more time to myself. It's been ages since I did any card making or used my filters and photo apps to take arty photos of Mrs Webster. She's a very old spider now. I want to make sure we get to spend some quality time together before she eventually passes. I know other spiders may come along, but it won't be the same. There is only one Mrs W.

I've just left messages for the social wonder to pick up on Monday, and hopefully she'll know who I should call to get a new care company on my case. Otherwise it will be the usual pass the parcel between the council, DWP and NHS, all suggesting I'm the responsibility of someone else.

I've cleared up the cornflakes and jam that was on the bench. I know it might sound a bit gross, but I can't really afford to waste that cereal, so that's today's breakfast. Not the ones that are on the floor though. I can't reach those. I can't manage the hoover while walking with a frame, so they'll jut have to stay there, getting crunched underfoot. Hopefully having a cat means they won't attract mice.

When I looked in the fridge to retrieve an open half can for Arthur I found the can was still there, but it was completely empty. Either someone loves cat food with their cornflakes and jam, or they fed Arthur for me. At least there's some milk left for my cereal and tea, even if it smells like it might be slightly on the turn. Perhaps that's why they left it. There's also a used coffee mug in the fridge and a dirty plate. If I was Sherlock Holmes I'd deduce that the person who left them there comes from a home with a dishwasher but isn't the sharpest spine on the hedgehog. In other words, Grace.

Shaun answered when I called Mum. He said she was still asleep. It was by then nearly midday.

"What jetlagged is she? It's hardly a long-haul flight from Marbella."

"Actually we came back on Thursday."

"Thursday? I thought you were returning on Saturday! You mean to say the two of you have been back all this time and neither of you has even thought to pick up the phone to see if I'm okay."

"I'm sure you'd have called if you wanted something. You always do."

"Excuse me? What's that supposed to mean? I'm the one who's been sitting here worrying, that you've been in a plane crash, or are 'banged up abroad', got food poisoning or whatever. I mean no arrival text! Not even a poxy postcard! Just how long does it actually take to write 'Wish You Were Fucking Here' even if you don't mean it?'

"The world doesn't revolve around you, Maisie."

"Or you, you selfish arsehole."

I didn't really mean to say that. Okay it was fully deserved and an accurate description of the guy, but I didn't mean to blurt it out. Usually when I'm gobby to Shaun he just 'f's' and blinds back. He's quite capable of standing up for himself and giving me a right old mouthful, so don't go feeling sorry for him or anything. But of course when that's happened we've been in the same room so he's not been able to cut me off. That's what he did this time – put the phone down on me, the bastard. I tried Mum's mobile but it was switched off as per usual. Typical.

Someone keeps ringing my door buzzer. I left it the first few times, because if Mum's in bed and everyone else seems to be able to let themselves in and come and go as they please, then it's probably not somebody I want to talk to. Also I remember Reuben's warning about letting people I don't know in. Finally though, curiosity got the better of me, as it always seems to do. Honestly I can't help myself.

"Hello?"

"Open the fucking door for fuck's sake."

"Who is it?"

"Look... just open the door right..."

I didn't. I mean I'm a lot of things, but stupid I'm not. I went down and knocked on Reuben's door. There was no answer. Back in my flat I decided to ring Tom. He wasn't at home either but he did at least pick up. His first question, without even saying hello to me was was "did the man at the door have an accent?" When I said he did, he wanted to know what kind. He seemed a little less stressed when I said it was the local one, but he still sounded a bit on edge. He then repeated Reuben's advice about not letting anyone I didn't know in. As if.

****

Now the buzzer has been buzzing again, but I'm just ignoring it. At the moment I'm feeling a little torn. I like getting on with my new neighbours and their friends, well some of them at any rate, and I still like this flat. I've a cat and Mrs Webster seems very at home on a sheltered window with plenty of sunshine and I must say the partial sea view, when I can look out the front, is very nice indeed. I am though beginning to find it all a little bit stressful, if I'm being completely honest with you. With my online friends, we're all there for each other when we need company, but when I want some private time, when I just ache or want to get on with some sketching and card making then in the old days, I could just switch everyone off. I liked living at home, and living on my own after Shaun moved in with Mum, wasn't as bad as I'd thought it would be. I'm not sure I like this kind of constant open-flat situation, with people coming in, trashing the kitchen, drinking, smoking and worse, while half the time acting as if I don't exist. I need to find some way to tell them this is my flat, not theirs, that sometimes I welcome their company, but sometimes, especially at night I don't. I wish I thought one of those 'Do Not Disturb' signs you see in the movies would work, but I'm not sure anyone give a toss. Whether I like it or not Chez Maisie is 'Open All Hours'.

I'm writing this rather than making a video or recording my thoughts with the mic. as currently Grace and a couple of people I don't know are hogging the sofa and channel surfing on my telly. I had been in the middle of 'Antiques Road Trip' but now they can't decide what to watch. Hopefully in a few minutes one or other will get a message and off they'll go. It's like a dentist's waiting room without the fish tank.

There's the bloody buzzer again. Nobody has even glanced up from their phones or channel hopping. I've realised the crisps they're eating are from my limited edition exotic flavours multi-pack, even though I'd hidden them away at the back of the cupboard. I've had enough. I don't care who's at the door. It could be a mad axe killer for all I care. I've had enough. I'm not even going to answer the soddin' intercom. I'm pressing the button and I'm letting them in.

****

Maisie no!!!! I just read that and I'm like OH.MY.GOD. DM me to let me know you're okay. @AbbyAtHome

Yes sorry, Abby, I'm now lying dead on the floor in a big pool of blood, or should that be strawberry jam? It's really fortunate that there is wi-fi in heaven. Surprising how far the signal reaches eh? No, seriously it wasn't an axe-man or even fingers-for-a-gun man from the nightclub. It was a homeless guy. He came up and stood there in my doorway, partly wrapped in a blanket, woollen hat pulled down over his eyes. He seemed to be wearing at least two coats but the top one had damp marks on it, and what looked like mould. He was also shaking or shivering slightly.

I didn't know what to do or say so we stood there looking at each other. Then he mumbled something and staggered. I thought he was going to fall so I invited him in and ushered him to the sofa. Grace and her friends vacated, but Arthur who was lying on the back stayed put. He gave the bloke a kind of bored look before turning to wash where his balls should've been, so I figured if the cat wasn't scared of my visitor then I shouldn't be either.

I offered the man a cup of tea. He mumbled again and I took it as a yes. The coffee and hot chocolate had all been used up by my ungrateful flat-guests, but I made two mugs of tea and was even able to rustle up a couple of malted milks. Unfortunately when I sampled one myself, I found they were a little bit soft as someone has left the lid off the tin. At least they were not seriously stale.

The bloke took off his hat. He had sticky-up hair as grizzled as his beard and his eyes reminded me of those of a cuddly hippo toy I'd had when I was younger. Since you've not seen Hugo the hippo, I'll try to describe what I mean. They were big, sad and with huge bags beneath. His face was quite pink and craggy apart from at the corners of his eyes. He had no laughter lines. For a few minutes we drank our tea in silence. I was wondering if I had anything else I could offer him, or if in doing so, since he hadn't asked, I'd offend him. I was only assuming by the blanket that he was homeless, after all. It might not actually be the case. For all I knew too, he was some undercover police officer or spy. Though if he had been he would probably have started asking me questions by this point. Finally the man spoke:

"I..."

I waited. He took a big glug of tea.

"I'm back."

I wasn't sure how to respond. Never mind where he was back from, where did he even think he was? I waited, but he seemed to have said his piece for the time being at least. If he'd spent much of the day ringing my doorbell, you would have assumed, or rather I would have assumed, that he would have some urgent reason for being let in. Perhaps though this was it. Maybe he just wanted a sofa to sit on and a cuppa. If that was all, then he was welcome to it. As the silence between us was becoming slightly awkward, I left him to his thoughts and started checking my socials. Mrs Webster has lost 47 followers since yesterday. Why? What is wrong with you people? She won't be posting for ever you know and she's already survived the first frost of this autumn. As soon as the temperature goes much below freezing, it'll be lights out, goodnight, and thanks for all the flies. So please, if you can, stay with her. Let's celebrate her long and unique journey to its very end.

"Alright Maisie? Oh hello, John." It was Karla. As she spoke to the geezer on the sofa he looked at his feet and hunched up as if trying to move away from her. His name was John. A common enough name, probably the most common name of all but surely this was *the* John. This was the mysterious tenant of this flat who had left before I moved in. This was the bloke who may or may not have left a gun in the meter cupboard. Before I could start to get to the bottom of that mystery however, I had to deal with Karla. "Got any plaster, Mais?"

"Only on the walls."

"Like hello? Sticky plaster."

"Like hello yourself. You mean sticking plasters and no for your information I'm allergic to them."

"Fat lot of use you are."

"I may be fat but I'm not meant to be of use, Karla. And it's no good you opening the fridge door, you've cleaned me out again."

"Wasn't me right? Don't start making accusations!"

"All I'm saying is there's no more food until my allowance comes in or someone else actually buys some."

"I don't have any money."

"Well perhaps you shouldn't be spending it all on drugs then."

"I don't do drugs."

"Yeah whatever. Just like sticking syringes in your arms for fun do you?"

"I'm dyslexic, you sad bitch!"

"Are you trying to say 'diabetic' you thick slapper?"

Karla charged at me. I lifted my walking frame like a lion tamer with a chair. She pulled up short, and eyeballed me. I stared back, unblinking. If we were going to fight, my weight, my leg and my asthma were against me, but Karla is so stick thin, I could probably make a reasonable attempt at snapping her like a fresh Twiglet. After a moment she said, "Got any Diet Coke?"

Life in this flat is weird and getting weirder. Karla, upon discovering the only things to drink were tea or tap water, disappeared off out again, without seemingly giving me another thought. When she had gone, John seemed relieved and I judged if there was a good time to talk to him, then this might well be it.

"So John, you used to live here right?"

"The social... social..."

"Social services?"

"I was given it. This was my flat. When I came out..."

"Came out?"

"Yes."

"Out of prison?"

"No, no. Not prison. Out of Roseview." I didn't know what Roseview was.

"You were given this flat?"

"They said I was responsible. It was my responsibility."

"For the flat?"

"For the flat. I just did my thing you know? Had a few beers, played my music. Didn't hurt anyone."

"I'm sure you didn't."

"But they said... I had parties, like drinking, druggy parties. People hanging out the window screaming. People trying to set fire to the place. It wasn't me. None of it was me. Yes I liked a drink. Hands up I admit I like a drink, but I don't like to party. I don't like that. That's not me."

Somebody, possibly the housing association had at this point starting sending John letters and people had come round to see him "Officials" he called them, though he didn't seem sure where exactly they were from. He stopped opening the letters but they started phoning and threatening him with eviction. John had been terrified by the thought of being evicted. It had stopped him sleeping. It had made him drink more, which seemed to be why he had been in that 'Roseview' place to start with. So scared had John been of being evicted, that one day he had had enough. He couldn't live with all the stress and anxiety. He had just left everything behind and walked out. He'd made himself homeless as he'd been terrified that some official had been about to do it to him. He explained that sometimes if you see something coming you need to stand up and stare it in the face. It was better to have abandoned your home than to be evicted, or it was if being evicted was the thing you feared the most in the whole world. That's how it seemed to have been for John.

I wanted to ask him a lot more questions, but it was difficult. I had a strong feeling now that the gun in the meter cupboard had nothing to do with him. John's hands shook constantly. I suspected that was to do with his past heavy drinking. I couldn't imagine him holding a gun. He'd clearly known Karla, and I was keen to know if he knew the rest of the neighbours. When I mentioned Adelina a little light came into his eyes and he said yes, he knew Adi. About Reuben and Tom he had nothing to say, just looked down at the floor.

I asked if he had paid his rent and he said "yes, mainly" stressing again that his problems had been mainly due to parties which while he had sometimes been present, had never been his idea in the first place. I managed to get him to mention the names of some of the people who had been at the parties, and the only one I recognised was Carol. He added that like many of the others she had only turned up to score. I suppose he meant drugs, not in the relationship or football sense, but he didn't really want to remember what had been a not altogether pleasant time for him. Although he was now sleeping in a shop doorway, he felt he could at least "hold my head together" there.

"Then there was Adi. Lovely Adi," he said, that look coming into his eyes again, as he remembered her. "They used her to hook me in you see? Not that I had any real chance. Is she still here?" I confirmed that she was. "She wasn't the only one then. There was Alex. She was... does up your house... an interior designer..."

Suddenly he was talking and there was some kind of story here. Maybe it would explain a few things for me. I nodded and prompted him to go on. "Well she'd got money. Running a business. She used to take him everywhere. Openings of galleries, society weddings, all that bollocks. Course she looked down her nose at me, like she was so clever. But I thought we're just the same. We're both hanging on a hook, it's just you don't know it yet. Course the cash was all being washed through her business, and when the funny money people came looking, well the shit hit the you know what. The buck stopped with her. They couldn't get no further than that, see? Lost her shop, lost everything. Think I heard she's ended up in Shetland. Trying to make a go of an organic wool thing. Broke her he did. Broke her."

I think I've got this tale down right. I tried to discreetly take a few notes as John told it. He didn't spell out who the 'he' was, but I think we've all got a fairly good idea.

My immediate concern however was not the money worries of some wool-weaving posho, but John himself. I didn't really know what to do. If he'd decided he was going to move back in, I don't think I'd have had the heart to stop him. I wondered aloud why he had come back. It turned out he had expected to find a few personal belongings here, including a little notebook he'd kept for drawing in. That shook me a bit. The ways in which our lives here had been similar, and the fact his had ended on the street is a thought I can't now get out of my head. This could be me. Is this where I'm heading?

I told John to take anything of his from the flat he wanted. Anything at all. He looked under the chair cushions for his little notebook and mentioned a jacket with a military pin on it that had belonged to his father. I told him that I hadn't seen anything like that and I hadn't chucked out anything that had been here when I arrived. I assumed the housing association had cleared most of his possessions. Perhaps they were still holding them somewhere for him, I suggested, though knowing a skip was probably their most likely destination. In the kitchen he picked up the mugs and smiled in recognition. Of course I didn't let him know I'd had to tip wee into the sexist one in an emergency, but it had been properly washed up since. I said I'd a cardboard box from when I'd moved in that he could use, to take his mugs and anything else that was his away in. He had no interest in the old kettle or toaster. Perhaps they had been part of the flat's furnishings when he'd moved in too.

John sat on the window seat looking out at what to him must've been a familiar view. Then almost unconsciously, he began to write with one finger in the slight dust and grime on the pane. H E L P. The slightly shaky letters were the same as the imprint left when I'd moved in. Then he seemed to rouse himself, stood up and headed for the door. I told him he didn't have to go, but it was as if he didn't hear me. He was halfway down the stairs before I remembered the box with his cups and called him back. He took it and headed out, without looking back.

I called Mum. She answered this time.

"Mum, you've got to help me."

"Why what's wrong?"

"I just met the guy who lived here before me. He's homeless now and he just left."

"I thought you said something was wrong."

"It is. It is! With this place. With everything." I heard her sigh.

"It's a nice flat. Much better than Mrs Latimer's..."

"No, it's not where I want to be. It's not me. I'm gonna end up kicked out. It's all going wrong."

"Nothing is going wrong. "

"Look can you come round? Like now? Straight away? I don't feel like I can talk on the phone because people might be listening and they keep walking in and out unannounced. I've no privacy. I need to see you."

"I can't come round now."

"But you've not been round since you got back. From your soddin' holiday. I didn't even get a postcard. You didn't even say you were back."

"I'm back."

"I fucking know that! I know that alright? But you might as well be still away. You might as well go and join my sister in fucking Australia..."

"Austria."

"Australia, Mum! You might as well fuck off there, for all I matter to you."

"Stop shouting, it's exhausting. Don't you ever think about that? Don't you ever think about how tiring it is for me, dealing with your 'me, me, me' attitude, day after day?"

"What? You haven't had to deal with me? You've been in fucking Marbella? Look fine, if all I am is a burden, well don't come round then. Don't call me. Don't fucking bother, alright? I'm sorry you think I'm exhausting. I'm sorry I was even born!"

****

I was going to ring Masoud for a pizza. That's what I usually do when life goes tits. Before I could dial however, Tom walked in with one. It was like he was psychic, or it would've been if he'd brought one I really like. Actually it was ricotta and olives, which isn't my favourite, but I'm not one to look a gift pizza in the box, if you know what I'm saying. He said Karla had let him know I'd run out of food. He was going to leave the pizza in the fridge for anyone who came in hungry. I said that was a very good idea. When he'd gone I ate it. Pretty much all of it and I stashed the last piece where they won't think of looking either. Anyone else who comes in and is hungry – tough. My flat, my pizza. If nobody cares about me, then I'm not going to care about anyone else. If Karla, Avery or anyone asks about it, I'll blame it on one of the others. That seems to be what they do. Whenever you try to get to the bottom of anything that's gone wrong here it's always someone else who's to blame. It's started to rain now, and I can imagine John sitting shivering in a damp shop doorway somewhere. John is a victim – of the system, or of people who took advantage of him. Nobody is going to take advantage of me.

I was going to ring Masoud and request a dipping bar and a bottle of fizz to go with the pizza. I know it would've been slightly disloyal as the pizza had not come from his shop, but then I haven't seen him since the party. It would've been a good excuse to catch up. In the end I didn't ring. I'm not sure ricotta and a dipping bar mix. Also I'm slightly offended that Masoud's not been in touch at all. Especially as when we last spoke, he was going to send some photos for me to give my opinion of. I know he didn't stay long at the party. He'd said at the time he'd another deliver to make, but I didn't see him check his phone to discover that. Perhaps he hadn't liked the look of the party or some of my guests, invited or non-invited. Alternatively, he might just currently be very busy. I don't know if certain times of year are more hectic than others in the pizza business, but it's probably true. I know when his boss had an advert made for the local radio stations the guys were rushed off their feet for a while. That's despite it having one of the lamest jingles I've ever heard. *'We're Pizza On The Pier. When you need us we'll be here.'* I might send him some of my photos of Arthur later and ask if he's any tips for photographing cats. The world of feline influencers is, I suspect, gonna be harder to crack than the spider one.

****

I felt miserable about rowing with Mum and I've spent most of the evening wondering whether to call her back or not. Trouble is, I know she'll act like I'm bothering her and making a nuisance of myself again. It sounds like Shaun has persuaded her to finally cut me loose. Perhaps that was the whole point of the holiday – get her on her own, and loosen her ties to me. Mum and me used to be so close. We loved spending time together. When Mia moved out Mum said she was so glad she still had me there with her. "You'll never leave me, will you, Maisie?" I would probably still be living with Mum if she hadn't met Shaun. In fact I know I would. I'm sure we'd have fought and bickered and got on each other's tits. But we'd have had some great times too. We'd have had a right laugh, like we used to when Dad was alive.

I'm not going to call Mum. I'm going to let her miss me. She will eventually I'm sure. Well I hope she will. If she doesn't, I'm better off without her, I suppose.

I decided to have an early night, but I couldn't sleep. Adelina hasn't exactly given herself a breathing space between her last relationship and her new one, despite Reuben's sensible advice. First of all it was all squeaky, squeaky, squeaky, oooh, ahhh, baby and then his car revving off into the night. It's amazing how she's found a new guy so quickly. Perhaps she uses that Tinder app where you swipe left or right. I mean anyone who sees a photo of Adelina is going to want to be with her – she really is fairytale princess beautiful. Trouble is a Prince Charming isn't the type to shag and rev off into the gloom. If you ask me she's let herself be taken in by another wrong 'un. Probably a geezer with pots of money and a wife and kids at home. She deserves better, she really does. It sounds like she might've had a little fling with John. I couldn't work out whether she had or whether he'd just had a crush on her. It would've been rude to ask. I know John looks like a bit of a scarecrow now, but who knows what he looked like when he still had a roof over his head. It's possible that him and Adelina were involved. I think he might have been good for her too, well better than her most recent conquests at any rate.

Shortly after Adelina's latest flame had withdrawn, so to speak, I heard a key in my lock, and Karla and Grace came in. I cursed myself. I could've put the bolts across if I'd remembered, or at least left my own key in the door. If I hadn't been distracted by my call to Mum and felt a bit groggy from bingeing on pizza, then I would've. That's how I usually prevent late night visitors from making an entrance. Anyway they went straight into the kitchenette without putting the main light on or checking whether I was awake or not. Sometimes I'm the invisible woman in my own flat. I heard the usual giggling, whispering, the fridge and cupboard doors opening and closing. I thought to myself that they wouldn't be here long. If they were expecting the cupboards to be replenished they are sadly mistaken. I checked my banking app earlier and I'm pretty much out of money until Tuesday at the soonest. The remaining biscuits are now stashed under this bed, as are the tea bags, a can of mushy peas, the remaining cornflakes and a blackened banana.

****

The whispering, rustling sounds and giggling in the kitchen is going on and on. I've just called out to Karla and Grace to keep it down, but after a moment they've started nattering again. I've rolled over to face the wall, and pulled the duvet up around my ears to give me a bit of peace and quiet, but it's not working. I wish they'd be on their way. It's past midnight. Don't they have homes to go to? Grace is surely young enough to still be living at home. Someone, somewhere must be worried about her. Even as that thought crosses my mind, I know it's unlikely to be true. In all likelihood nobody cares where Grace is or what she is doing. Perhaps her mum's got a boyfriend she puts first too. Or she lives in a care home or something. Maybe, like me there's no one at all she can turn to if she gets herself into trouble.

I can't help thinking about John again. I'm brooding about it as

Mum would say. This should be his bed. This should be his home. It was his home, until other people turned up, got drunk, threw parties and caused him hassle with the housing association. Now I admit my party was my responsibility, and although it did get a bit out of hand, it was a one-off. There has been quite a bit of noise in here since then though and loads of comings and goings. I hope the neighbours haven't been disturbed enough to put in any complaints. I have tried to stop my visitors smoking out of the windows and shouting down to their friends in the street at all hours, but it's just impossible sometimes. If they won't listen, they won't listen. Most nights I've been able to chivvy everyone out by one am at the latest, but not every time. It's not as if next door are having to live beside one of those party houses with hen night crowds arriving every Friday night though. They're pretty lucky in that respect cos those places are everywhere in Brighton now. None of my guests runs amok in their undies with inflatable model penises or sings 'I Will Survive' in the back garden. If there had been any complaints about my place, the social wonder would have told me, wouldn't she? I'm not sure how much longer I want to stay here, but if I move, it has to be to somewhere, not nowhere. That's the tricky part.

****

The noise just went on and on. Finally I couldn't take any more. I hauled myself out of bed, threw my dressing gown on and grabbed hold of my walking frame. In the kitchenette Karla and Grace froze when they saw me, as if I'd caught them doing something they shouldn't have been doing. Only the very dusty up-light by the cooker was switched on, but it was enough for me to see that the two formerly empty biscuit tins were open. These were the rusty tins from the high shelf that had been there when I moved in. Tonight though those tins weren't empty. They were full of little polythene bags. Those bags were all filled with something that from where I was standing looked a hell of a lot like pills.

It was one of those situations where nobody wants to make the first move. I was absolutely fuming but I didn't know what to say or do. Karla and Grace were drug dealing, that much was plainly obvious, and it appeared they were keeping their ecstasy, acid or whatever it was, stashed in my flat. Absolutely bloody perfect if a new carer came in this week, or even someone from the housing association making a snap inspection of the premises. So now I'm responsible for running a drugs den. I'm being evicted, going to court, and being sent to fucking prison, because frankly who's gonna believe I knew sod all about it? Whose gonna believe I'm really that stupid and trusting?

It started snowing. Snowing hard. Little white shapes dropping down from the front sash window and pinging off the brickwork below. Then it was more like hailstones as the pills rattled down a handful at a time onto the concrete outside Tom's window.

"Maisie, stop! Stop now!" Karla moved forward to grab the packets from me. In response I just slung more pills, these ones still bagged from the window.

"Maisie!" she screamed. I lifted my walking frame, putting it between myself and the wild-eyed banshee.

"Don't," Grace said simply. I don't know which of us she was addressing.

"Look, give me the tins. Just give the tins right?" I scattered another handful of snap bags from the window. "I'm warning you." I saw a flash of silver. Karla had grabbed one of my dinner knives from the washing up bowl. Fortunately I knew they weren't that sharp. Even so as I saw her move I swung my frame. She screamed and there was an almighty crash and then a loud bang. I didn't know it then, but I'd actually missed Karla and hit the toaster. As it landed on the floor it had gone off with a bang. In the moment I don't know what I thought the bang was. Maybe I thought it was a gunshot. It was however the thing that made me hurl the first biscuit tin out of the window. I threw it as hard as I could. It sailed through the air, cleared the pavement and landed in the road, bags of pills spilling out everywhere. I threw the second one after it. It bounced off a parking meter, as its contents slid across the tarmac.

Karla was standing beside me, but she was not brandishing the knife now. Instead she was gawking outside, open mouthed at the packets of pills strewn all over the deserted street.

"You idiot. You fucking idiot." She turned to Grace. "Come on!" I heard them race down the stairs. As they did so I watched as a taxi drove slowly up our street, it's front wheels, almost in slow motion crushing the first tin. The car stopped and the driver got out to discover what he'd run over. Karla and Grace rushed out into the street. The driver was holding up a snap bag of pills to the light on his phone. He looked at the mess beneath his tyres and all around. Then he began making a call. Meanwhile Karla and Grace had started gathering up as many packets as they could, scrabbling in the kerb. The taxi driver though was having none of it. He shouted and ran at them, causing them both to back up, cursing him.

"I'm calling the police!" he shouted. Karla looked up towards my window. I shrank back behind the curtain.

"He'll kill you! He'll fucking kill you!" I didn't know for sure who 'he' was, but once again I could hazard a guess.

CHAPTER 11

I got dressed and went back to bed in my clothes, after checking my door was bolted on the inside of course. I heard voices in the street, cars pull up and their doors opening and closing. I didn't know what was going on though, and frankly didn't care. It was all-quiet in the house at least. No one seemed inclined to come up or down and start a confrontation over what I'd done. There were no drugs left in my flat, of that I was pretty sure. I'd checked everywhere I could think of, after Karla and Grace had gone downstairs. I'd even looked in places like the toilet cistern and the icebox, like you see on the true-life cop shows. Truth be told, I fully expected a visit from Sussex Police before the night was out, which was the main reason for changing out my jammies, but nobody came.

Pulling back the front curtains this morning, disturbing Arthur in the process, I could see a few pills scattered immediately below, around the basement flat's window, and a couple on a ledge above Reuben's. The street itself now looked as though nothing had happened however. All the little bags, stray and crushed pills and both tins had gone.

****

"Maisie are you there?"

"I'm not seeing anyone today."

"That's a shame. I've just made some coffee.

"Have to drink it yourself then won't ya?"

I've a tea with definitely off milk in it, and a brown over-ripe banana. I'm writing this without checking your messages dear followers. I know you're all going to say I should've called the police last night. It was my first thought too, believe me. Then though I realised it's a little more complicated than that. I don't know who cleared up the pills in the street or who the taxi driver called. Maybe it was the police, but I'd been awake for hours after, and I hadn't seen any blue lights flashing through the curtains, or heard the chatter of police radios. If I called them now, I could tell them what Karla and Grace had been doing, and mention my suspicions about other members of this household, chiefly the two individuals who live below me. However you can bet, if Karla and Grace are dealing drugs for either Reuben or Tom or possibly both, neither of the guys will be stupid enough to have drugs in their own premises. Clearly the idea was for me to take all the risks. So while Karla and Grace might be arrested, Reuben and Tom are likely to escape all blame, while knowing I've tried to drop them in it. To be honest I don't see much point in getting Karla and Grace arrested, and if I do I have a bad feeling that they'll be let go in hours. Then things could get a lot worse for me. A lot, lot worse. It's never safe to be a grass, I know that much.

I've thought of calling a cab and legging it, with just Arthur and Mrs Webster, but I can't get down the stairs at any speed, and Reuben is sure to be listening out for me. If I call Mum and Shaun I'll put them in danger. With Shaun I'm not fussed, but Mum doesn't deserve to be dragged into this God-awful mess. It's entirely my fault for allowing my neighbours and their friends to see my place as their place, before I'd got to know them properly. I was too keen to meet new people, too keen on the idea of living like they do in 'Friends'. Nobody in 'Friends' deals drugs from their neighbour's flat, or did I somehow miss that episode?

I've been looking online to see if I can find anything out about Reuben and Tom. I thought they might have made more than the odd appearance in court reporting articles from the local papers, but I can't yet find anything. At least Reuben's name is slightly more unusual but searches on anything to do with drugs offences have so far drawn a blank. If I knew for certain that either of them had been in trouble with the law I would probably have a better chance of persuading the police to take me seriously. At the moment, I'm just sitting here with my imagination running wild, not knowing what might happen next. The pills most people seem to get caught in possession of are something called MDMA, which was ecstasy when their parents' generation was taking it and dancing to Acid House music. That was in olden times of course, before a yellow smiley face became the first emoji.

It feels like I'm under siege and I do need to get some food at some point today. I don't really fancy pizza again so soon, and again if I call Masoud, I might be putting him at risk of harm. I don't want to put my real friends in danger.

****

Tom keeps trying to ring me but I'm not taking his calls. I've just had a call from a number I don't recognise too and it's gone to answer. I will give that one a listen.

'Hello Maisie, it's Glynis from your Primary Health Team here. We understand your independent care provider is no longer able to provide the services you require, so we are wanting to send someone out to assess your needs as a client before we assign your case to a new company. If you are able to call us back today...'

"Hello Glynis? It's Maisie. It would be really, really good if you could send someone today. Err two people if that's all possible."

"Okay, Maisie, would you be home say between two and five?"

"Oh absolutely, I'm not going anywhere."

****

While I'm waiting for the care team, I'm packing a bag. I've washed out and carefully dried the jam-jar ready to scoop Mrs Webster from her web when the time comes. I still have the box with the air holes in it for Arthur. I've put a comfy sweatshirt in the bottom instead of the newspaper he came with. Hopefully he'll let me put him back in there. I think I'll have to leave the rest of my stuff behind. I've no idea where I'll end up, and I can imagine the housing department giving me all sorts of shit about making myself intentionally homeless, but I don't really have much choice in the matter. I have to escape.

****

I let in the care assessor and she was just one middle-aged woman who was about 5 foot, two and could be accurately described as petite. Now I'm the last person to be sexist or smallist but I could've really done with a couple of big, muscular men to escort me out of here. I was in the middle of explaining that we both needed to go and go now, when Adelina came down from upstairs and with a pleasant smile joined us. Well I don't know how much she knows or whether she's in on the whole thing, so I clammed up at that point. The care assessor said she can't help me with my wish to move or travel anywhere today. She wasn't insured to take me outside of the flat, she explained. I said that was fine. All I needed was for her to help me down the stairs and gave me a hand pulling Delores from her alcove and a leg up so I could clamber on board. Of course she wasn't authorised to do that either. Then Adelina piped up that I've recently hurt my leg, and so she'd "really worry" if I went out at all. I shot her an evil glance. Traitor. No more games of Hungry Hippo for her.

The assessor had a quick look at my limb of many colours and expressed the view that although she wasn't actually a medical professional, I probably need to see a doctor and a qualified physiotherapist. Is there another kind of physio, and if the person accessing my needs is just a general dogsbody how on earth will

I get the right kind of care? In desperation, I asked her to phone an ambulance, but she said that while my still swollen leg was 'of concern' it didn't appear to be that kind of emergency. I could always ring 111 later and see what they had to say. Hmm, that's a long and winding road I've been down many times before. Alternatively she might be able to book me a physiotherapy appointment, but if it needed to be a home visit there is a waiting list of over six weeks. There didn't really seem a lot of point. I'll be dead by then, off the end of the Palace Pier, feet encased in concrete. I'm sure that'll impact on my next mobility assessment.

I managed to eventually get rid of Adelina, by saying that I had to talk to my care assessor in private. The assessor agreed that it should be a private meeting unless I specified any particular person to sit in and perhaps assist, such as a carer or family member. I told her I could cope by myself. While I was still answering mostly pointless questions and a form as long as bog roll was gradually being filled, in came Grace with a bag of rather random groceries. "Sorry if we were a bit annoying last night. Won't happen again."

"Daughter? Niece?" smiled the care assessor.

"Read my bloody case file," I muttered under my breath.

Grace started tidying the kitchen and putting the groceries away. The care assessor having clocked the mess here on arrival was now making a note. No doubt it was to say that I actually had a horde of happy helpers at my beck and call, and wouldn't need any official care provision at all. Grace was across the room in the kitchenette, and mainly crouched out of sight, so I couldn't use the need for privacy excuse again to get rid of her. On the few occasions I looked away from my official questioner to see what she was up to, she appeared to have her phone in her hand.

Was she using it to record or relay my conversation to someone or other, or was I now going completely paranoid?

The form was filled, the assessor from the Primary Health Care Team said someone would be in touch, cleverly without saying who or when. Apparently though my care visits should soon be restored. I would've preferred a 'would' rather than a 'should', but I'd done my best to express my ongoing needs. I still felt though, that if what Karla had shouted at me last night had even a smidgen of truth in it, I might not have ongoing care needs, or any needs at all for much longer. The assessor said I needn't get up, but I decided to show her to the door. There without Grace ear wigging and possibly bugging my conversation, I could try to explain once more about my immediate need to be removed to a place of safety. That was the term I had been looking for – 'place of safety'. I rehearsed the line in my head, as I stood up.

Upon reaching my flat door shortly after the care assessor, I was not at all surprised to see a twinkle appear in her eyes, and the flicker of a smile on her lips. I knew exactly who she had just encountered on the stairs.

The front door closed behind the care assessor and Reuben slipped into my flat before I could close and bolt the door. He sat down on the sofa without being asked. As he did so Grace stood up and scuttled out. Of course she did. I don't suppose she much wanted to witness what was bound to be coming. Reuben's eyes were hard and cold.

"Cup of tea?" I gasped hoarsely. I was reliant on my own mugs now that John had collected his.

"No, ta." He stretched, cat like, cracking his knuckles. I found myself staring at his rings. The one I had previously thought to be a shaped like skull was actually more like a head screaming in anger or pain. "How you getting along with Arthur?"

"Fine. Err yeah, he's settled in well." I wondered how long it would be before he got around to the huge, stonking, white pill-shaped elephant in the room. Should I leave it for him to say something, or should I try to get in first with my excuses, I wondered. Trouble is the only excuse I had, which was of course that I didn't want anyone stashing drugs in my flat, was not I sensed going to wash. I think I should've kept quiet and said nothing at this point, but as always, when I'm this close to shitting an entire house brick, I started to gabble away.

"Err about last night..."

"Last night?" He said it as though he had no idea what I was talking about and wasn't particularly interested. I was willing to bet however that this wasn't true.

"Yes err, erm, about what happened?"

"Something happened?" Damn him, damn him. There was an uneasy pause. I kept my mouth tight shut. If he wasn't going to admit to knowing, then I wasn't going to admit to what I'd done. "Look Maisie" he said at last, "what I really came to ask is, do you think you could do me a little favour?" – Like voluntarily stick my feet in that block of concrete, my mind answered back, but I simply found myself nodding mechanically. "Carol. You know her right?"

"Carol?" I wasn't still trying to play his 'deny all knowledge' game, I was just slightly thrown by the question.

"Yeah... she was at your party."

"Oh her? Yes she did. Uninvited, I must add. I've no idea who she is."

"She was my plus one."

"Ah." I suddenly remembered I had offered Reuben the opportunity to bring a plus one, but they certainly hadn't arrived together. It wasn't worth splitting hairs about though, especially as it was keeping us away from the subject of the avalanche of pills.

"I was wondering if she could come and stay with you for a day or so." My heart sank. I hadn't warmed to Carol. She was an odd one to say the least.

"Well... there's not much room in here..." I said, actually meaning, "if your weird older woman plus-one means so much to you, why don't you let her stay in your own roomy and very tastefully decorated flat?"

"It'll be fine. She'll sleep on the sofa. And she loves cats. We used to have loads." I noticed the 'we'.

"Doesn't she have anywhere else to stay then?"

"Not where she feels safe. She doesn't feel very safe at home at the moment."

"I know that feeling." Shit. It had just come out. Big gob strikes again.

"Well then, that might be what you both need. I think she just needs a few cups of tea, some chat and a bit of reassurance."

"If I had any tea bags."

"You'll probably find you have. Didn't I see Grace popping upstairs with some shopping for you?"

"I didn't order anything. And I've no idea how I'm even going to pay her."

"I wouldn't worry about that."

I heard car doors banging outside. Reuben walked over to look out of the window. I noticed he did so from the side, almost warily. I sense Carol and myself are not the only people currently living with a certain sense of fear.

I reached for my inhaler. I always get breathy when I get nervous, though I was now starting to think I'd over-reacted, over the concrete boots. I didn't much fancy having Carol to stay, but at least by doing so it looked like I'd avoid any blowback from last night's activities.

Tom came in with Carol, who was wearing a red cape that made her look a bit like the wolf that had eaten Red Riding Hood. He put her broken suitcase and a tote bag with a recycling slogan on it, down on the floor and went over to speak to Reuben quietly.

Whatever Tom had said appeared to have shook Reuben, as he left abruptly, without even speaking to Carol or giving me so much as a departing glance. Tom followed him hurriedly, closing the door behind him.

"Ladybird, ladybird," said Carol. She wasn't looking towards Mrs Webster, and even if it was possible to mistake a spider for a brightly coloured beetle, it didn't seem likely that was what she was talking about.

"Pardon?"

"Lady, ladybird fly away home. Your car is on fire, your children are gone. Kids eh? You try to tell 'em. Keep out of trouble! Keep out of fucking trouble, you hear me?"

Mum used to recite that rhyme when I used to try to make pets of the ladybirds in our garden, and I'm pretty sure it's the house that's on fire rather than a motor vehicle. I stuck the kettle on. Carol sat down on the sofa and took a can of beer from her bag and ripped it open. It was the strong stuff too. I wasn't sure she was going to need the tea.

"I was scared it was gonna be me. My caravan that got it. Just tip a bit of paraffin – slop, slop and that's poor Mummy gone up in flames. I saw them parked down the track. A black merc with tinted glass. I asked Jill and Jeff, they're my neighbours, to take a look, but the car drove off when they knew they'd been spotted. How do I get caught up in this thing – that's what I wanna know! I ain't involved. I ain't done nothing to nobody!"

"Biscuit, Carol?" A whole luxury biscuit selection box had appeared in the cupboard now, so I had creams and chocolate ones and even those long cigar-shaped hollow ones. Not only were there tea bags, there was an expensive brand of coffee. Carol too, I reasoned, might turn out to be the gift that kept on giving. I sensed that she liked to talk, and would do so without much prompting. Finally, I might get some answers.

****

Okay, that was a tad optimistic. I'm getting a bit tired of Carol and her semi-pissed yammering on now. What I have found out is that she lives in a mobile home on a holiday caravan site, having lost her council home for some reason. The big news is that Reuben is her son. He tends to neglect her and keep her short of money, or so she says. His dad isn't on the scene but he's both rich and a bad lot. Carol likes a drink or ten and she used to smoke crack, though insists she's almost given it up as it's bad for her teeth. She doesn't actually seem to have that many teeth, so this is probably true. The bad news that sent Reuben and Tom on their way is that Reuben's car has mysteriously caught fire, and is apparently still blazing away in a nearby street. It was by all accounts a top of the range model, though I didn't catch the make. Carol insisted it was his pride and joy.

Carol is sick of Reuben bringing trouble to her door, as she put it. He has been in trouble since the day he could walk, according to his mother. All opinions expressed here are Carol's own and I have no independent evidence to back them up. Mind you I did see a glimpse of a fire engine, lights flashing and siren blaring, pass the end of the road, and I did hear Reuben and Tom rushing out, so I'm inclined to believe the information about the car at least.

A few minutes ago I was taking a leak and I came back in to see Carol bent over the frame of the now open front window, her bony arse in her faded denim jeans sticking up in the air. I thought for a moment she was trying to escape and was about to point out that my door was unlocked and she could simply use the stairs, when she straightened back up. "Can't quite reach the dratted things." Her chipped varnished nail pointed towards a couple of pills still nestling on the ledge below. "Didn't I see you had one of those grabbers, when I was here before?"

"Err they're just aspirin. Out of date aspirin. They do say to throw away out of date medicines don't they, Carol?"

With a grunt, Carol left me to close the window and headed back to the sofa. She started talking again, not really caring if I was listening or not. This time it was about some programme on the TV that had been crystal clear about the fact the end of the world was coming later this year. We are all going to be wiped out before climate change even had a chance to get going properly. "It's coming from the sky!" I'm guessing she means an asteroid. Then she said that we personally probably wouldn't even be around long enough for the TV predicted disaster to happen. "He's gone too far this time. There are some toes you can't tread on. Everyone's got their own thing going on, y'know? Try to muscle in and take a piece of that and they don't like it. Up 'til now he's been lucky. But you can only stay lucky for so long. Is that quiz on? The one with the millionaires?" She'd already found the TV remote and started searching for something to watch. I fed Arthur. His cat food supply had also been replenished.

I wasn't in the mood to watch a quiz show but it seemed to mesmerize Carol. I put my headphones on and found a local radio station. They were playing Donna Summer's 'State Of Independence'. I might still be in receipt of a Personal Independence Payment, but unless my leg will bend enough to board Delores, I'm anything but independent. Am I minding Carol or has she been sent to mind me? I feel as much a captive as my house-cat, supplied with food, attention and a place to sleep but no freedom.

Before I make my escape, I need to find somewhere to go. I need allies to help me with my getaway, and most of all I need a plan. So followers out there, send us any tips, ideas etc. that'll help me with that. In the meantime I'm going to order some over the counter anti-inflammatories and a cream with arnica in it, to reduce bruising and swelling. I don't normally take anti-inflammatories cos they give me guts ache, but they do bring down swelling. If I could bend my leg just a little bit more, I'm sure I could ride Delores. There's a pharmacy nearby that offers same day deliveries so that's perfect. I might have to whisper though, as if she knows I'm calling a chemist, I have a nasty feeling Carol will want to add an item or two to my order. I've just noticed all the pots of pills and bottles of this and that, which she's dumped in my bathroom. I think her bowel problems might even be more chronic than my own.

I've taken out my phone twice to give Mum a call and then put it away again. I hate that we've rowed but I can't really apologise when I'm not the one in the wrong. Also I don't want to involve her in any of the murky stuff going on around here. Mum's a bit gullible at the best of times. She always thinks she's going to win those prize draws that come through the door, and the bungalow has draughty double glazing cos she let some chancer rip out our perfectly good windows. Plus, when she's been over here she's clearly thought Reuben was the bee's knees. See a few muscles and she's anyone's. It seems like I'm the only one who can see right through him.

Mum is always telling me I need to stand on my own feet and

she's right, I do. I need to sort out this problem with my neighbours by myself. There must be places I can contact to get help and advice. It's not like Carol's watching me like a hawk or anything. I mean she is watching me, but she's more of a drunken gannet, necking her extra strong beer and chewing on my biscuits with the last of her teeth. I can get out of here. I can find myself somewhere else to live. I know I can and I will. It's just easier said than done that's all.

****

Carol being here hasn't stopped the usual suspects rocking up and expecting to eat my food, drink my drink, smoke out of my window and sprawl across my bed and window seat, scrolling their phones. In fact Karla, who else, still seems to think it's okay to smoke actually inside the flat. I snatched her lighter and threatened to stamp on it. I wouldn't have risked a confrontation if it had been just for myself, but I don't want Arthur passively breathing in her noxious gases. Surprisingly Carol backed me up, telling her to "smoke out the fucking winder or sling yer fucking hook." Couldn't have put it better myself. Ten minutes later though Carol herself lit up and she had no intention of obeying my flat rules, certainly not while the prize on the umpteenth quiz show of the evening was still going up. Arthur and I retreated into the bathroom. I put the loo seat down and perched precariously on its top. At least there's an extractor fan in here. One of the lads did burst in, in the process of unzipping his flies, but upon seeing us, well me in particular, he shot back out into the room. Other people in this block have toilets, why does mine have to be the public convenience?

****

It's one am and Carol is still watching the telly with the volume loud enough to wake the entire city. 'Kin 'ell! Even worse, she still somehow through the din, hears every tap on the door and has been letting everyone into my flat, despite my pleading with her to keep it bolted. Tonight there seems to be more people than ever, mere shadowy shapes half the time, their phones glowing in the darkness as they await instructions. Occasionally I get a whiff of dope smoke, perfume, aftershave or BO as they pass to go into the kitchenette, or huddle on the front window seat, now the sofa has been commandeered as Carol's temporary resting place.

Arthur had been sleeping in the front window, but after someone sat on him in the dark, he has wisely moved to the end of my bed. Wisely, as long as I don't roll over in my sleep that is, though at the moment sleep isn't looking very likely. I wonder how many nights you can lie awake before you actually die. Please don't DM and tell me. Sometimes ignorance is bliss. I'm hoping Carol won't be staying here very long. Did Reuben say only a couple of days? I hope he's not one of those people who say that meaning a couple of weeks, or years. I have learnt my lesson where leaving food in the kitchenette is concerned. Everything edible or drinkable is in bed with me, under the duvet. I've got my cool bag so hopefully even the milk will survive. I'll have to switch to long life milk though, 'afterlife' as Donal called it, if I can't find a new home soon.

Thanks for all the escape plan tips and advice. Digging a tunnel out is a tad ambitious being as I'm on the first floor, and anything involving a rescue helicopter is hardly do-able. There have been some useful, practical suggestions too which I'll certainly take on board. Thank you also for the suggestions of organisations and charities that might be able to offer me somewhere to go. I've started having a look, and though I haven't found one yet who can help with my exact situation, if I really knew what my exact situation was, I'll keep looking.

'Maisie – I think I know what your exact situation is. I've been lying awake too and I've found lots of references to a thing called #cuckooing. @AbbyAtHome

****

Fuck me! I've just had a bit of a google and this cuckooing thing Abby mentioned does indeed sound like it might be what is going on. It also sounds a lot like what happened to John, before he chose life on the streets over this bedlam.

'Cuckooing is a form of crime where drug dealers take over the home of a vulnerable person in order to use it as a base for drug dealing.' So says wikipedia. Who knew eh? Who knew? Not your poor old Maisie that's for sure. Apparently it's a growing problem particularly in the South of England. Okay – drugs check. South of England – check. It's named after the birds – cuckoos – that lay their eggs in other birds' nests and then leave them to bring up their babies. It doesn't say anything about anyone who drops his alkie mother into somebody else's nest, but the rest does sound similar to my situation. It also says the people who let this happen to their homes often do it in return for free drugs. I mean what!!! I do not and have never taken anything but prescription medication. I'm as clean as a... as a car that's just been cleaned. Cleaner in fact.

Wait... I don't suppose receiving a few groceries, a night out, and a cat – that wouldn't mean I'm like allowing this shit to happen would it? Would the police say, "well you accepted posh coffees and an animal companion, and CCTV has you out in a nightclub with said suspects"? It does sound a bit like bribery, or grooming even, now I've thought about it.

I've just found an account of someone where the gang who had cuckooed her insisted she was involved in their drug dealing and so she was evicted. It wasn't true either. Now she can't get anywhere else to live because of that conviction. Like John she's in a doorway and begging. There's another case where the man was like me and had no interest in doing anything illegal. He just thought he'd made some new friends. Someone else had been honey trapped into a one-sided relationship with one of the people taking over their place. Does that sound a bit like John and his feelings for Adelina? A lot of people have suffered violence and beatings for getting on the wrong side of the people who have taken advantage of them. Is that gonna happen? Could that happen to me?

Across the room, Carol is sitting on the sofa puffing away at some kind of pipe. Not the kind the men all smoke in old, black and white films and not one of those big hookahs they have outside the Middle Eastern restaurants in Western Road. The TV is on a shopping channel, and in the kitchenette I can make out the shape of someone dancing alone in the light of the open and empty fridge. He or she doesn't appear to be grooving along to the man on the telly who is selling cubic zirconia jewellery for all he's worth. Perhaps the mystery dancer is wearing headphones that I can't see from here in a kind of silent disco way. For all I know the shadow is getting down to beats that can be heard in his or her head alone. I'm watching the endless boogying in the faint hope it makes me nod off.

CHAPTER 12

There's a bit of a tense atmosphere here again this morning. Only Grace and Avery have turned up for breakfast so far, so I've relented and shared the last of the old cornflakes and the still reasonably fresh milk. They both checked their phones even more constantly than usual.

Tom and Reuben are out in the backyard, with Tom's dog. They seem to be having a few hushed, but urgent exchanges. Reuben in particular looks very wired, as alert as a fox raiding a dustbin. He's never got back to me about the snake tattoo. Probably has too much else on his mind, after the torched car episode. Carol is watching the telly and again smoking what I've discovered from Avery is a crack pipe. Happy days! I pretended I was studying Mrs Webster, but with the back window slightly ajar, to try and catch a little of what the guys below were saying, but I didn't have much luck. Reuben did definitely flinch when a police car screeched by along the coast road. I get the feeling something else has happened, maybe overnight, but I don't think Carol knows anything about it, if indeed there is an 'it'. I'll try to make a few discreet enquiries.

"Avery, is everything alright?"

"I'm good, Mais. You?"

"I mean has something happened?" He looked at Grace, she shrugged.

"Nah, nah, all's good. Nothing for you to worry about anyway."

I'd like to get a gander at the local news, and with the TV occupied and not private enough, I put my headphones on and go online. There's a fleeting mention of a fight near Churchill Square last night. A number of people were involved. The police are saying it appears to be gang related. The incident happened after a short car chase when the occupants of one car got out and attacked the occupants of the second. A baseball bat and a knife are mentioned. A guy is fighting for his life in hospital. A bystander said that some, but not all of those involved, spoke in what he described as 'heavily accented English'. The police have issued the description of two men they would like to trace in connection with the incident. One is described as being over six foot tall and thick set, the other of slim build with long blond hair.

I'm sitting at the window looking down at someone with hair as described, and the other bloke sounds a bit like Jonas the man mountain. Oh here's Karla, running in, eyes glued to her phone.

"Maisie, have you pigged all the bleedin' food again!"

"My food."

"Oh you bought it yourself then did yer?"

"Don't you get any breakfast at home?"

"I eat here."

I retrieve the box of biscuits and offer it. She tries to grab the whole lot, almost pulling me over in the process, but I keep my grip. She has to content herself with filling her pockets.

My mind though is still with that street fight. I wonder whether if it was Jonas and Tom, were they being chased or doing the chasing? Karla is already on her way out, rucksack on her back. "Be careful out there today," I find myself saying.

"Yeah, Mum," she sneers back at me. She is so young, barely in her twenties at a guess. This shouldn't be her life. Carol lets rip a gigantic fart that is fouler than even the white smoke she is exhaling. This shouldn't be any of our lives.

****

I spent the morning watching Youtube videos on my tablet. Ones with animals doing cute things mainly. I'm sure you don't blame me. Trampolining foxes and duck on a slide are good for my stress levels. Unfortunately, a comic one about an owl twisting its head around until it fell off a branch, led me to a clip from a wildlife documentary about cuckoos. Having hatched out of its egg, in the nest of a couple of tiny warblers, the cuckoo chick proceeded to heave the other genuine eggs and the couple's much tinier and weaker real babies up onto its broad shoulders one by one. Then in each case it arched its back and flipped them out of the nest. They fell from the tree and that was the end of them. Sometimes it took the cuckoo chick many attempts to remove a single chick or egg, but it stubbornly kept going. It was that single-minded. Then the parent birds came back and meekly accepted the situation. All the food they'd gathered for their own children was willingly fed to the interloper. Meanwhile their own eggs and tiny babies grew cold and died beneath the tree. There weren't many biscuits left in the box when I'd finished watching that one.

Donal rang, to check I was okay, but as soon as she heard me on the phone, ruddy Carol had to come over and sit next to me. Suddenly the life of Maisie was more interesting than 'The Chase' or whatever it was she'd been gawking at. I ended up saying I was fine now, and we just chatted about music and stuff. Hopefully he'll twig the situation and check back in with my blog later.

What I love about the generation gap is that none of the youngsters take any notice of what an old thirty-something like me is doing online. They're not remotely curious. As far as I know, none of them has discovered any of my own socials at all. I'm so glad I restricted my sharing with Avery, to Mrs Webster's Instagram.

I didn't mention I had any other accounts and being a spider she doesn't post anything controversial or comment on the activities in the world inside her window. Although you can see I follow her, it seems no one has clicked on that link, as my own followers haven't grown in number for some time. The other reason I shared Mrs Webster's site with Avery, was because her followers far outstrip mine and I was trying to be 'down wiv the kids' and show I owned an account with proper influencer numbers. Today, I'm taking down a few things from my own profile and probably belatedly, altering my privacy settings. I'm sure I'd know by now if Reuben, Tom and the rest knew I was posting about them, and I'm now going to make sure they definitely stay in the dark about it. Don't worry, my loyal following – you'll still be the first to know anything and everything that happens here. Right now though, while Carol is in the land of nod, I'm going to tippy-toe over to the telly, switch it off and hide the remote. Then hopefully I'll get a little afternoon snooze while things are relatively quiet.

****

Oh God! Oh my God... fucking hell... Some young guy, one of the Vogue boys... has come in and collapsed. Just came walking in and crumpled. And blood... blood is literally pumping out of his leg. Carol is on her knees screaming, holding her head and screaming. I'm recording this live, as everyone; everyone from the house is rushing in. I don't know what to do? What should I do?

****

They're all here now. Reuben, Tom, Adelina. They've wrapped a belt around the leg to stop the pumping, and they're using one of my shirts to tie around it. I can't bend down so there's nothing I can really do but call 999. I'm doing that now.

****

I'm writing this on my tablet, but Jonas has taken my router and my phone, so I don't know when, if ever, you'll get to read this. But I gotta do something. To keep myself from losing it. I'm really breathy and I can't find my inhaler. I hope they didn't take that too. I'd only got as far as the emergency switchboard when Reuben realised what I was doing and shouted to Jonas. Jonas then snatched my phone and cut the call. He handed it to Tom who pocketed it, along with his own. Then without a word he unplugged the router and took it away. Reuben said he was dealing with the situation, though from what I could make out of his and Tom's hushed conversation, they were actually going to dump the young guy, still bleeding out, in a street near the hospital. I said, "you gotta take him to hospital! Someone needs to do that. Or let an ambulance come here." They ignored me. "I don't understand," I said. "Why can't an ambulance come here? What have you got to hide?"

Anyway, now they've all gone apart from Tom. Jonas picked up the stabbing victim and just carried him out. The lad was either unconscious or in shock. He didn't make a sound and his body was all floppy. Tom's currently sitting on the window seat looking at his phones. My phone is in his pocket and my router is God knows where. He has the flat keys too and locked us both in before sticking them in one of his many pockets. I can't help staring at the huge pool of blood on the floor. Can a slim teenager lose that much blood and live? I hope Reuben and others haven't just left him in some alleyway or side street where no one will pass by in time. They must be serious about wanting to save his life. I have to believe they've enough humanity for that.

I can't imagine Avery would let his friend die, or the other Vogue boy – Billy or Bailey, for that matter. They were here when the stabbed lad struggled in, and were the first to rush to his aid. I wish I'd taken the time to learn everyone's names, to get to know them as individuals instead of naming those two lads after a dance at a party. I wish I hadn't had that bloody party. It was the start of everything. Or was that the fuse blowing on my first night here?

Has everything happened because of one dodgy fuse? Followers, if you learn one thing from my crazy life, check your lighting circuit. Shit. What am I saying? I'm rambling. You're probably reading this... if you ever do get to read this, and thinking, does she actually know the danger she's now in? If her neighbours can't trust her to be left alone and if they're ruthless gangsters which they might well be, then they're going to dispose of the silly cow before too long. It would be so easy to inject her with something. Poor lonely fatso, of course she overdosed. Must've wanted to end her miserable existence. Coroner's verdict: suicide. I shouldn't let myself think like this. It's making me get breathier. I'm starting to feel light-headed.

"Tom, have you seen my inhaler?"

"Nope."

He's not even pretending to be concerned. It's not down the side of the bed or the sofa. Those are the two places I usually lose it. Usually when I need a puff I stop thinking really clearly, but I'm actually thinking very clearly now. Very clearly indeed.

****

"What are you doing?"

"Sorry, I thought it might be down the back of the window seat. I sit here sometimes watching the world go by. Looks like rain again eh?"

"Huh?"

"Is that car anything to do with you?" He didn't look up from his phone. "The Merc with the tinted windows that's just pulled up outside." As Tom leapt up, his head collided with my walking frame. I'd swung it as hard as I could. We both collapsed, me only because I'd lost my balance. There wasn't a Mercedes outside.

It was a lie. I'd simply put two and two together from the stuff Carol had told me about being watched. Tom groaned. I hadn't hit him hard enough. He was dazed but moving. I needed to do it again. I had to, but I couldn't.

I hauled myself to my feet. I heard a key in the lock and my door opened. It was Karla. She'd been somewhere else when it all kicked off and judging by her expression on seeing the blood the news hadn't reached her yet. Tom was still moaning but starting to sit up. Karla glanced from the blood to him to me, then back again. She looked absolutely gob smacked. I imagine she thought at that moment that the blood was Tom's and that I'd been the one who had stabbed him. Before she could say or do anything, I used my frame to rush to the door. There I picked up the box I'd quietly lured Arthur into moments earlier, while Tom had been engrossed with his phone, and the jam jar which now contained Mrs Webster.

From the door I headed down the stairs. It wasn't easy. I had to chuck the walking frame down ahead of me, and steady myself on the rail with one hand, whilst wrapping the other arm around the box. The jar hung dangerously from the pocket of my fleece. Bracing myself against the bottom banisters, I pushed Delores out into the hall. The key was still in the ignition. No one had imagined I'd get this far, or perhaps they hadn't known Donal had fixed her. He'd done so before Reuben arrived at my party and while Tom was busy Djing. I used the elasticated ropes that had come with Delores to attach Arthur's box securely to the luggage rack. I put the jar in the front shopping basket. As I opened the front door I fervently hoped that whatever Donal had done to get her motor going again, it was going to be enough. As I dragged her down the steps and gritted my teeth while I hauled my still partly swollen leg across her saddle, I heard Tom yell from upstairs.

It was dark outside and cold, but being primed to try to make my escape today, I'd been wearing my thickest fleece indoors. If it rained I'd get soggy but at least I wouldn't freeze to death. Delores started first time and I was off, at top speed. It felt like the thirty miles an hour she was supposed to be able to achieve at full throttle with her maximum load, but realistically carrying someone who is well over her carrying capacity, not to mention a cat and a spider, well we were probably doing around 10 mph, at most, and that was downhill towards the coast road. Looking back I saw Tom rush out into the street behind me, but lost sight of him as I rounded the corner. Now I wasn't entirely confident that Delores could outrun Tom for long, so instead of racing along the coast road, or indeed the prom, I cut up into the maze of criss-crossing back streets. As soon as I could see an opening leading to a small mews of houses I drove in there, and parked up behind the communal waste bins. Thank God Brighton has communal waste bins. You probably won't hear many people saying that, but I'd never been happier to see and hide behind two of those great hulking things.

Miaow.

"I know Arthur. I know. But you better keep still or your first ride on my disability vehicle might well be your last." He mewed again more plaintively. "What I mean is they may well do me in, not you. I don't think Reuben would harm you, Arthur. He might be a lot of things but I think he's definitely still a cat person." I couldn't really reassure Mrs Webster in the same way. If they caught me, she'd probably starve, trapped in glass jar with a lid with air holes in it. Perhaps I should've left her behind. It was in hindsight probably selfish to involve both the animals in this high-risk situation. The trouble with me is that I can't bear to be alone. With Mum and I feuding, you my dear followers temporarily cut off, and my neighbours becoming the absolute opposite of good friends, I had run out of people to rely on. For the first time I truly had to depend on me.

The place I need to reach is Mum's. Unfortunately Brighton's a big place and her bungalow is too far away and up way too steep a hill for me to reach on Delores. My best bet for now is getting to Pizza On The Pier. That as they say, will hopefully be a place of safety. It doesn't have bulletproof glass or anything, but unless any of my housemates have read my socials, they won't know of my connection to the place. If they have they'll know where it is, cos there's only one pier still attached to the land. The other is just a blackened seagull perch left on its own in the middle of the sea. Mum has a photo on her wall of the West Pier when it burnt down. I think that's a bit grim really. It's not how it would like to be remembered I'm sure.

Perhaps I should be thinking how I'd like to be remembered. I was very impressed by a biker funeral I once saw pass by Mrs Latimer's. Perhaps mine could all be people on disability vehicles, and involve cats in some way. Even a spider shaped wreath or two. I'm sure Abby, Davey and Paige could arrange that for me. I'm hoping however it doesn't come to that. Now I reckon Tom is currently out looking for me, and being skinny as a greyhound, he can probably run like one. The current plan is that when, any time now, Tom has stopped running up and down the coast road in either direction, he will call Reuben and tell him he's lost me. I don't know what they'll do at that point. Hopefully, knowing that eventually I'll be talking to the police, they will return to their flats to dispose of anything there that links them to anything incriminating. I mean if you're some kind of drug gang kingpin, you're bound to have something, either a phone, or financial details – something that you need to dispose of. I expect that's what they did when that interior designer got in trouble. Had a paperwork shred or bonfire and then it was all "Who me? I don't even know the woman." Destroying evidence, even if you've done it before would I imagine take time. That should, with a bit of luck, give me time to travel at top speed all the way to Pizza On The Pier.

****

I was almost at the pier, whizzing along the pavement, when a mini cab slowed down so it was travelling along level with me. To my horror, when I turned my head I saw that Reuben was in the back. On the coast road, other cars beeped and drivers gesticulated as they pulled around the crawling cab. Clearly having his own car burnt out wasn't going to stop Reuben finding me. I'd severely underestimated him. He grinned, finding the somewhat unfair chase amusing, and made a gesture at me to pull over, as if he was a highway cop in a TV show. He was enjoying this way too much. I wasn't going to slow up. It wasn't as if I was going very fast in the first place but that's scarcely the point. The strains of that old Spear Of Destiny song 'You'll Never Take Me Alive' played in my head. I know I've watched one too many movie car chases, but if I gave up and stopped, I dreaded to think what my fate would be. Instead, I pulled a tight corner and headed up Ship Street. The cab followed, but I knew as I turned off again into the pedestrian only alleyway that is Black Lion Lane that it couldn't follow me into the maze of The Lanes. They are too narrow for cars and all motor vehicles are banned, apart from of course, mobility scooters. I heard the car door slam as Reuben got out, but I didn't look back. I used to love running around these twittens and back doubles when I was a kid. It's where my dad and I played hide and seek, while Mum visited a friend who worked in one of the shops. Like today, I'd dodge the courting couples gazing in jewellery shop windows, the beggars, the buskers, and the little groups of tourists. There'd always be a doorway to skulk in, a gap between buildings to squeeze into. On Delores though I found it wasn't so easy to make myself invisible. If only I could have turned back time and become a smaller, younger, lighter Maisie. Then I could've ditched the scooter and ran, spider in my pocket, cat in my arms. Instead I almost ran over a man sitting on the ground selling clockwork animals and caused a toddler on reins to fall over and bawl his heart out.

On reaching Dolphin Square, I realised Reuben had arrived there too, though from using a different combination of the narrow streets to me. I zoomed around the fountain, with him sprinting after me. He was on his phone meanwhile, shouting to the rest of his crew as to where we were. As he cut across and grabbed onto

Delores' handlebars, I managed to snatch his phone and throw it as far as I could. It hit the ground near a shop window and broke apart. I wasn't however fast enough to stop him switching off Delores and taking her key. Her engine stalled and died. He stood panting, but only slightly. After all the press ups I'd seen him do in the backyard this was no surprise. I took a few painful, wheezy breaths.

"Well?" said Reuben.

I wanted to scream. I tried to shout for help, but nothing but a wheeze escaped my lips. I looked at my hands. They were red like raw beef from gripping onto the scooter. I could now hear my heart pumping hard as my breath squeaked and hissed its way out. There were quite a few people who had watched our chase and were now standing in their little clusters looking at us. By their expressions they couldn't decide if it was all some kind of prank or something more sinister. One woman handed her dog's lead to her partner, while she took a photo of us both. Someone else used us as background for a selfie. Honestly if it had been Brighton Festival time you can bet some enterprising person would've started selling tickets.

Reuben had immediately clocked that we were now a public event. He wasn't at all fazed by the attention, in fact I think he rather enjoyed it. By appearing relaxed and smiling at the onlookers, it made people continue on their way, convinced it was all good fun. "Ever wanna be famous, Mais?" If I'd had the breath to answer him this is what I'd have said. "I am famous, Rube, old son. More than you'll ever know."

CHAPTER 13

Reuben retrieved the two pieces of his phone from the ground and found when reassembled it was no longer working. Passers by had completely lost interest in us by now. Eccentric occurrences are after all one of the things this city is known for. I could only watch on though as Reuben charmed a passing young women into lending him her phone. He made a call, starting to tell someone, presumably Tom, where we were, but the person at the other end clearly had more urgent news to impart. Reuben rang off, ran a hand through his hair, seemingly suddenly agitated. When he didn't immediately respond to the girl's request to return her phone, she simply took it from his hand and moved on. He didn't even seem to notice. With legs feeling like jelly I climbed off of Delores, propping myself up against the wall. I felt slightly sick.

"We've gotta go, Mais."

"I can't." I took a step, leaning heavily on the shop wall. "Just can't." Across the square, an elderly man was walking with a stick. Reuben quickly crossed and spoke with him. I willed the man to refuse to hand it over and to put up a fight, but the old gent took a look across at me and fell hook, line and sinker for the sob story Reuben was obviously telling him about his poor disabled friend's mobility scooter breaking down, and her needing to get somewhere urgently. At least that's what I guessed he was saying. The old man took out a pen and wrote something, probably his address for the stick's return, on a scrap of paper, before handing Reuben his precious stick. That scumbag could charm the birds from the trees and I had no doubt he actually would do that if he needed to. When the elderly guy went on his way, with a cheery wave in my direction, he seemed to walk nearly as well without the stick than with it. Typical.

Reuben offered me the stick. "Come on now."

"No." I stood my ground. I had just enough breath to speak now.

"Maisie..."

"No." I steadied myself on the stick but I was going nowhere. Not with him. Reuben took Mrs Webster's jar out of Delores' basket.

"Much as I hate to harm any living thing, if you don't come with me, or you shout out or speak to anyone but me, Mrs What's Her Name goes under my boot."

"It's Mrs Webster!" I took a step forward. "Alright, I'm coming." He unzipped his leather jacket, and tucked Mrs Webster's jar snugly into the inside pocket. Having undone the hooks of the elastic ropes that were holding Arthur's box on top of Delores, he lifted it into his arms. We walked very slowly out of The Lanes towards the bus stops at Old Steine.

"I'm afraid I can't easily get a vehicle out that you can travel in at this short notice" he explained, almost apologetically. "So we'll just have to get a bus."

We stood at the bus stop. A man already waiting there didn't glance up from his phone for even a moment. If he had, I wonder if he'd have sensed that something was seriously wrong. I seriously doubt it. He would still probably not have noticed that a woman, a man, a cat and a spider were taking part in a life and death drama bigger than anything that had happened in his whole life. A bus arrived and departed with the man boarding it. Reuben hadn't even glanced at the departure screens. I imagine he knew where we were going.

"If you're going to shoot me..." He raised a hand to stop me speaking, not in a threatening way, just as if to say he didn't want to hear it. I was only speaking quietly and we were alone, so I continued. "If you're going to shoot me, I want you to let Arthur and

Mrs Webster go, okay? They haven't done anything wrong. And I know you like cats, even if you're not keen on spiders."

"I don't mind spiders," he said softly. "My old bedroom at my mum's place was full of them. I even used to give them names. Like your Mrs Webster."

"My mum can't stand them. And I'm starting to think she feels the same about me too."

"Nah, I've met her remember? Like two peas in a pod you are."

"I don't really know what to say about your mum."

"She's a crack whore."

"I'd noticed. She's alright though. In small doses."

"Very small ones." He stepped forward and flagged a bus. It came to a stop, and the driver, clocking me, automatically lowered the floor to make it easier for me to board. That small act of random kindness brought tears to my eyes. The decent, honest driver, didn't know he was transporting me to almost certain death. It was a bit like being a farm animal. When you see their little faces peering fearfully out as you pass a lorry on the motorway, you always get that feeling that they know. It kind of makes me hope that animals believe in an afterlife. I know I don't. Reuben probably does. After all he does have the wings of an angel, even if he has the heart of a devil. He paid for us both, which wasn't really so generous in the circumstances. Single tickets I heard him say, rather than returns.

The bus was empty apart from us. I couldn't sit down and be confident of getting up again. Reuben put Arthur's box on the floor and sat on the front seat meant for pensioners, with his buckled boots on the rail in front like a rebellious teenager. We were pulling away, leaving the pier and Masoud and Hadi behind. I imagined a fresh pizza coming out of the oven, being slid into a box and the box zipped inside a case and carried outside by whoever was making the deliveries. It was unthinkable that I'd never taste one again.

"I'd like a pizza." Reuben was looking out the window. "Did you hear me?"

"Kick off now and you know what happens." He indicated the jar.

"I'm not kicking off. I'm hungry and if tonight is the night I'm gonna die, I'd like a pizza in my belly."

"No one's dying. I'm just taking you home. You can't be wandering about out here on your own at night. It's not safe for you." Maybe what he said was true and he didn't plan to kill me, but anyone who threatened my spider wasn't someone I could trust at his word. Also being taken 'home' as he put it, meant being a prisoner in my own flat again, with no way to communicate with the outside world. It hardly seemed like a better option.

"I don't want to go back there."

"You need someone to take care of you."

"And that's what you do is it? You take care of people? By making them deal drugs or sell their bodies." There was no point now in pretending I didn't know. He clearly felt that at this point there was no point in denying it either.

"I never ask anyone to do anything I haven't." He said it as if that was justification enough. It might have been to him, but it wasn't to me.

I wished I could think of a way of escaping. For most people getting off the bus and making a dash for it would be a possibility. I cursed myself for being me. Reuben was fiddling with his phone.

The screen was badly cracked, but as he pressed the two sides together, suddenly it came back to life. He pressed a button, held it to his ear.

"Tom?"

Bang! It was a small explosion, just in front of us. I thought the bus had hit something. Then I saw the shattered glass on the roadside window. Someone had shot at us! Somebody had actually fired a gun, presumably trying to kill me, or possibly Reuben. The bus stopped.

"What the hell was that?" The driver was out of his cab. Reuben ushered me off of the bus. I walked as quickly as I could, but it still seemed to take an alarming length of time.

"Up here!" He indicated a side street. "Before they come round again." I assume he meant we had been shot at from a moving vehicle. I think they call it a 'drive by'.

"Was that a shot? Were they shooting at us? Err at you?" We were heading off of North Street, into Bond Street, one of the smaller shopping streets that run off of it. I could see Reuben was scared and also frustrated at needing to wait for me. Suddenly they were there, leaving their car in the middle of road and spilling out. It was the guys with the jackets and jeans from the club. There were four of them. The one with sunglasses on his head, still had them up there. Perhaps he even sleeps in the poncey things. We shrank back into a shop doorway, hoping the shadows would render us invisible. The guys headed up New Road, which runs in parallel to where we were hiding. I guess they thought we'd probably fled into the dimly lit Pavilion Gardens, hoping to hide among the trees or escape by one of its several exits. I knew though they were going to comb the whole area and I knew at my speed of travel, they'd certainly find us, or they would if we stayed together.

"Give me Mrs Webster?" I hissed.

"What?"

"Give her. I'll cause a distraction. Give you a chance to get out of here, but I want my cat and my spider." He looked at me startled for a second, then handed the jar over.

"Oh and the key."

"Key?"

"To my scooter."

He rummaged in a back jeans pocket and found it.

"What are you gonna –"

"Just go Reuben. Now." He hesitated, then reached in his pocket. I thought he was going to take out the fuse-box cupboard gun and shoot me dead. I thought that it was all over. But it was his phone. He pressed it into my hand. Then he turned and sprinted away, fast and light on his feet. At the corner, he vanished from view.

I waited. Accented voices told me the armed men were returning. Slowly, painfully I turned to face the shop window behind me. I raised the stick. I hit the glass. It didn't break. Shit! Bollocks! Shit! I tried again, harder, much harder. The glass finally smashed. An alarm started ringing. I moved to the next window – a vegan café. I've nothing against vegans or cafés as you know, but again – smash. Lights came on in the flats above the shop block, as a second alarm started to shrill. I wasn't sure what the next shop sold, but I didn't care. Smash! By now people were coming out into the street. The guys in their jeans, jackets and conspicuous jewellery stopped and starred at the broken windows then at me. Now though we were not alone. Several people had come from nearby homes or had been walking by. A man with a posh accent, a checked cap and a hipster beard said, "I say, what on earth are you doing?" I looked around to warn him about the suit-jacketed gangsters but they had melted away. Clearly they didn't want to waste their time killing me in front of trendy witnesses, when their real quarry was still at large and no doubt getting further away by the minute.

"Fuck knows," I said. "Fuck knows what I'm doing." Then I remembered the phone. I took it out and I rang Masoud. He said he'd come and get me. Hadi was there with him and he'd go and collect Delores. I mustn't worry.

I stopped worrying. A few more people were coming out on the street now. Despite the ringing alarms no one tried to detain or argue with me as I walked slowly and stiffly away. I heard someone mutter "Best let her go. Probably care in community". That almost made me smile. *Care*, they didn't know the half of it.

****

There is nothing like the aroma of a cooking pizza, especially when you know it's going to be coming your way. I'm typing this on Reuben's battered phone, looking out on the twinkling lights of the big bad city from the cosy interior of Pizza On The Pier. Arthur's still in his box as I wouldn't want him running out onto the pier deck and possibly taking an accidental swim when a take-away customer opens the door. Mrs Webster is sitting on the bottom of the jar, grooming her palps as though she hasn't a care in the world. In a way she hasn't. She knows it's up to me to find her somewhere to build her next web. Why should she worry about it, I've not let her down so far? Tonight though I've no idea where any of us is going to stay. At least we're all still in one piece. For that I'm grateful.

After he had found me, Masoud had immediately ordered one of those big taxis with the sliding doors. We had waited for around twenty minutes for it to arrive, sitting in the window of a bustling pub in the North Laines area. It was fine apart from a French Bulldog called Amelie sniffing at Arthur's box, although I'd nearly choked on my orange juice when I heard the wail of sirens.

"They're coming for me! I'm gonna be charged with criminal damage. I'm never gonna be able to pay for those windows, not in a zillion years!" Masoud coolly sipped his cranberry and ice and said that the police would be far more interested in the bus driver's report of his vehicle being hit by a bullet, than a woman breaking a few windows. In his experience when Pizza On The Pier had had windows broken by random vandals, the police had only bothered to phone him back two days later. I still worried that there'd been witnesses and the fact that I'd be extremely easy to identify in a line up. In fact they wouldn't be able to find any even near look-alikes for the line up. For all I knew I'd been caught on CCTV too. Masoud however thought it would all blow over. I hope he's right.

Hadi had collected Delores' key from me and ridden her back here, while Masoud and I took the cab. I told them I was going to abandon all of my belongings left behind at the flat, but Hadi said he and Masoud had a group of friends, including a rather scary sounding chef. If they all stormed in there to collect my things he doubted anyone would stop them. I didn't want them taking that kind of risk on my behalf, but he wouldn't be talked out of it. Masoud was of the opinion that my neighbours wouldn't much care anyway. "It wasn't your stuff they wanted, it was you living there, Maisie. Giving them an address to run their drugs trafficking and other bad business from. Then if the police came round, they could blame it all on you. And trust me, they won't care you've gone either. They'll hope the next person who moves in is someone whose life they can take over too."

"That's what I let happen, didn't I? I let my life be taken over."

"Only for a while. Then you fought back. You escaped."

"Eventually."

"You still did it. You must not see yourself as a victim. You are not, Maisie. I have known you long enough to tell you that. You won, Maisie. You won."

It was a kind thing to say, but had I really won? I felt I wasn't really in a much better position than John. I no longer had a home. True I have friends, really good friends, and had a beautiful steaming pizza before me, just waiting for me to pick up my knife and fork, but I still had some big problems to solve.

****

I'm going to make some very necessary and long overdue changes in my life. The first was refusing the dessert menu after the pizza, in spite of the offer of a Death By Chocolate on the house. I think I've had enough of Death By Anything tonight. When I get my stuff back I'm going to dig out the A4 sheets left by my last dietician, and stick them up on the wall, as long as I end up somewhere that has walls that is. I'm going to start that diet again, and this time I'll do it publicly so all of you dear followers can make sure I stick to it.

I didn't know what to do with Reuben's phone. Hadi said I could put it in an envelope and send it anonymously to the police. I suspected they wouldn't find anything incriminating on it though. All the 'bad business' as Masoud called it, had as far as I was aware been conducted by Tom via a multitude of handsets. They would all be Pay As You Go and not tied to any user, no doubt. I found myself staring at the cracked phone as I ate my pizza. I kept expecting it to ring, and it to be Reuben. Maybe he even had a tracker app on it and would come here looking for me. I decided that perhaps I should throw it in the sea, or rather ask Masoud to do it for me. I didn't really feel up to walking out on that slippery wooden pier deck, with the biting wind above and angry waves below. Masoud took the phone, went to step outside, then came back to me.

"Why don't you use it first? Use it to call your mother."

224

CHAPTER 14

It was the last thing I wanted to do. Calling Mum in the middle of the night to say that I was in trouble. How many times had I done that in the past, and the 'trouble' that had dragged her from her bed and in many cases out to Mrs Latimer's had been anything from an ingrowing toenail to a slight smell of gas, when the place only had electricity. After all I'd been through, I felt like I ought to be able to finish sorting this situation out for myself. The problem was that the pizza place would soon be closing for the night and I really did need to find somewhere to stay.

Shaun answered, half asleep and with that groan in his voice that's always there when he speaks to me. I couldn't and didn't want to explain anything to him, but with Masoud washing the last of the trays and plates and Hadi trying not to look at his watch, as he swept up, I knew I had to tell him the situation.

"Err Shaun, erm listen I've kinda been made homeless. I've nowhere to go. I need to come and stay with you and Mum..." I heard him mutter a swear word under his breath. There was a pause. Then he asked where I was and said wearily he was coming. He rang off without even saying goodbye.

"Was that your mother?" I sighed. The guys seemed to think the fact that Shaun was coming meant all was 'happy ever after', but I suspected even as he put his coat and shoes on, no doubt slagging me off to Mum as he did, he was already plotting how he could stop me coming back to the bungalow.

****

Shaun turned up in Mum's neighbour's work van. It was possible to get either me or Delores in the back but not both of us. Hadi solved that one by offering to ride Delores to Mum's if I gave him the address.

He admitted he had quite enjoyed the trip on her back from Dolphin Square to Pizza On The Pier. He joked that perhaps getting old might suit him very well. That's when I gave both the guys the biggest hugs of my life. I promised I wouldn't stay out of touch with them for more than a few days at a time in future. Masoud said he was glad of that, though I mustn't use it as an excuse to eat more pizza. When they'd both had time to go home and have had a few hours kip they'll call their friends and go and liberate my stuff from the flat.

"Thanks Masoud. You're a true friend. And you, Hadi." Masoud still isn't a great one for showing his emotions, but said he'd send me over a new batch of photos to discuss in a couple of days.

The back of Mum's neighbour's van isn't exactly comfy. Every time Shaun goes over a bump my piles end up colliding with my tonsils. Also as I had to sit in the back it involved bellowing at him to be heard, and then craning my neck painfully to hear what he was yelling back. First he seemed to think the situation was that I'd just had an attack of the late night munchies and Delores had conked out, leaving me stranded at some random fast food place. I'm sure Mum tells him about my life and my friends, but it all goes in one ear and out the other with Shaun. If my exploits had involved a sport of some kind no doubt he'd have had some notion of what was going on. Instead he was clueless as usual.

I'd managed to explain about my flat and why I couldn't go back there, while he was moving things like the neighbour's tool kit around so they didn't slide into me. He always does lots of harrumphing when he's doing that kind of thing, just to ensure I get the message that I'm an unwelcome waste-of-a-huge-amount-of-space. I thought he was going to tell me my emergency was all in my mind, or I was exaggerating, but instead he nodded.

"County lines by the sound of it. It was on the news last week, before the footie."

As we set off, Arthur, who'd been almost worryingly quiet, miaowed loudly. "Is that a cat?" hollered Shaun from the front seat. I wondered why I had just credited him with being in possession of a brain cell.

"No it's a small dog that does really accurate impressions."

"God, it looks like something's going on there, Mais." There was police tape and blue lights galore at the corner of the Old Steine and North Street. The bus Reuben and I had been travelling on was still parked where it had stopped after the gunshot. Someone was photographing the shattered window and a policeman was inside it, talking into a phone or radio.

I used Reuben's phone to check the local news. I'd completely forgotten about throwing it into the briny. Twenty minutes previously, a short article had been posted about a report of a shot being fired at a bus. Witnesses including 'a couple believed to have been travelling on the bus at the time' were being asked to get in touch. I wasn't too thrilled with that description to be honest. I hope it didn't make the jeans and suit jackets guys think I was Reuben's plus one, in any sense of the words. There was no mention of anyone breaking shop windows, at least not yet, and nothing else of note seemed to have happened. I mean I was pleased someone had found their lost dachshund and somebody else had organised a nocturnal litter pick in Preston Park, but mostly I was glad to see there'd been no more incidents involving gun shots or other disturbances. Despite all that has happened I kind of wish Reuben well. I sincerely hope our paths never cross again, but he did, to be fair, make a bloody good cup of coffee.

At this point I realised we were not travelling towards Mum's bungalow. Even taking into account the detour around the police road closure this was not the right direction.

"Shaun – where are we going?"

He didn't answer. For a moment I considered it might be an out of the frying pan into the fire kind of deal. Had Shaun somehow been in on what had happened to me all along? Was he actually one of the gang? Could he even be some kind of underground crime boss who was behind the whole cuckooing, drug dealing and God knows what else racket? It would make sense in a way. Those types of people do spend a lot of time sunning themselves in the Costas. At least they do in those cockney gangster movies. I don't have any real life examples to back up that statement though. Also those kind of twists might always happen in TV dramas and those novels with the severed limbs and dead kids you're supposed to read on the beach, but do they really occur in Brighton?

"The hospital," Shaun said.

"Eh? Pardon?"

"We are going to the hospital," he bawled back over his shoulder.

"Err no thanks, I don't need to. Apart from back ache and the fact this crappy van's pancaked my piles, I'm pretty much okay, considering."

"Your Mum's in the hospital."

My mouth went dry. My stomach lurched.

"What? Why?"

"She's got a bit of a cold...."

Mum was in hospital with "a bit of a cold". Typical.

****

Sitting at Mum's bedside, I realised how long it had been since we'd really talked. Or rather she had really talked and I'd listened. We'd got into the habit of me telling her everything, and her holding things back. Then we'd bicker, joke around and play the odd board game. That was how we were. How we'd always been. She'd been holding back anything she thought would cause me to over-react, panic or get breathy since I was a kid. She'd always done her best to avoid letting me know anything that might worry me. I think to be fair, she'd also realised years back, that when she tells me about something that affects her, my first thought has always been 'yeah but how does your problem affect me?' That's what I'd always concentrated on. If Mum sprained her ankle, who would collect my washing? If Mum was having lunch with friends, who'd take my returns to the post office, who'd darn my bed socks, sort out my prescription mix up? I know that makes me sound really selfish, and it's true to a certain extent. I think it's also what happens when you end up relying on someone too much. You take them for granted without meaning to or even noticing.

So Mum hadn't told me she had cancer. She hadn't told me that Marbella trip had been during her short break between chemotherapy sessions. She hadn't told me that while arranging my bariatric rescue, visiting me in hospital and moving all of my belongings into the new flat, she herself was actually pretty ill. She'd had the diagnosis shortly before my fall and had been delaying telling me, waiting for the right time. When I'd toppled off the bed at Mrs Latimer's and ended up needing winching from the window, she had decided that now was not the time to burden me with any more worries. That was typical Mum.

Now she kept apologising. She lay there looking pale and waxy and sad looking, and apologised to me, as if any of it was her fault. She seemed to think she'd let me down. By going away, by keeping her illness from me, for catching a cold while her immune system was in such a weakened state it could lead to something more serious, without monitoring. I told her it wasn't her fault. Nothing that had happened to either of us was. How could it be? I needed to make her believe it though. Really believe it.

So here I was – voluntarily homeless, with possibly still active links to organised crime, plus a house cat and my spider. Once again needing something, once again leaning on my poor Mum for support. Instead it should've been me looking after her, dropping everything to run, well okay, walk slowly, to her bedside. Mum admitted she hadn't told Mia she was ill either. She didn't want her having to jump on the first flight home, when she was having the time of her life in Australia or Austria – neither of us could now remember which it was.

"And I thought that was what you were having too, Maisie. The time of your life. Finally. With your new place and your friendly seeming neighbours. Those people popping in and helping you arrange your party. I didn't want to spoil that. I thought that, at last, things were starting to go well for you. Both of my daughters are living their lives the way they want, and whatever happens to me, I've got them this far."

"Mum... Mum don't talk like that."

I'd been all ready to tell her about me. Everything that had happened since we'd last spoke, but I didn't. I didn't say a word. I decided not to even tell her that I had wanted to move back in with her. The last thing she needed at the moment was me coming back and being a gigantic burden once again. I had realised upon walking in, that Shaun had collected me without speaking to her in the meantime. Mum had no idea why I was there at the hospital, other than the fact Shaun must've told me where she was, and brought me there.

"Maisie... look love, Shaun's finding it hard to cope with this thing. Very hard." Shaun had gone off to the café downstairs to find us both a cup of tea. "He's not really managing. It's all a bit much for him – all the stress. And with me currently not able to do much at home, or with organising things." She propped herself up on the pillows and felt for my hand. I found and squeezed hers. It wasn't the one attached to a drip.

"Look... I don't suppose... I know you really love your independence... but there isn't any way is there, that you could maybe come round a few times a week just to help me out with things? It would only be for a few months. While I finish my treatment. Or you know, you could always move back in if you wanted? Your old room's still like you left it. Well once Shaun's moved out all his clutter. I've mentioned it to him, and to be honest, he'd be relieved... he could then go back to working full time and it would take some of the strain off him. Plus help with the bills."

There's loads of stuff I should've said at this point including "I love you," but for some reason all I did was blurt out, "Can my cat move in too?" Clearly my listening skills and empathy need a bit of work.

****

I thought a blog would be something you could read from end to end, like when you download a book onto your Kindle thingummy. Course nothing's ever that straight forward when it comes to my daughter. There're bits you can read, then there's a link to somewhere else. Then you click on a button or something underlined in another colour and you can hear her chatting away. Then it goes back to being written down somewhere, and then she's let loads of people comment and unless you can work out who they are, or know them, it's just like a load of nonsense. That's without all the links to her videos. I mean if you were going to make a little film using that camera thing on your computer, you'd do it properly wouldn't you? You'd talk clearly and slowly. You'd have planned what you wanted to say beforehand. And you would definitely have changed out of your pyjamas and combed you hair before you got started. I mean, who wouldn't – except my Maisie? I mean when do you ever see a newsreader gabbling away through a mouthful of cornflakes and spitting them everywhere when they're trying to tell you something important? And don't get me started on taking the camera into the loo. There're a lot of funny people out there on the online and I'm not talking about comedians. Really she ought to know better.

I hope people don't blame me. I never brought her up to use all that bad language. Me and her father weren't ones for swearing. And farting on camera, really? Even that ruddy cat's got better manners than her, even though it can only be called house trained in the loosest possible sense. I hope they don't think the rest of our family behaves like my daughter, because we don't. She's showing us all up, that's what she's doing. There is only one Maisie, believe me.

When I started off reading her blog and watching the little clips I wasn't sure I'd work my way through the whole thing. It's certainly not to my taste. Far, far too much about bodily functions and other stuff no one in their right mind would want to know.

But although at times it made me cringe with embarrassment, for her as much as me, in the end, I've looked at quite a bit of it. Cos what else can you do when you're feeling seriously rough, and you've read all your detectives from the library?

I haven't got much past halfway yet, and already I'm horrified by the things that went on in that house. Poor Maisie! Next time she lives on her own, and in the spring, when I'm fully recovered, she insists she will, I'm gonna keep reading this ruddy blog. I did know she was blogging, but as she's told you, I'm no fan of the online and I'd never looked at it until now. If I had, I'd have got her out of that place pretty sharpish, I can tell you.

Anyway, this is my first and last contribution to it. I'm only writing this post, if that's what you call it, to keep her quiet, while she's making my dinner and putting the washing in the tumble dryer. Maisie has this idea I might want to start a blog of my own. 'Shel's cancer diary'. She even came up with a front page with silly photo of me pulling a face in the hospital, but really, I'm not a diary person. Or someone who wants to share their every thought with the world. Perhaps it's my age. I didn't grow up with all these smart gadgets, and I think I'm probably smarter for that. And I don't want to share my "experience of cancer" as Maisie puts it. It's not me at all.

There was this woman I met on the ward though, called Debbie, and she showed me this website called Pinterest. You can go on there, start a page, and pin on photos of your favourite things. I've already started my first virtual pin board and I'm finding it really addictive. I'm looking for photos of places I went with my late husband and the kids when they were at school. Or things we shared together, like bags of Revels, making hedgehogs out of teasels and that whole yo-yo craze that came back for a while. I remember Mia giving Maisie a black eye when she tried to show her a stunt with one of those things. They were bloody dangerous.

Anyway this is Shel – Maisie's mum, saying don't worry if you don't hear any more from me. I'm not about to pop my clogs – everything's going in the right direction. But I won't be blogging again, definitely not. This one entry – do you even call it that (?) - is a one off. I'll leave you, Maisie's long suffering followers to my daughter, and she can continue to tell you all the latest ins and outs of her life, in far more detail than I think any of you really need to know.

So Maisie will be back with you shortly I'm sure, but that will be after she's brought me my dinner – which would've actually been ready half an hour ago, if she hadn't spent so much time at the kitchen window, yammering on to that ruddy spider.